FLAME & SLAG

PARTHIAN
LIBRARY OF WALES

FLAME & SLAG

RON BERRY

PARTHIAN
LIBRARY OF WALES

Parthian
The Old Surgery
Napier Street
Cardigan
SA43 1ED
www.parthianbooks.com

The Library of Wales is a Welsh Government
initiative which highlights and celebrates Wales' literary
heritage in the English language.

Published with the financial support of
the Welsh Books Council.

www.thelibraryofwales.com

Series Editor: Dai Smith

Flame and Slag first published in 1968
© Rob Berry 1968
Library of Wales edition 2012
Foreword © Leighton Andrews
All Rights Reserved

ISBN 978-1-906998-48-6

Cover Image: I.C. Rapoport
Cover design: theundercard.com

Printed and bound by Gwasg Gomer, Llandysul, Wales
Typeset by Elaine Sharples

British Library Cataloguing in Publication Data

A cataloguing record for this book is available from the British Library.

FOREWORD

You won't read another novel like *Flame and Slag*. Unless, of course, you quickly turn to another book by Ron Berry or one of his many short stories. Novels which describe life underground, or life in coal-mining communities in their heyday do exist, of course, and several of them are written by writers from the Rhondda or the South Wales coalfield more generally – though few enough give you as much of the detail of the work. But there is a breathless urgency to this writing – an awareness almost in the richness of its language, the similes piled high on one another and so closely together – that life is short and hard and things need to be said both sharply and evocatively, but concisely too, before the lungs give way. This is a demand heard from within a cacophony of voices.

Flame and Slag carries two stories – the marriage of Rees and his wife Ellen and the twists and turns of their relationship, often darkly comic, and the journal of Ellen's father John, recording the development of the Caib colliery from its sinking in the 1920s. The sinking of a colliery in the 1920s seems almost counter-intuitive, since we know the story of the rapid growth of the Rhondda and its population, from barely a thousand in 1851 to 152,000 in 1911, and its population peak at 167,000 or so by 1921. Then the decline sets in, with over 200 mines closing in South Wales in the interwar years. But there was still a brief burst in places in the early 1920s, and the new Glenrhondda Number 2 pit was sunk in Blaencwm. Ron Berry describes this in his defiantly existential autobiography, *History is What You Live:*

> For two years before I started in Infants' School, pit sinkers wearing black oilskins like the Skipper sardines advert filed past Upper and Lower Terraces.

So despite the distancing sentences in *Flame and Slag,* suggesting the Rhondda is somewhere other ('Hard times, good hard times which nobody can recapture, every man in Daren completely ignorant about THE MINERS' NEXT STEP passing from lodge to lodge over in Rhondda'), Daren is in the Rhondda and is probably Blaencwm, or Blaenycwm as Ron would have called it.

They still remember Ron Berry in Blaencwm. I am writing this foreword at the end of July, 2012, the year of the centenary of *The Miners' Next Step.* Five days ago I was in Michaels Rd, Blaencwm, four doors down from Ron Berry's old house, looking across the Selsig river at the Glenrhondda tip with my constituents Pat and Tom Brunker. 'As boys, we all looked up to Ron,' said Tom, 'marvellous footballer, good boxer.' Tom's uncle's death in the colliery is mentioned in Ron's autobiography. Pat, former Chair of Welsh Labour, remembers Tom showing off his muscles by the pool – and you can see a photograph of such a pose in *History is What You Live.*

I have a soft spot for Blaencwm. My quest for the Rhondda selection began in Pat and Tom's house, ten years ago. They still remember Ron in Blaencwm, and maybe that's not surprising for, as he says of his fictitious Blaencwm in *Flame and Slag,* 'if there's any glue in Daren, it's memory. We remember everything.'

And here, at the top of the Rhondda Fawr, you have a real sense of the complexity that Raymond Williams wrote about, reviewing the Welsh industrial novel:

> In any Welsh mining valley, there is the profoundly different yet immediately accessible landscape of open hills and the sky above them, of a rising light and of a clear expansion, into which it is possible, both physically and figuratively, to move... it is a shape which manifests not only a consciousness of history but a consciousness of alternatives, and then, in a modern form, a consciousness of aspirations and possibilities.

Ron's life was, of course, one that reflected this – contrasted with the working life underground were the active physical leisure pursuits like football, swimming, cycling and a love of the outdoors, someone who could write in detail about peregrine falcons as well as the intricate mechanics of mining. But sometimes the contradiction is spat out as a hatred of the conditions imposed by mining and the consumer capitalism that depends upon it – '...you're a blackened man eating whitened bread under artificial light in a manufactured airsteam.' Ron himself wrote of his own desire to return to the Valleys' countryside when he was working in a factory in England during the war: 'I felt *hiraeth* for mountains, for space, for green silence.'

As I said there is richness in the language, a vivacity and a grasp for an appropriate local simile – 'Ike himself governed by mining economics like a truant officer is ruled by the miching boys who justify his job'. There is a natural occasional use of the colloquial domestic Welsh that has remained strong amongst many families in the Upper Rhondda Fawr. Sometimes language is used to sardonic effect like a more engaged *Under Milk Wood*: 'My wife Ellen, Mrs Selina Cynon's willing pupil for every Shwmae and familarising idiom that binds tight the work-, bread-, bed- and pavement-bonded people of this bloody Wales of ours.'

A foreword, of course, is not a review. My task is to encourage you to read *Flame and Slag* – and so you should, for the story, for the quality of the writing, and for the history it contains. This is the Wales when coal was still powerful, when mobile chest X-rays could trigger referrals to the Pneumoconiosis Unit in Llandough hospital, where the trains until the early 1960s still ran through the tunnel linking Blaencwm and Blaengwynfi, and where Remploy and countless other factories had just started up in the post-war wave of reconstruction.

But above all, this is a perspective from a Rhondda after the closure of the Glenrhondda colliery in 1966 – and a Wales after the Aberfan disaster the same year. You will find in the book the bitterness directed at the National Coal

Board and its Chairman, Lord Robens, a strong target of criticism for that tragedy – and for his delay in visiting the community of Aberfan:

> 'I got four brothers working over in Brynywawr, doin' as much for the country as Lord Alf in his little white aeroplane.'

(One of the trappings of power enjoyed by the Chairman of the NCB was a corporate aeroplane.) The political agenda, if there is one, is a simple assertion of the battle between 'Us' – the workers, the members of that Rhondda community – and 'Them', not only the owners of private capitalist enterprise, but the state bureaucrats and their apologists. The stance is one entirely in line, arguably, with the Ron Berry who in the war-years read anarchist newsletters 'over sausages and mash, mesmeric articles under the editorship of George Woodcock, sermons on penultimate values from Bakunin, extracts from Peter Kropotkin, Proudhon and Emma Goldman'.

So there is cynicism about politics. This picks its targets, and hits them – the municipal councillors who control jobs for teachers, the MP who 'piped up in the House, was duly recorded in Hansard and committed to limbo' and the 'lucidly bland' Minister, in this case Cledwyn Hughes. But in this novel, published in the era of the Caerphilly and Rhondda West by-elections when Plaid ran Labour close seriously for the first times in the Valleys, Ron's narrator Rees is caustic not just about Labour and its 'deck of cardboard Nye Bevans remembering old Tredegar in the plushness of Berkshire' – but also of Plaid:

'Selina Cynon teaching you Welsh?,' I said. 'Next thing you'll be joining Plaid Cymru. What's your ticket, Mrs Stevens, a poop-stirring bureaucracy in Cardiff like the one in Whitehall?'

It is also a book of its era. Some of the attitudes recorded, on race, for example, reflect a language which might have been accepted as neutral in its day but would be seen to be questionable now. And in terms of the sexual politics of the novel, while Ellen is allowed her own space and establishes herself in her own realm, ('women are always short of the right men') the attitude occasionally displayed by some male characters towards violence against women will strike many today as being as casual as a chorus of Delilah.

At times, then, this is a raw account. Certainly an angry account of what is happening to the Valleys in the 1960s. But there is humour in it, and passion, and hope in the people and what they make of the conditions in which they live. Earlier I called Ron's autobiography existential. Read that after you have read this novel, for the background to the place and its historical context. What endures, at the end of *Flame and Slag*, is love. Ron Berry's fierce clarity – remembered today, unprompted, in Blaencwm – is tempered in this book by the possibility of human love and the hope that future generations could learn and move forward.

Leighton Andrews

FLAME & SLAG

1

Then, between the heyday and ultimate dissolution of Caib
colliery, Ellen came. Remote Ellen Vaughan, my seventy-
five per cent silicotic grandfather urging her up the steep
backyard where he harboured racing pigeons in a blue and
white loft perched on a ramp of railway sleepers.

My grandmother stamped life into her splayed feet.
"What's he doing now? The girl's not int'rested in his old
pigeons. *Nefoedd, nefoedd*, there's no rest for the wicked",
and she slip-slopped out after them, rotundly shapeless,
dratting under her tongue the way of pure grandmothers all
the working world over. I had a Sunday mood to warrant
the passive June morning, fuzzy anticyclonic mist spread
motionless below the mountain skyline and greenfly crinkling
our postmaster's roses—he came complaining, borrowed
my grandfather's brass spray pump, sucked lips prowing
his Graeco-Roman nose at the ammoniac pong of pigeon
droppings.

"This is Rees, my nephew," Grancha said. "Don't remember Ellen Vaughan, do you, boy?"

"I remember him, Mr Stevens," she said.

"Course, o' course she does"—old Gran, distrusting frankness, barging possessively into the kitchen. "Now come back inside, *merch*; make yourself at home."

They talked about Winchester, about Daren names, family pedigrees, the pigeons droning crop-happy in the loft; Grancha's beloved homers. But Ellen and I were strangers, formal in the silliness of Sunday morning, Caib screens hanging low, silent over the railway sidings. Another Daren Sabbath. From inside the open kitchen door I watched Grancha's droopy old ex-Bordeaux, ex-Nantes winner squatting puffy feathered as a squab behind the loft window, saw him cuffed by a young mealy cock chasing a red hen, the hen's bill nibbling the worn-out old champion's frayed primary feathers while the mealy trod her vagrantly fast, inevitable as electricity.

"Is Winchester *nice*, though?" asked my Gran, pinning down the ancient city once and for all.

"Beautiful walks," approved Ellen, "up along the river banks. And, of course, the cathedral. Everyone wants to see Winchester Cathedral."

Granch said, "But Shon Vaughan has come home, and I don't blame him. Born and bred in Daren your dad was. Come home, Duw-aye, I should say. Me, I wouldn't leave here, not after the misery..."

"Glyndwr Stevens, mind your own business," my grandmother said, old Granch sensibly hacking the little death cough he'd lived with for twenty years.

I thought, hup, sweet gossip, sweeter salacity, dirty

2

bedclothes somewhere in Ellen's family. Past tense dirt. Mystery Ellen Vaughan, tranquil. She out of the past. I couldn't remember her in Daren infants' school. Four hundred bleating nonentities, the village swarm, singing, *There's a young lad up the hill there, with his white coat and his bright hair, he comes to court me.* Infants in our rickety land of song, the time my father used to tramp into the house from Caib pit, nigger-minstrel black, rising half-white out of the zinc bath in front of the kitchen fire, soiled suds wrinkling, left drying below his navel before he kneeled cooped as a devout oriental in the bath to wash his lower half. Couldn't remember this jet-haired Ellen, dream-laid girl, woman, violet-eyed for sorcery, for illusion more than for beauty and grief, her white hands like unused blessings in her lap.

"Where will you work, gel?" said my grandmother, pitching that inbred, trustless Welshy wheedling, servility cored with unbreakable arrogance.

Ellen smiled complaisantly saccharose, responding to Gran. "Mr Harding has offered me a job."

"Nice," said Gran. "Stamps and savings, is it?"

"Book-keeping, Mrs Stevens, and serving behind the counter."

"Indeed, isn't that ever so nice. You'll do good with Dicko Harding. Influence, see; *merch.*"

"Our cadging old postmaster," I said. "The creep makes a man's stomach heave."

"Reesy, I'll *give* you!"

I said, "You know him better than I do, Gran."

"Well, there's no need, outright in front of visitors and all. More tea, Ellen bach?"

3

"I really must go now, Mrs Stevens. My father is rather weak these days. He'll be pleased I've called to see you and Mr Stevens."

"Any time!" Grancha yelping, gasping; he'd taken enough excitement, stillness coming on him, his shrunken grey head stilted stiffly on his scragged neck, reaching for air.

"Show the gel out, Rees. Sitting there like an ignorant thing"—Gran creaking a regardless smile at Ellen before bundling across to comfort the old man. "Leave the door open! You hear, Reesy, wide open!"

Wasteful, the pity spent on old age. Endless pity shredding to cobwebby remorse by the time death wins, guilt and failure yoking the unity of man.

"Where are you working?" Ellen said.

"Over the tump, Caib colliery."

"I remember you," she said again. "But I don't remember your parents."

"Both dead. What's wrong with your father? Is he ill?" Then, crowding the nation's flaw at her, enjoying myself: "Know what, Ellen, there's more sickness in South Wales than anywhere else in the country. You name it, we've got it. If South Wales was tropical, we'd breed mad dictators faster than gnats."

She said, "My father suffers from bronchitis and bad nerves. He's emotionally disturbed"—calmly dismissing him, the night-thrashed calm of oblivion, of peace, peace acquired, fanned to the quick.

"Daren might bring him around," I said. "It's quiet enough here, and besides, I suppose he knows most of us. That helps."

"You don't have to walk home with me, Rees,"—her pale

face wearing evermore scaled inside a harmony of bone, blood and flesh.

"Do you mind?" I said.

"I suspect you're an exaggerator, Rees,"—glossy hair hooding her lowered eyes, then suddenly thrusting exposure, nakedly frank. "Of course, it was my mother; she deserted him a long time ago. My father won't recover, not fully, not this side of paradise."

"Or the other place, Ellen."

It came from her like a mask speaking: "What do you know about love?"

"Nothing. You have no right to ask, either. It's like whatever grows in stone. There's no reason for it in the beginning."

"Exaggerator and liar," she accused. "Like him."

"Your old man? Hey, girl..."

"He can't, *won't* take life as it comes, so he's sick. I'm sick of sickness. I didn't want to come back to this place,"—her mouth smiling, spurning disgust easier than her doom-quiet eyes. "My father has come home to die; it's as simple as that."

"And I'm the same as him, as John Vaughan? Much obliged," I said. "Anyway, while we're on the subject, what do you know about love? Do they call it lurv up in Winchester?"

"Love can turn poisonous, destroy people; at least, a man like my father."

"Hard luck on him," I said.

She showed her teeth. "You're so tough, hm?"

Caib pit-head banksman buzzed three, the huge side-by-side wheels spinning, their fifty-eight seconds blur crowning

5

the summer-green tump, slowing until the spokes appeared to run backwards, then the final precise joggle, cages landed, the clanging gate echoing all over Daren if you listened for it. "They're still rising muck," I said. "Big fall in the face where I work. More than likely we'll be on the muck again tomorrow, after the argument."

She swanned her dark head, gazed immobile, as if she didn't have to breathe.

"See, Ellen, they'll be compelled to pay us," I said. "It's a question of coming to some arrangement for loss of wages, abnormal conditions... no matter, you would't understand."

"My father often talks about Caib colliery. He remembers the first days, when they began sinking the pit."

"Nineteen-twenty-three," I said. "We were sparkles in our mothers' eyes. The storks that brought us weren't hatched out."

"The institute, too,"—heedless again, gesturing. "He talks about the time they built the 'stute"—smiling at her flashback —"over there, in front of Daren woods. Wasn't he on the committee?"

I thought, the burden of it, paddying to a wife-wrecked ex-miner. Ellen's olde Winchester is on another planet. "Correct," I said. "Your father's photograph is hanging in the committee room. John Vaughan, lodge treasurer, nineteen-thirty-two. If there's any glue in Daren, it's memory. We remember everything, all the bread-and-scrape of bygone years, like a deck of cardboard Nye Bevans remembering scabby old Tredegar in the plushness of Berkshire. With only piffles left to fight for, the next best thing is to remember memories. Quarrel about bloody memories. Tomorrow morning we'll bring our lodge chairman before the Caib manager; they'll argue seven kinds of manure out of each other and eventually we'll win. They'll agree on maybe two-thirds of what we should be getting for clearing muck instead of filling coal. Arguments are beautiful when you're not involved right down in the guts."

Ellen blew, "Ugh,"—disinterested, familiar as a guerrilla girl whiffing hand-rolled fags in the company of righteous bandits, and I thought anxiously: John Vaughan, what have you done to your strange daughter?

"Starting in the post office tomorrow?" I said.

"Tuesday morning, Rees."

"Queer day to start in a new job, Ellen?"

"I shan't be here tomorrow."

Shut it, I thought, leave the girl alone—Caib's banksman buzzing three signals again, the aerial muck-buckets floating up Waunwen like a brochure glimpse of Switzerland, trip-levered at the last pylon high up on the mountain, regular spews of muck showering down, the quadruple-humped slag tip itself older than any man in Daren. Older than Caib pit.

"I've arranged to go shopping in Swansea tomorrow. Shopping and visiting some relatives. We'll probably spend the evening in Three Cliffs if the day is warm."

"Last fling before old Dicko Harding puts your nose to the grindstone." I said.

"Tal Harding is driving me down, actually."

"He's married. Old Dicko gave him the bungalow behind Caib institute."

Ellen said, "Married! Tal seems to be having the kind of experience my father had with my mother."

"But Tal's wife, she always bounces back. It's been going on for three or four years. Like cat and dog they are."

7

"Not any more, Rees. He's divorcing her."

I said, "Ah, you can't go wrong working for his old man. Dicko owns about ninety houses here in Daren, and he won't last much longer. He's too crabby to draw breath."

"Come inside," she said. "You've walked this far."

"The Daren tongues will be after you and Tal Harding. Better wait until he's divorced," I said.

"Tal Harding doesn't mean anything to me. In you go, tough guy"—impulsively butting my shoulder with hers, harmlessly vindictive, like a Brownie's revenge.

Riven as a burnt-out aesthete, vitality siphoned up, drained away from inside his skull, John Vaughan lay baby-limp on a small, brand-new settee in Number 9 Thelma Street. You wouldn't recognize him from the stark, owl-faced photograph in Caib institute committee room. He looked petrified, petrifying, his tiny dog-fretful blue eyes ambushed below white, furry eyebrows. His lamby curled haircut belonged to Arcadia, bulked milkily white behind his ears and on his neckline. Rivose creases dug into the putty-grey flesh of his jowls and brow, like the drying-out carcass of a hairless, foetal mammal.

"Some other time," I whispered. "Don't disturb him."

She called softly, pleasantly sarcastic, "Dad, do you remember this handsome fellow?"

Pleasure seemed to groan into his dog-beaten little eyes. "Well, well, mun, it's Dai Stevens all over again. Ellen, my glasses... ta, bach, ta", and I heard the light knock of his bony nose against the spectacles. "To the tee!" Ululant conviction smoothed the raspy anguish from his voice. "Dai Stevens will never die while you're alive, boy! Glad to meet you! Your father was the best butty a man could wish to have. Duw, aye, now you've made my day. Sit down, sit down by here," feebly swinging his legs off the settee. "Shake hands, Rees, there, put it there. Well, *myn Jawch*, Dai's son, the living image."

"They say I resemble him more than my mother"— conveniently agreeing, glancing up at Ellen, sharing something, the *power*, contracted and shared from that exact moment. Because then it came, was there, soaring like a needle of smoke through a stitch-hole in Time, her pale face inscrutably gentle, lightening, trysting the moment; John Vaughan sitting stiff-armed with his workless hands on his thighs, his fleecy head bent, mouth tucked, huhrring and hissing emphysema. Bronchitis: her white lie.

"Please lay down again, Mr Vaughan," I said, senselessly cursing to myself, knowing he'd break, die, never survive the wet, the snow and fog of Daren winters. "I'll call in again; we'll have a chat when you're feeling better."

Ellen followed me outside. "You're welcome to come to tea this evening. He'll be quite chirpy later on."

I said "What time you meeting Tal Harding tomorrow?"

"Why?"

"Let me take you to Swansea; anywhere out along the coast, too, if you like?"

"It's rather awkward, Rees."

"It's simple, Ellen. Eleven-o'clock bus from the Square."

"All right, but somewhere else, somewhere less obvious."

"Brecon town. Ten-o'clock bus from the Square."

"What excuses can I make? Aren't you the least bit concerned about Tal Harding? I'm sure he respects you, but you, why are you so tough?"

9

"Tal might grow up after they bury old Dicko," I said. "The money'll be his then, unless his wife fiddles it out of him."

"That's typical Daren big talk. You haven't had any personal experience whatsoever. I told you Tal Harding's marriage is finished."

"Ellen," I said, "good weeks I make eighteen quid and poor weeks don't come often, not in the Caib."

"Interesting," her murmur faint, condescending as a turning-away oracle.

"What do you mean *interesting*! Listen, girl, eighteen quid a week's enough to get married on!"

Grave, incisive, like an off-throned bitch empress, she said, "Men weren't born to work underground."

"We're all born to be anything. I saw the look you gave me in the house. For Christ's sake, Ellen, I'm not a fool."

"I must have been, coming back to this place after all these years."

"Be glad about it," I said, insisting. "Ellen, I'm glad, glad all over! See!"

"And I'm a pessimist? Phu. Bye-bye now. Tea at seven o'clock,"—her pale face gone empty, promising nothing, the price of nothing.

Afternoon warmth lifted the mountain fog, dark green Forestry Commission firs frizzing the flat-edged summit of Waunwen, and I thought, Tal, you misbegotten son of a penny-brained Cardi, I'm not letting you take Ellen Vaughan. She's mine, claiming her, claiming the future, zombie-stalking Daren's Sunday-resting backstreets, Grancha and Gran snoozing when I arrived home, pigeon crooning lulling over them. Obsessed now, unconsciously jockeying some archetypal mating dream while hooking my shaving-mirror over the kitchen-window latch, I noticed Caib's aerial muck-buckets coming to a stop in the glaring sunshine.

Tonight, I thought, bulling head-on, blurting out, "Ask her tonight! Aye, for God's sake, tonight!"

And Grancha wheezed, "Ah, whassat, boy?"

"Nothing, Granch; go back to sleep," I said.

2

Monday morning four weeks later and I didn't even have a clean shirt to wear. Old Gran muttering over the sink, mulish as a man-faced hilly-billy woman, dabbing the collar of my dingy *Double-two* with a stained cake of white blanco. Forgetting to send our wash to the laundry, she remembered that tin of blanco; probably kept it tucked away since my summer plimsoll days in junior school. Our wedding morning was an omen of time unspent, sometimes not having a respectable shirt at all and Ellen similarly skimped for clothes being merely part of its spending. Aye, *charismata* for ever on its backside, more or less, due to the selective code of the Welfare State.

"If your father Dai heard this carry-on, he'd knock some sense into you, Reesy, yes he would. But what I say is, make your own bed and lie on it. Don't come back here when she scrags your hair out by the roots. Kate Minty wasn't her mother for nothing. There, best I can do at short notice. Air it by the fire first,"—a round-arm jerk flinging the smeared *Double-two* into my face.

I borrowed an outsize shirt off my best man, Percy Cynon.

"Gran, don't forget," I said, "the reception's at twelve o'clock. I'll send a car for you and Granch. Where's he now, out with his pigeons?"

She screeched through the open window, "Glyndwr! You change them durr-ty clothes!" Her animosity mumbled on, ingrained, fruitless, 'Ach, ach, him and his messy old pigeons, stink the house out they do"; then again, "Glyndwr!"

She was crone-humming the old Will Hopkin's ballad, *Myfi sy'n fachgen ieuanc ffôl* when I said, "Cheerio then, Gran, wish me luck," and for the first time since wiping my snotty nose in her sack apron old Granny Stevens pressed a tight-lipped sign on my cheek. Her gift, having abandoned cause for kissing.

My grandfather was still sitting on the wooden steps outside his pigeon loft. We shook hands, tears wetting down alongside his nose, his moustached mouth wabbling, croaking, "Rees, always remember, boy bach, a good wife is better than bread," so I swallowed throat-burn jogging out to the white-ribboned wedding car, the whole main street length of Daren blurring past the window before I lit a cigarette, relaxed, less for awareness than submission, admitting defeat. I felt agreeably conquered, another ready-made man.

All the earth under the stars can only behave as earth, but people wed. Marriage the essence, each pair unfolding its own pantheon of bliss, purgation, righteousness, blasphemy, penultimate heavens and hells of perfect necessity. Ashpit ascetics carry howling marriage traces in their cells; neither can death always, not even the bloodiest, sever matrimony, unpick the wedlock between outwardly humdrum Tristrams and Isoldes, Darbys and Joans, the Romeos and Juliets of our for ever spreading fringe.

The eight minutes registrar's ceremony passed in mindlessness, a kind of alien truce from living, Ellen perfectly at ease with the middle-aged spinster civil servant, sharing small, shyly connected maiden smiles, the minutiae of affectionless affinity welding them together. Afterwards we crossed the road to a pub, drank champagne and journeyed the ten mountain and scrubland, tip-flanked and village-wriggled miles back to Upper Daren.

We rented the long smoke room in Waun Arms, fifty guests eating off vestally draped trestle tables, Percy Cynon's mother in charge (her tablecloths, too), Percy reading a speech we'd manufactured together—the least bonhomie infectious best man, fifteen stone of covenanted bachelor, almost compulsorily elected best man due to Mrs Selina Cynon's guaranteed worth as catering organizer, as queen of protocol at weddings, funerals, socially promising births, anything intrinsic to female morale, emancipatory or of precedent in Daren. Percy and I worked neighbour stents in Caib colliery. His grandfather, Thomas Ivor Cynon, threw the first sod, beginning forty years of steam-coal production, his photograph also hanging in Caib institute. A bearded man, diminutive Viking with rolled-out lips and swollen eyes: original chairman of the Federation lodge.

"Speech," whispered Ellen. "My love, it's your turn."

A group from the pit were singing, "*Sixteen tons and what do you get, another day older and deeper in debt*"—they'd hogged the bar since before Gran blanco-ed my shirt collar.

14

It's a man's world, underground, virtuous history having driven out women and children.

I said, "Ladies and gentlemen..."

"Luvhah!" they bawled. "The great luvhah!"

"... I want to thank you all for making our wedding day such a wonderful success. In particular I want to thank Mrs Cynon and her helpers. If any of you blokes happen to mention this occasion in twenty years time, you'll remember more about this good feed than anything else. I now call upon my wife, Mrs Ellen Stevens, to say a few words."

Mrs Cynon led the 'Hear-hears', the rowdies from Caib yelling, "Mrs Stevens Stamps!"

She didn't blush, John Vaughan sitting beside her, crying like a peeler of onions, poor sick man. "Friends," she said, and you could hear the colliery screens clanking far enough away to sound like toy hurdy-gurdy music, "this is the happiest day of my life. I never, *never* expected to wear a wedding ring six weeks after returning home to Daren, which only goes to show"—flashing white teeth at the girls—"that where there's faith there's hope."

Safe on his boozy freedom road, Tal Harding rocked to his feet, whisky slopping over his snazzy waistcoat. "Three cheers for the bride! Hip-pipp!"

The smoke room windows pinged, Tal huzza-ing up the roar like a bacchanalian Nazi.

Ellen sat down, smiling, murmuring cruelly dry as sand, "Fool, the man's a fool."

I said, "Tal lost. He's suffering."

She stood up again, saying, "Thank you, thank you everybody," calmly beckoning forward some Caib mates carrying another firkin of beer.

15

Private in the happy hubbub, I leaned to her ear. "You're a wicked one, Ellen, marrying me for my income."

"For love, my love. In sickness and health, for better or worse, to honour and cherish for as long as we both shall live," promising serenely, her square hand coming down on mine. "I'll be a good wife, Rees."

"God, you make it sound like penal servitude," I said "Don't dout the flame, girl."

"We're mates for always."

Thirsty strays were coming in from the closed public bar, my half-canned, breathless grandfather haranguing a Caib packer whose young face shone from rich food and beer. "Your nationalization," contended the old man, "is bound to create more pneumoconiosis. I'm telling you, *bachgen*. Look, all those machines throwing out dust, mun, see! Not the stone-dust like I got, *pneumo*! Mark my words."

"We must keep up with the times, Mr Stevens"—the packer smirking like a cream-fed cat.

"Aye, boy, and suffer young!"

Struggling under his sickly halo, Ellen's father cried, "The finest steam coal in the world. Us miners put the great into Great Britain, that's a fact. Carry on, Glyndwr, I'm listening."

"*Gwaith, gwaith. Gad 'e fod. Paid a gwneyd dim rhagor!*" —my lavender-doused grandmother hammering a stern bomp-bomp with her fist on the table. But Grancha croaked his judgement: "Oh, nice and lovely for you now, boy, but bad later. Very bad. Wait till later on when they don't want our coal and the old pits close down. Oil, *bachgen*, oil tankers coming across the seas."

16

"Atomic power!" hailed John Vaughan, his curly white mane quivering like primped fleece.

Ellen caught his arm. "Hush, dad, you haven't worked underground for fifteen years."

"Coal is bound to lose in the long run, it's plain for anyone with eyes to see!"

"Shh, you'll make yourself ill." She grimaced, less chagrined than resolute: "Rees, I'm ready to leave now."

We went around the room, Ellen pacing our farewells, unflinching when she came to Tal Harding, poor Tal's unsweated body stranded in a massive black-varnished armchair (this left-over piece from rustic times, when Daren folk were obedient to seasons and the weather), solitary at the far end of the long room.

"Go home and sleep," she said, patting his hand. "Rees and I are leaving now. Goodbye, Tal."

He appealed from his wet, helpless eyes. "Gaw-bless, Ellen, Gaw-bless both... Reesy", the light fading out from him, his jaw failing on gapes, all holds slipping, then Tal's head gently, safely rolled him into unconsciousness.

"He's a loser," I said. "I feel sorry for him."

"My mastermind husband, you're a philosopher," remarked Ellen like sealing dubious goods. "Right now, darling, we've been round them all."

Continuing philosophically crab-fisted, I reckon honeymoons are rendered to us by way of revelation, I mean in contrast to the wasteful commitments of nature. Meaning NATURE, natural selection's slavery, whether it be nits breeding in Elizabeth the First's wig, cow hippos in heat, rut-mad spiders, the deathless morality of grass, space-flight virus,

17

anaconda dialogues, sturgeon idylls, more than all these multiplied to excelsior, whereas for people everywhere, it's honeymoons. Wedlock fidelity. Our honeymoon edifice two thousand years old, via Deuteronomy 24:5. *When a man hath taken a new wife, he shall not go out to war, neither shall he be charged with any business: but he shall be free at home one year, and shall cheer up his wife which he hath taken.*

Pressing on then, collier-fisted by heritage, we spent our seven days' honeymoon caravanning in Horton on the Gower coast. Courtship habits prevailed that first afternoon, but thereafter we were proven. Proved each other, I mean, but still I failed to understand my brand-new wife, couldn't possibly except in the sanctimonious way of bachelors blinkered by pseudo-Christian rearing, slippery books, Rinso-ed films and the buttoned dialectic of Daren. Wales is agog with Daren counterparts, none of them worse than Detroit, hinterland Africa or Llasa.

Between love-knotting and living we strolled and swam, mister and missis blindly happy as nectar-drunk midges inside a hyacinth and all day long the blue sky curved above Horton bay to the sea horizon. What people do, they are. We were lovers.

A dozen caravans were parked in this cow-patted field overlooking the bay, others by the organized drove spaced out below the headland and right around to Port Eynon. In Port Eynon we drank light beer in a pub where *verboten* notices hung everywhere. This old pub had dogs, big dogs, slavering as Nansen's huskies. Sometimes we carried small flagons to the beach and waited until after dark for sea-mating, undertones snickering all around the summer-night bay, wails dissonant to the purring tide, twined couples stumbling or sculling away from other couples. A hidden world of twos, but during day-time you'd see the inevitable sand plodders, shabby roamers, often elderly, lonely men and women with dead mahogany complexions and the shifty glances of retreat, of inadequacy, of soul-frost.

We strung fossils and shells on nylon thread and posted them off without a cover note to the spinster registrar who read the rites over us. One morning I wrote lewd fantasy mottoes, to the unknown Mayor of Weston-super-Mare, to three image-famous gossipers pin-stabbed from an old copy of *Television Weekly*, then two fabricated confessional pages by Dior (Ellen fancied herself as a fashionist), and a requiem for my grandfather's long-distance champion homer. These samples were sealed in our collection of empty beer bottles and launched off Worm's Head, the whole campaign amusing Ellen, but I considered myself hellish clever. Penman Reeso from Caib pit operating under licence. Poetastry territory, the Gower peninsula. Gene-land for silly pit-boys.

Rain came on the sixth afternoon, scuds drumming our caravan, Ellen sluicing off yesterday's brine and sand, posed like a caryatid at the wash-basin, laughing through splutters. 'I'm not ticklish! Stop! Stop it... ugh, you greedy pig. Pig," she said, "pig, pig, pig!" her breasts heaving, dun nipples glowing shiny, and I thought, good God Almighty, my wife. Rees Stevens's beaut, her pretending whimpers, whooping, yowling temptation. "Don't! Let me finish washing!"

Warm-wet, biting, loving.

Rainy evening in Horton, drowsy Ellen smelling of Lifebuoy, yellow skinned under the creaking, tinted lampshades, cows lowing, gulls screaming, the beach deserted as prehistory, and next day we came home to Daren, to the house below Caib railway siding, where limp John Vaughan marooned himself on the settee.

Sickness helps to cripple the healthy, but that first year brought maiming and mort in too many shapes.

First shift down under, swarming August rain feeding the young evergreens on Waunwen, and straightway a walk-out from Number 2 face, Andrew Booth the manager waiting for us at pit-bottom, angrier than he could afford to be against four dozen men who had the "working agreement" ready behind their tongues.

Percy Cynon said, "You know it as well as we do, Mr Booth. We won't fill enough coal to cook chips. The face isn't water bombed."

"You'll have coal by nine o'clock. I'm warning the lot of you. Now get back in there! This is one case you're going to lose."

"What about the two hours, then, Mr Booth?"

"*Iesu Grist*, you'll make it up before the end of the shift. Now bugger off back in there. Some tired wasters in this pit want coddling—well, they won't get it from me, not while I'm in charge. Useless bloody shower ... men, by the Jesus, men they call themselves." Squirting small spits to right and left, the brave little Caib autocrat rapped his steel toecap with his safety stick.

Percy said, "That kind of talk won't do, Mr Booth. See, we can nail you for abuse as they call it. Question is, these two hours from seven till nine. We'll go back to the face all right, only there'll have to be some allowance for the stoppage, as in the agreement."

"Day-work, and consider yourselves bloody lucky. Listen"
—choking on temper—"I want this pit-bottom clear! So
move, get in, move!"

"Cheeky old sod you are, Mr Booth," one of the colliers
said, another undersized little tiger, shorter than old Booth
himself, swaggering gimp-shouldered from the weight of the
water jack in his coat pocket.

Percy wheeled around, doing a pacifying shepherd act with
his big arms. "Come on, boys, it's a fair arrangement. We can't
argue against two hours' day-work for sitting on our arses."

A couple of borers were already in our Number 2 face,
water infusion busting out the coal, front slips anyhow, but
towards the end of the shift we were using punchers on the
hard stuff, the pace fallen off by now, beer steam rising
from the regular club-men boozers, all of us waiting for the
shout to pack it in. And then at five past two (and he'd
done this a thousand times before) Percy Cynon rode the
scraper chains out to the gate road, but he stayed on a
second too long, one of the cross-bars taking his left leg
over the cog at the gate road, the slack under-chain mashing
his ankle, calf, knee, finishing him for good in the Caib.
Finishing the Cynons as well—their family name in Daren,
I mean—Percy's one leg dooming him lifetime bachelor, no
longer sworn, the tetchy brag of a sex-shy young man.

Every evening until Christmas we visited him in hospital.
After the year turned they transferred Percy to Talygarn, the
miners' hospital for rehabilitation. The big hard collier took
life's chopper early; he was only twenty-three.

By February Ellen was six months pregnant on Lydia.
Batched snowdrops whimpled outside Percy's ward in
Talygarn, and back home in Daren we were four feet under

21

snow, borough council workmen earning their double pay keeping the roadways salted for local bus services.

I said, "Perce, it must feel good to move around. You seem to walk fine."

"Aye, I'll master it," he said, smiling, hiding his mind from himself, Ellen sitting composed as a summer dove, Percy standing sloped away from his artificial leg, his bomper-round liquid eye-balls staring confused isolation. He belonged underground with grafting men, team workers, quarrelsome, brotherly, sullen, insular as monks. Among miners Percy had tact, courage, sympathy, the strength to be and do, but Talygarn, the official goodness of Talygarn, aseptically cranking minds to fit broken bodies, the place desolated his spirit.

"We're having a baby in May"—placid Ellen communicating with him as if he were the ear of the world.

Percy said, "I bet my old lady'll be there, performing," and he grinned over his fattening shoulder. "Us two, Reesy, we'll have a drink that day, right?"

We never did though. Daren lives ended like trees falling, leaving spaced filled in with essential duties, with exact compulsions cultivated against havoc.

Before the great spring thaw Grancha Stevens died in his armchair while my grandmother scraped clean the pigeon loft and chipped ice out of the drinking bowls. Returning indoors, she banked up the fire, threw *Old Moore's Almanack* on to his lap and demanded to hear what the stars foretold for February 1960. Three hours later Ellen found her nursing old Glyndwr to her vast dropped bosom, rocking him to and fro, keening like a vent, the clump sole of her broad shoe slapping tap-tap-tap on the fallen *Almanack*.

The day before his funeral Gran wrung every pigeon in the loft, harrying the frenzied birds, trampling corpses and cursing all the living world in Welsh. Her wits regressed fifty years, sending her trudging up Waunwen to the abandoned drift above Caib tip, Waun Level, where my grandfather contracted silicosis in hard headings, climbing up through the snow like a Khirgiz peasant woman, cheese sandwiches and a pop bottle of cold tea clutched beneath her cardigan, screeching at the mouth of the drift, "Glyndwr! *Dere mâs o fyna!*" stale warmish air fan-driven from Caib pit dripping the snow around the mossy, stone-arched mountainside hole.

Lashed prone on a seven-foot corrugated sheet, we sledged her downhill, skirting the bulging north side of Caib tip, wallowing chest deep in snow and hidden bogs, the old lady unperturbed, stretched out motionless as a log, singing quavery, "*Beth sydd i mi yn y byd, Ond gorthrymder mawr o hyd*" (What is there for me in this world, But great tribulation all the while) as we carried her into the house, repeating this old Welsh hymn for two days, the coma pressing, lifting behind little tots of whisky, only Gran's heart and the thin, broken tassel of lament staying alive.

Glyndwr and Margaret May Stevens, herself resting above him in Daren cemetery before rust blemished the nameplate on his coffin. After each burial, Tal Harding merely glanced at his father's snowbound grave, Percy following behind Tal to the car rocking purposefully on his bright alloy stick— Percy's car, new, paid for out of his compensation money, and nothing else, only softer living to which he never adapted himself. His leg for the car.

Andrew Booth sent wreaths, and Mrs Cynon graciously

overseered Ellen at both funeral dinners. Watching Ellen, unable to feel grief-stricken, simply sadness, dull sorrow like illness, I saw her sociable ease, everyone at level with my timeless wife, dispensing not tolerable, necessary authority *vide* Mrs Selina Cynon, but calm, naturally serious equality.

3

We moved into my grandparents' house early in March, shortly before Ellen's absent mother appeared. Kate Vaughan taxi-ing from Daren Halt one mild slushy evening, a strange blue-rinsed woman, urbanely un-Welsh, yet determined to retrieve her deserted past, pecking a formal kiss at Ellen's cheek, announcing like purified echo, "It's marvellous to find you married and settled down, Ellie, it really is, darling," turning on three-inch stilleto heels, meaninglessly familiar, "Rees Stevens, how do you do," her grasp limply loose as the wearied hand of royalty. She had Ellen's violet eyes, but searching blind, glittering, dervished from within.

John Vaughan wept, taking his wife's chiding like thanksgiving. So we left the house in Thelma Street for the neglected, smaller house where my grandfather was born and died. Blissfully alone, erringly green, we planned together, Caib pit-wheels visible from our bedroom window, Grancha's pigeon-loft site destined for a rockery, clean turf instead of the dirt backyard, a bathroom extension beyond our kitchen, built-in cupboards, new doors, plastering, painting. Even a goldfish pond expertly constructed by Rees-jack-of-all-trades. Meanwhile Ellen served her notice in Daren post office and bought herself a second-hand treadle sewing-machine. Eight months showed on her like six, said the clinic nurse, Mrs Cynon guaranteeing all's well, too, on account of Ellen's shape: "Just right, *merch*. I've never seen a mis coming from that sort of behind. Keep going till the very day; start laying-by and you'll bring a lazy baby."

Ellen's callisthenics, the inescapable euphoria, stallion pride from witnessing her deep breathing, whoofing and panting at the open window. Her tip-toes, her rotations, Ellen's intense confidence, and outside the window Caib's wanly greening tump foreground. Behind her, myself in bed on Saturday and Sunday mornings.

"Rees, go downstairs and—ahh-hwp—light the fire."

"I'm doing all right at the moment, my love."

"Most mornings I'm sick—ahh-hwp—but it's wearing off now."

"Well done, my love," I said.

"Light the fire, Rees, please."

"In a few minutes."

"Yesterday I bought some—ohh-ohh-ohh, ahh-hwp— some material for a dress. Think I'll get back to size by next summer?"

"Sure to, Ellen."

"Light the fire, boy."

"I'd sooner burn something else, my beaut. What I mean is you're shining like a Christmas lantern through that nightie."

"Easter egg more like."

"Lovely egg."

"Eggy, that's what you are. Light the fire—ahh-hwp—you loafer."

Pretending one of those old pulpit threateners, I said, "Five days a week shalt thou labour under the NCB, leaving Saturday and Sunday for playing the white man, for soldiering on, for ding-dong, for cultivating the mind..."

"For sloth," Ellen said. "Are there dry sticks in the oven? You can stay there, I'll light the fire," swaying herself elegantly to the dressing-table, where she shed her nightdress casually fast as an eel and brought her blue-traced belly back to the foot of the bed for her day clothes. I felt like Abram plus his bequeathed extra ha, leaping downstairs, lighting the fire, slick as a metropolitan chef preparing two British bacon-and-egg breakfasts while Ellen projected into next summer, cutting out the new pale primrose material to her maiden measurements, committing herself: the complete wife.

"After breakfast," I said, "I'll start barrowing stones from Daren river. Build up the rockery in three tiers. Won't take long to bash down the old loft, timber's all rotten. Once the weather comes warmer I'll do the digging and scatter the grass seed."

"I want a path from the back door right around the house,"she said. "For the baby's pram."

"All in good time, my love. Seen your mother lately?"

"My father does the shopping. He looks ghastly."

"He always has," I said.

The downpipes gurgled melting snow, snow four weeks dirtied, and thick mist came drifting over Waunwen as I hauled river stones into the backyard, Ellen sitting inside the living-room window, cutting a pattern out of a long-forgotten, unread newspaper, scissoring through a calculated song of praise to Welsh miners from the Duke of Edinburgh, some moribund charter speech: *It is hard to compute the contribution which this mining community has made to the power and prosperity of the United Kingdom. Since then, there has been much hardship and distress, enough to break the spirit of lesser men, but your people, to the admiration of their countrymen, have triumphed over it... building a new life ... looking forward with confidence to an age of peaceful industry and steady employment*—this stupefying extract helping to light the fire on Monday morning, the remainder in Ellen's dress pattern.

"Take care of yourself," she said. "Meat pie and veg for dinner when you come home."

Climbing the red ash pathway up Caib tump, I looked back at old Grancha's blue and white loft, thinking, next weekend I'll have all that lot scrapped for firewood. Save me humping blocks out from the pit for a month. But the loft stood rotting quietly all summer, dock-weeds nourished on acid pigeon droppings bursting up through the broken floor boards, burgeoning inside the windows like greenhouse plants. Our plans and the loft stood still, because six days after Ellen designed her dress, five after Andrew Booth successfully modernized Caib, running a conveyor belt right back to pit-bottom (the first of its kind in Wales), nature undid a century's work, Caib tip breaking away, erupting from the steep breast of Waunwen, hitting Thelma Street like a black tidal wave.

One inch of our annual eighty-one average rainfall poured over-night; first to cop on that drenching Saturday morning, the silent shunting yard jigsawed around Caib washery and screens. Niched into the base of Waunwen, three small culverts trapped half a dozen spate stream feeders to Daren river. These culverts were blocked simultaneously, greasing the tip already fallen a hundred yards, the black eagre bearing trucks across the siding, deep-riding and rolling dinosaurian in the softly roaring crushed shale, the undertow bulking heaviest, faster than the surface prow of the tip, carrying it clunking and chittering, unbroken almost like scum, a joggling froth of fresh-tipped muck, stones, bass coal, ancient tram ribs, derelict timbers. The over-all effect was of gargantuan stripping: green Waunwen flayed down to the clay and all the granite ballast chippings gulped off the railway sidings.

Ellen's parents were having breakfast, Mrs Vaughan wearing a pink brocade dressing-gown and chipped glacé silver mules, remnants along with the blue rinse of her emancipated years living common-law in Hampshire. John Vaughan dutifully read the *Daily Mirror* on his lap, not being allowed to prop it on the table, a clean, tidy, semi-invalid man, adamant only against having his hair cut, shaved neck and temples as in the days when he worked under-ground.

Kate Vaughan's scream: "Get up, run!" as daylight cut out of the window behind his bent shoulders, easily racing him to the back of the house as the room filled—a month later we found a century-old powder tin trapped in the firegrate, this Waun Level relic from the belly of the black slurry. Ellen and I were racing across Daren in Percy Cynon's car, Caib pit hooter blowing S O S nonstop, Percy savaging the car up a dirt lane, rounding the left-hand corner towards the intersection, then crashing fast into reverse as the outer spreading muck came at us, inches deep, gently swilling like summer sea-water. We climbed out, Thelma Street forty yards away.

Ellen moaned, twenty feet of tip muck shifting seething-topped down between the corner houses, leaving dripping tide marks on each gable end, three houses on the upper right-hand side of Thelma Street overwhelmed to their eaves, huge soft black curds dolloping from front windows, screams, madman shouts, squealing, grinding timbers, moans, Ellen moaning, incoherently moaning shock, Percy floundering on his one knee, unable to stand in the thickening slurry. We drove back down the lane to the next lateral road level, the same black tide riding between the uphill houses, and now we could see it pouring through the left-hand row where Ellen's parents lived, squeezed gouts heaving out from the downstairs windows and doorways, Mrs Vaughan borne thigh-deep at the bottom of their garden, momentarily transfixed in her pink brocade against the chicken wire fence. But she climbed over and waded down the adjoining garden, hands grabbing for her, bundling her safely through the house and into the crowded road-way down below.

"My father," moaned Ellen.

"Upstairs, safe, he's safe, it's only the ground floor this side of Thelma Street. We'll have to wait till it stops moving," Percy said, rigidly convincing, like a man bred for catastrophe, the roiling tide of soft muck spreading out towards us again. Ourselves, hundreds of Upper Daren people, all retreating agonized as nightmare victims on both flanks of the fallen tip.

I said, "Stay here, Ellen. I'm going across the roof-tops."

"Best wait till it stops moving," Percy said.

They were ape-walking the ridges, men, youths and young women, then sliding the slates sideways on their buttocks down to the guttering, calling for relatives and children inside the bedrooms. Gangly against the washed sky, a solitary youngster crab-walked the roofs of the right-hand row, above the three houses buried to their back-garden caves. Caib hooter lowered to a mooing groan as ambulance and police sirens broke fresh tones and all over Upper Daren you could hear wailing, rise and fall sustained, on and on.

I left my shoes at the bottom of a ladder in somebody's garden.

"One at a time! Let him get up there first!"

"Have you seen John Vaughan?" I said. "Number nine, this side of Thelma Street."

"Nuh. My brother's living in number six, Josh Evans-North. Anybody seen Josh North?"

"Climb, man," I said. "I'll hold the ladder."

There were fourteen of us spaced along the unbroken roof ridge. Counting chimneys, I yelled down number 9. "John! John Vaughan!" the echoes dulling to silence. I side-slid down to the eaves. "John, you all right in there?" — falling ten feet as the guttering pulled away from the rotted fascia board so that I dropped clean, landing safely below the bedroom window-sill. Knee-deep in softish muck. Safe. Empty bedrooms, and as I climbed my legs free the level-stretched shale in the garden forced entry somewhere down below, a sucking gutter falling away beneath my feet where I clung scrabbling to avoid dirt more than danger, number 9 back door suddenly bursting outwards and John Vaughan floated free buried neck-deep, his grey corrugated face aghast, dead, the white hair trailing smudged, matting

31

weedily in the coiling surface muck. Clawing fingers and toes, I tried to reach him, half a dozen other men goat-jumping up alongside the sluggish gutter, waiting for it to stop moving, and as it slowed to standstill the final wet roll of top slurry creamed remorselessly over his white head. While we dug out his body, Ellen gave birth to Lydia on the oak table in Caib institute.

By Monday afternoon eleven men, women and children had lain hidden under blankets on the billiard-hall floor.

Nobody sang. Neither music nor singing came from Daren all that summer. Looking up at Waunwen, for the first time in living memory you could see the old stone-arched soft coal drift where my grandfather drove hard headings, where silicosis began caking his lungs even before they squared and pegged out the turf for Caib pit-shaft.

4

We found them in a Peak Frean's tin on top of his wardrobe,
the sixpenny exercise-books wrapped in brown paper, green
passe-partout binding scaling the tin itself.

"Looks private," Tal Harding said. "In my opinion you
should take them home to Ellen."

Percy Cynon rocked around on his heel, fleshiness
uglifying his features. "Ellen's business is his business. See
what's in the bloody books, Rees," grinning at Tal, "and
we'll mind ours. Right, Tal? Downstairs, c'mon, let's sweat
some of this fat off."

"Mrs Vaughan would have first claim, only she's not here
any more," Tal said.

Percy shouted, "Oi, Post Office, come and bend your back
over this shovel!"

Thelma Street people were flinging muck out through
front doors and parlour windows, a small NCB bulldozer
fanning up and down the roadway, filling it into lorries at

the intersection. I heard Percy bantering Tal, calling him a bladder of lard-gutted obscenity, Tal sniggering his rare tenor laugh. That laugh belonged to hysterical adolescence. I replaced the exercise-books in the biscuit tin; they were clean as new, maroon, numbered 1 to 10, John Vaughan's scrupulous signature balanced on each front cover. Private diaries, I thought. Ellen's now; she'd better have them.

Much later, June twilight softening the wreckage left by the fallen tip, I remembered the biscuit tin and told her about it, grieving pooled dark in her lovely eyes.

"They are diaries, sort of," she said. "My father wrote them before we came home. Year after year, tales and news about Daren from the old days."

"Shall I fetch them, Ellen?"

"You're not tired, Rees?"

"Not unless you want to go to bed," I said, hugging hopefully, bargaining the only living defence against death.

"Bed, already, this time of day?" her smile impenetrable as music to a deaf mute. "Strikes me you'd like to bathe in it, matey."

I said, "What, my love?"

She breathed, chilling the word in my ear.

So I brought the tin from Thelma Street.

"Rees," she offered, "I'd rather listen to you reading these notebooks."

"Okay, here, this is number one; we'll start here. Anything specially private in these, I mean concerning yourself or your mother?"

"Doesn't matter any more. Read," she said.

"It's about the Caib, yeh, seems so. Listen: *ACCOUNT RE SINKING OF CAIB PIT & OTHER MATTERS RELATING*

34

TO DAREN & LOWER DAREN. By John Vaughan, Treasurer of Number One Lodge 1932–'42. Treasurer of Daren Miners' Cottage Hospital 1934–'39.

"It was Twmws Ivor Cynon who cut the actual first sod on April 21st 1923. Mr Joseph Gibby the owner put the shovel into Twm's hands for him to have a go, make the start of Caib pit & the reason we called it CAIB comes from Twmws's grandfather who was a blacksmith very clever at making a caib, which is the Welsh name for mattock. Well do I remember Twm & his wife Charlotte Cynon, as smart a pair for looks & good nature as you could wish to meet. She in her sky blue frills promising Twm the world if only he would come straight home instead of calling in the WAUN ARMS. Unless I am badly mistaken Mrs Thelma Gibby befriended Charlotte in the hope of chancing her arm with Twmws, not that he would try anything underhand to upset his Charlotte. As for Mr Gibby I must say he did not seem the kind of husband for Mrs Thelma Gibby, her being so all on edge to join in any social affairs. That is how life is with many partners as I have found to my personal cost. Mrs Gibby was dressed all in white like some gay bride. Gay she was true enough, gayer than any girl in Daren at that time but she & Mr Gibby only stayed about six months in the beginning. I am referring to 1923, exactly 23 years after they drove the railway tunnel under Waunwen but long before the senior school & the Earl Haig & Daren Cooperative on Harding's Square, actually Daren was only quarter as big with gas lamps no farther than Dicko Harding's stables. It was like another kingdom in those days as compared to these days, any honest man would say there are vast differences. For instance until Caib raised steam coal we were still working house coal seams half-way

35

up the mountains & every summer you would see brown squirrels in the Avenue trees. What I can claim without fear of contradiction is that we were happier. Much happier all round as regards being neighbours sharing & sharing alike. Nothing resembling what came after, for instance the Schiller Award in 1933 made even brothers enemies to each other."

Ellen went, "Eh?"

"Schiller Award, never heard of it I said. "I've heard about Mabon's Sliding Scale, the Minimum Wage and the Sankey Award. I'll find out, though, make inquiries in the pit tomorrow."

"It's too far in the past. My father loved gossip, didn't he?"

"This is news for us, Ellen, that white woman chasing after Percy's grandfather."

"Tempted to, you mean. Silly Mr Gibby, whoever he was."

"Silly? Him? He was one of the bastards who lived in country mansions anywhere except near the pits they owned. Right, all right, we'll get back to your old man."

"Yes, read," she said.

"Another thing," I had to say, "our output per man in the Caib is higher than any bloody colliery in the area, so this Gibby bloke started a gold-mine not a coal-pit. Him or his bloody descendants are still coining off our backs."

She said, "Don't expect justice given to you. It's taken, Rees, taken. That's right, my love, read."

" ... even brothers enemies to each other. After Mr Gibby left Daren seven new men came from Merthyr Tydfil followed by some Irishmen & about a dozen sinkers came tramping from Gloucester & Forest of Dean way. More than two dozen all told with Twmws Ivor as overman. Smallest among them

*in size & the cleverest. The rest were big men, strong as bulls.
Once a full grown black bull escaped from Hopkins'
slaughterhouse, dogs & boys chasing it right up through Daren
into a bog where they built the colliery dam in 1927, the year
Mr & Mrs Gibby arrived to officially open Caib institute. They
shot the bull's head almost off in that bog & borrowed horses
from Watkins Main Level to drag him down to where Harding's
Square now is this present day. Crude as anything you will
see in places like Spain. Another time the sinkers chased a
fox through Upper Row, farm dogs as well & killed it on the
doorstep of Number 4. I think Sarah Price Widow lived in
Number 4. A hard life but food & beer were cheap. My own
mother took in three Forest of Dean sinkers as lodgers, named
Sid Lawrence, Jake Rimmer, & Bert Burgess. They could live
on bread & Caerphilly, no manners or etiquette as we learned
at home & at school. The Irish Paddies were worst for
drunkenness. They upset Daren. There was a lot of Band of
Hope here eventually. Five new chapels, Band of Hope & Siloh
Male Voice in training for eisteddfods. Rain or fine the sinkers
never stopped working. One main reason why I am making
this Account is the hope that it will be handed down, perhaps
show future colliers that we have not always had cutting
machines to do the donkey work. Memorizing back, it is a
mystery & a miracle how we survived. Winters in particular,
everything transported to Daren by horse & cart & no roads
worth calling, only parish roads like the famous one over
Waunwen. Many new arrivals came over Waunwen with
nothing more than the clothes on their backs. Well do I
remember Mike Minty coming down Waunwen with Mrs
Minty & Kate ..."*

"My mother," Ellen said.

I said, "Irish?"

"My father was. Didn't you know I'm half Irish? Go on, Rees."

" ...*Mrs Minty & Kate a hundred yards behind him. Hot summer weather it was & Mike came off the parish road & straight across to Twmws Cynon. Being myself thirteen years old then, miching from school top class, I set eyes on Kate Minty for the first time. Twmws says to Mike Minty, 'Aye indeed, there's a start here for any man who can do a fair day's work. Five & fourpence a shift. You will have to buy oilskins from Harding's Stores. On tick, is it? Never mind, butty, meet me in the WAUN ARMS tonight.' The shock Twmws had when Mike held out a fistful of sovereigns. 'Goodness me, bachgen, richest man in Daren you are. Pleased to meet you, Missis Minty. Come to the right place you have. See down by there? Mr Gibby is going to build twenty houses for his Caib colliers. Only too glad to put in a good word for you to Mr Gibby. You will have a brand new little home to call your own. Settle down here in Daren.Very nice it is in the summer.' Afterwards I never miched school, Kate saw to that. We were boy & girl sweethearts, which is not a good sign for later on in life, therefore I hope & pray the same thing does not happen to our daughter Ellen.*"

She tongued her lips, cool disgust ill-matching the rife post-natal laxity of her body. "My poor sick father," she said. "He couldn't forgive himself for falling in love."

"Nothing can spoil ours," I said.

"The years he spent waiting for my mother to come back to him. He grew to relish the pain of waiting."

I said, "Not the way I love you, Ellen."

"I shan't ever hurt you, Rees. Read some more."

"Kate's father was a decent man sober. Dangerous in drink. Mrs Minty used to lock him out of the house, letting him sleep it off in Caib cabin. We always found sinkers sleeping in the cabin on Sunday mornings. There & laid out on the grass behind WAUN ARMS. They were greedy drinkers & fighters & always friends afterwards. Us Daren people could not understand this attitude, it was in contradiction to our long Federation struggles against the coal owners. Thank God they never stayed on as colliers in 1926 because those sinkers lacked discipline amongst themselves to negotiate for wages & conditions. Mike Minty stayed, one of the few. Colliers are generally primitive to start off but pit sinkers are lots more savage. Uncontrollable individuals. Tramping men dressed like the Skipper's Sardines advertisement. Rough diamonds as my mother used to say when we walked past them fighting outside the pubs. Thirty-six love children were born in Daren in 1924. Everyone blamed the Caib sinkers although of course it was not all their fault. One of the seven wonders is why Charlotte Cynon allowed her Twmws to spend night after night in their company. We had some negro men from Cardiff & Barry Docks come to Daren in 1924 & '25. They did not stay long. You felt sorry for them in the cold & rain. There was an elder sister to Dicko Harding who had a big say in Calvaria Chapel. I remember she died single, her contention being that negro men brought the pox to Daren. Trefor Wilkins caught the pox before he was killed under a journey on the main coming out from Waun Level. Mrs Wilkins had to wash him & lay him out herself for his parish burial. Hard times, good hard times which nobody can recapture, every man in Daren completely ignorant about THE MINERS' NEXT STEP passing from lodge to lodge over in Rhondda. The 1926 strike *was on before our Number One Lodge came to understand SOCIALIST ways & means of fighting for the CAUSE. As it affected Caib itself the strike finished in November, just in time for Mr Gibby to prove the Four Feet seam. One day I watched Mr Gibby & his surveyor riding up in a bowk. Soaked to the skin they were. Water in the Caib. Twm Cynon & his sinkers had struck water, but when you see Nant Melyn gutter running down the tump into Daren river what else should they expect but water. Common sense tells in the end. Pumps came up on the railway line to Daren Halt, Archie Booth in charge. He soon settled himself in Daren, married one of the Miskin daughters, Nathan Miskin Level-Crossing not his brother who sloped off with Mrs Pegler from the RED COW. When they struck the Caib Four Feet seam Archie Booth was pumpsman, those pumps of his banging around the twenty-four hours but nobody complained due to they had to get the Caib sinking finished & unless men keep going they will not succeed. That is the secret of life itself ..."*

Ellen said, "Dad, dad, dad, damn you," lullabying it soft voiced, the bitterness drawn fine, belonging to her pulse.

"Don't get upset, my beaut," I said.

"The horrible way he died."

"I know."

"Rees, why do we stay in Daren? The grief will always be here, even if they remove the tip and close the colliery."

"Hey," I said, "close the Caib? We're driving down to the Seven Feet seam, my love. There's enough coal there for a hundred years, and know what the next move is? They're bringing in a German firm to drive on the main roadways, mining engineers from Germany under contract to the NCB. We'll have Germans living here in Daren next January,

40

Germans, Poles, maybe coloured men. They're opening headings in plenty of other pits all over the country."

Ellen wasn't listening, her murmur fumbling tentative as the beginning of thought. "Yes, Rees, it doesn't matter. We'll have sons, more daughters"—rancour kindling, suddenly rasping raw, ferocious, too savage for reason, feline, a threshold surge, comingling of womb and mind: "Listen to me, you, you ... when Lydia was born I felt sorry for her! Do you understand? Sorry for *her* sake. They were all crying, crying and groaning in the next room. My father was dead! Lydia was alive! He was spying down at us from that old photograph, my daughter squealing like a rabbit, alive. Lydia, our baby, Rees, ours! Do you hear, ours!"

"I know, Ellen, please, I know! Jesus God, my love, as if I don't realize what you've gone through."

Swaying in anguish, her mouth and eyes screwed up tight, I felt afraid to touch her. Then patience came over her cold as winter. "We'll harden to it," she said.

I said, "We will, we must harden to it," confessing my own lost, submerged heartbreak: "We've got to stay, my love. As your father says"—waving that sixpenny maroon exercise-book, the old fashioned copperplate rambling without pause from beginning to end—"if we can't live with it here, find ourselves here, we shan't be able to anywhere else. Unless we cheat. All right, some families from Thelma Street are leaving Daren; let them run away, let them find comfort in new places, new faces. Let people talk, back-chat and bicker their bastard-born heads off about Daren!" And now it came out, out, out: "My father was killed in Caib pit, smashed, he was smashed, girl! He was smashed to bloody pieces."

41

Ellen's white face fell awry. "Your father? Why haven't you told me? Rees, why hasn't somebody told me?" — pulling my head down, pleading, sympathy dissembling her lovely frozen calm. "We'll stay, Rees, stay for always. Is it a secret? Why is it a secret about him?"

"I don't need to cry my bloody eyes out," I said. "It's so long ago, the shame, the stupid guilt. He broke one of the laws. My father climbed over crossed rails into old workings, that's when the fall caught him, came down on him in this old airway return road. He went there to relieve himself. One chance in a million, true as God, one chance in a million, but the Caib killed him. My mother died then, she soon died, she died in her own way. Granny Stevens brought me to this house, dragged me snivelling all the way. I remember I had hiccups from crying. My clothes were thrown in a washing basket slung over her arm. She dragged me like a lost pup. They never spoke about my parents. Even Saturday nights when Granch had a load on the guilt was there, deep as the bloody Caib. Can you understand the shame, Ellen? Why they put their son out of their minds, because he was killed with his trousers down? See how crazy they were? Ask anybody in Daren how Dai Stevens was killed. They'll say buried under a fall. Ask them when it happened. They'll say the day before Vesting Day. I was three years old and all the fucking houses" — Ellen grinned, thank God— "were plastered with flags and union jacks, speeches in the 'stute, on the Square, open tap all day in the pubs, old Granch too drunk to stand, Siloh bloody Male Voice Choir on the BBC, aye, and my father buried, crushed into his own mess. They brought out his remains in a feed sack. There wasn't a man's body left to plant up in Daren cemetery; they just went through the motions."

42

Ellen said, "Your mother suffered."

"She did," I said, failing to sneer, "worse than Granny Stevens. My love, you're married into a mad family."

"But your grandmother was old, feeble."

"My mother, Ellen—you won't hear about her either, not from any respectable woman in Daren. But they know, they know all right. In the snugs and back rooms they'll still gossip about my mother."

"More secrets, Rees,"—two fingers pressed against my lips. "You're no different, turning cruel with this hate locked inside you. We aren't supposed to carry the sins of our parents. It's you and me, Rees, and the baby. Now steady yourself. Tell me about your mother."

I couldn't say the words.

"You've seen me crying, often; why are you ashamed to cry?"—cheerfully aggressive, rolling her fist on my chin. "Big man, is that it? Too tough for tears? Rees-love, my father spilt his heart out in those notebooks. Wait until you come near the end, those years of sickness."

"Perhaps we should burn them," I said.

"Not yet, no. Tell me about your mother."

"She ran away. They say she went first to Cardiff, down the docks, then she went to Tosteg with some old man, living with him, one of those cracked old men who scrounge around ashtips. All I heard from my grandmother was, good riddance after bad rubbish. Just the right answer for a three-year-old kid. It's easier to understand Caib tip falling on Thelma Street."

From here I could tell it all, finish the story.

"She died in Sully hospital before I went up to junior school. That was the end, that was the very end for me."

Ellen raised one, two, three fingers. "From now on, Reesy, it's you, me and the baby. Shall I read, or shall we ..."

"Put Lydia in her pram and we'll stroll across to the woods. Afternoon shift tomorrow," I said. "Long lay in in the morning."

Deceptive as a summer iceberg, Ellen said, "The way you arrange our lives around the pit."

"It's easy, beaut, like facts and figures."

5

Concerning figures—apart from Ellen's 37, 26, 38. Try figuring Time and you're in a state of obstruction from the start. What I mean is you finish clogged around where you started, unless you form a Theory, become a brilliant artiste of manifesto squiggles. Theorist squigglers are responsible for sonic bangs and mental derailment; they're our Em Ones for strap-hanging right out of existence by the neck. They can't discuss murder or the cost of fags with a wagon repairer, not over a casual sort of man-to-man pint.

God again, where does one get in trying to measure the facts about God? Figure Him out for fair. You'll hear the sweetest talkers on earth assessing God. Language lemmings they are, and we reckon to ourselves, that's it, that's as far as he can possibly go. God-wise he's there, he's reached his Lordward limit. Then the wandering telly camera happens to poke at him when he's *listening*, someone else explaining (another Almighty statistician), and by the crucified Christ he looks bad, worse than poorly, he looks ill. He's unloved. Unloveable—like most of us. But unlike a child crying from belly-ache or napkin rash, his whole ontology bleeds, drip-drip-dripping away. Haemophilia of the soul. He's diseased by a faintish kind of evil perpetuated in the name of Godliness and holiness. Other talkers, natural preachers or what-not, those who sing cliché symbols instead of getting down to minting fresh facts and figures, they aren't really bothered about God. He's handy, up there out of the way. For certain you wouldn't trust them; you couldn't imagine them turning the other cheek, keep taking it (IT: i.e. adversity, animosity, hatred, love in reverse or the simple mayhem of thrombotic frenzy) left and right until altruism or the State interfered. As a matter of fact, the plain fact of any man feeling himself precious enough to tackle destiny, fate, free-will, conscience, life at his own pace in his own time, allowing leeway for neighbourliness, private diversions, sensible obligations, bouts of 'flu, climatical vagaries, genetical hazards, chance, any such self-identifying man, precious and paying the price for it, is fully armed against other men who figure out destiny, etc., and dictatorially (or governmentally, depends how you react) launch theirs as perfect, date-stamped forged for infinity. For the kind of painless history recorded in *Whitaker's*.

I'm recommending long-term trial and error disintegration, perhaps, as opposed to compulsory One-ness. Perhaps there's more information in disintegration, less need for the equivalent of another Christ. Savouring saviours usually chafes through to the marrow-bone, and sheer numbers clotting our homo calendar make the absolutely first saviour-bloke who vouchsafed 'I love YOU' sound like a gink, of

46

course, he wasn't at all, not even if he'd clubbed down a queue of panting beaux who couldn't posit 'I luv ya', let alone utter it. Besides, no doubt he, the very first, was probably addressing his mother or his sister. It's a healthy, starving thought. In keeping with feeling precious enough to pay the price.

Regarding figures. Someone or maybe hundreds co-ordinated altogether, calculated the Caib tip-slide problem. Working most weekends I spent months clearing the muck and rubble out of number 9 Thelma Street. Six houses opposite were written off as beyond repair, back-sides they were still buried up to the slates. We had assurances from the NCB; they were going to pay in full for repairs, redecorating, refurnishing, the lot. And all that summer walking-stick pensioners with waddling, patient old dogs stood watch and reported progress in the pubs and clubs. Huge yellow earth-shifters and red and black draglines clove a vast basin out of the tip, dumpers and lorries hauling it farther north around Waunwen, unloading the muck nearer the upper reaches of Daren river, where if it slipped again only the native trout population would suffer. Post-glacial trout, their progenitors miraculously arrived, spawning in the barren river—but no matter about the chewed residue of Daren ecology.

Various specialists came, judgement-gutted with integral calculus, experts qualified to estimate costs in terms of death and property. Not a soul in Daren queried the cost of hiring the draglines, earth-shifters, lorries from private firms; nobody balanced this cost against the coal filled out from Caib since 1926. Somewhere, obviously, button-tappers were wriggling the figures off machines in offices where a ramping human fart would dislocate the cerebellum. Somewhere records were mounting up, but overall old Daren boomed. Pubs, grocers, cafés, even the chapels had their dose of uplift. Then a new edict came in November 1959. The Coal Board offered cash payments for the twenty houses in Thelma Street, thus obliterating Mrs Thelma Gibby, too, Joseph Gibby's memorial to her after he proved steam coal in the Caib.

Consequently Mrs Kate Vaughan returned from Hampshire, collected two thousand quid—Thelma Street designated for clearance under Town and Country Planning in any case—bought Lydia a pink knitted suit and turned her back on Daren for always. Feckless, durable Mike Minty's daughter Kate, brought over the parish road; she left me the best of her life: Ellen.

Looters moved in. Once the rumour floated that extended colliery railway sidings were to replace Thelma Street, they went into action like locusts. Vans, cars, handcarts, prams, you'd see them trekking to and from the ruined street. Small boys marched the lanes with a couple of rafters, slates, or maybe a pair of water taps wrapped in *Daren & District Clarion*. Scrap merchants struck with acetylene torches on railings, front gates, guttering, downpipes. Wash-basins vanished, doors, window sashes, coal-sheds, baths, firegrates, floor tiles grained with slurry, with muck ripped, dug, shovelled out of the Caib by the thieves' grandfathers, great-grandfathers if they helped make the original slag-tip outside Waun Level.

Mrs Cynon was outraged. "Anybody'd swear nine out of ten families were living on the parish as we had to during the strikes," she said, Lydia cooped in her left arm, her

48

right hand sweeping disgust, a big florid woman, heavy boned, full mouthed as an innocent voluptuary, hacking at the morality of Daren.

"You expect people to change, Selina?" Ellen said, inquiring formally, finding it normal the way Thelma Street was attacked, denuded like a providential offering.

"Everything is changing for the better, *merch*," urged Mrs Cynon. "There's myself on widow's pension plus allowances, d'you see, Ellie, better off now than when my father slaved all hours, bless him, to keep a roof over our heads and enough food in our stomachs."

"But you've seen two wars, Selina," — the smile on Ellen's face evoking sanction, live and let live.

"Ach, wars didn't hurt us worse than Caib tip falling down. We mustn't expect plain sailing! Trials are sent to test us. What I'm against is carrying on like that!" — the old lady stanced in judgement, pointing across at Thelma Street, the baby gurgling up at her, Mrs Cynon squinting over her bulbous nose, queenly solicitous, *"Beth sydd yn bod arnoch chwi nawr, cariad?"*

The day of reckoning never came. Authorized NCB demolishers arrived, packed dynamite under the walls, warning sirens groaned and after the explosions bulldozers churned in, lorries behind them, Thelma Street site levelled off like a recreation ground within a fortnight. And about a month later coal trucks buffered and shunted beneath a new aerial bucket system that lifted Caib muck half a mile around Waunwen to the new tip.

Daren women were still wearing mourning headscarves. Plain squares of black nylon, shilling each, Marks and Spencers.

The boom continued when the German engineering firm, now registered in Great Britain—the same Deutschland capital that Adolf Hitler spent, feeling himself exceeding precious, poor driven gout-head-started the underground roadway to the Seven Feet seam. Hard-grafting men, these Germans, Poles, Ukrainians. Money-men, like the early ones in Daren who needed two and three generations to cultivate themselves, to feel they belonged, were homogeneous to mining and therefore privileged, entitled to respect if not adequate reward for their insular role, mining being a full-time role, more a way of life than other production jobs, carrying with it the paradox of self-sufficient arrogance and the unique fatalism that succumbs to change, is incapable of change. The principles of Change: evolutionary, devolutionary, involutionary, revolutionary, of progress and regress, of ingression, eggression and digression. Survival hurts poets—and miners, sailors, soldiers, slaves, for whom mining, the seas, soldiering and slavery is greater than themselves, as poets are governed by abstract language. London's Westminster and Daren's borough council, neither of these can leave scratch marks more significant than those on the cave walls of Altimara.

Rees Stevens doesn't have to blurb this piece either. Naked facts and figures are published every year in *Whitaker's*. Histories embalmed, egos preserved without a creak, flawless, bang-on as yesterday's weather. Anyone can use *Whitaker's* for anything, any year book, any chart, statistical record, any statement of accounts. *Vide Whitaker's* 1960, in terms of mining, first the destiny deciders: NCB Chairman, £10,000 a year plus £1,000 expenses; Deputy Chairman, £8,000 a year plus £500 allowance; six Board members at

£7,500 a year, plus £500 allowances; four part-time members at £1,000 a year. Secretary of the Board and under-secretary, salaries not given. Nine director-generals, salaries not given. Nine chairmen of divisional boards, salaries not given. Right then, these are the supermen, the long-heads, the brains, statutory and paid for, like we elect and pay for Ministers, panjandrum councillors, inland revenue wizards, the whole incendiary civil service galaxy. Then a little tailpiece in *Whitaker's* says: 'Estimated average earnings, including Allowances in Kind of all adult male workers in 1960 was £16.4.0 per week.' Observe the charming definitive, *workers*.

But what a calculation! The last penny accounted for, issued direct from Hobart House to *Whitaker's*. Disrespectfully compare this tailpiece with the nice round-figure salaries paid to Board administrators and the records of coal production and distribution. All those blind noughts frothing at the end.

Now, quoting from the Welsh press, Celtic culture's hallelujah horn, our upside-down, jock-strapped cornucopia:

'117 pits have been closed in Wales since 1946.'

Aye indeed, we were nationalized in 1947.

There are no publicized records of men (numbers, when and where) suffering from dust, no how, when and where record of the disabled, but the NCB annual statement of accounts does publish the *total* amount of money paid to disabled miners and ex-miners. Thuswise, pussy and hard-handed comrades, figures on paper determine self-preciousness and destiny, and bugger them about considerably, most often regardless.

51

Pardon the taint of spleen, of plebeian bile.

Back in 1960 we had no qualms about Caib colliery. The coal was there in the Four Feet, millions of tons of high-grade steam coal. Only two explosions in thirty-four years, the killed men forgotten, just about forgotten. Ours was a good pit. In 1960 we had a sharp lodge committee. Compo cases were looked after, we ran a tote for pensioners, gave them £5 hampers and a cheque every Christmas. Daren Dramatic Society was established in Caib institute. We had ten chapels and a Welsh Church of England, two cinemas, a film society, three pigeon clubs, a dog fanciers' club, four soccer teams, cricket and rugby teams, the Women's Guild was a power combine, Daren and District Angling Association, a bowls team, motor-cycle club, Barclay's and Midland banks were thriving on H.P. deals, and the railway tunnel under Waunwen was still open in 1960. We had a swimming pool. The Houghton Four X brewery flourished, serving nine pubs and two affiliated clubs, plus the Earl Haig and Daren Social and Welfare Club (bingo three nights, dances two nights, concerts two nights), and the borough council were planning their two-phase housing project costing three million pounds.

Two thousand Daren folk, mostly girls, worked in a radio and television factory.

In 1960 the NCB built new screens, washery and flocculation plants for Caib colliery. The Germans, Latvians, Ukrainians and Poles were here, those denationalized characters, couthless but without the bedlam innocence of roaming navvies, drilling, blasting the new underground roadway, shuttling in with their Eimco machines regardless of powder smoke and water, but they wouldn't handle a shovel if they could help it. In the site office on top pit, you'd see a photograph of Queen Elizabeth II on one wall and a doctored portrait of the owner's German wife on the opposite wall. Our Queen for patriotism, the other for money. Maybe the times were propitious. Times change. The German firm came without a blip of publicity. They simply arrived, rigged up their gear, sank pits, drove extensive link headings, built factories. Their men did not come to Wales to ease a labour shortage, they came to do business, make legitimate profit.

Tal Harding boarded four Germans in his empty bungalow, Tal himself living forlorn as any father-hammered son in the flat above Daren general post office. Mrs Cynon fostered a Pole named Fred Fransceska. When Fred married a barmaid from the Earl Haig club big Percy acted best man again, his mother in charge of the invitation list. Fred belonged. He'd worn Silesian coal scars on his face since boyhood. Ellen liked Fred. She befriended him. They both ignored questions unrelated to living from day to day. Ellen's ideas were governed by the assumption that we lived between waking and sleeping, easy when easy, greedy if necessary, scrimping without remorse, pleasuring without guilt. When Fred Fransceska got drunk in our house he showed us where a Russian bullet had ploughed through his buttock, and he was slavering sobs like a ruined behemoth, his underpants around his ankles, Ellen weeping sympathy, Lydia crying because they were, Morfed (Fred's new wife, half his age) sprinting down the street to *Waun Arms* for more whisky to dilute her first experience of Fred expressing the blues of his youth.

Early spring glorified Daren, warming inland from across the Bristol Channel, crazy yellow daffodils guarding the lawn outside Caib institute, the background trees, all hardwood timber, storming massed leaf buds, and Waunwen's huge black scar completely stabilized, prinking special grass seed planted by the Coal Board, who were still dealing with claims for injury and death. The tip-slide a full year behind us, Daren's solitary, deserted Welsh Church of England taking a glossy face-lift conversion into a supermarket, and weekly notices in the *Clarion* advising relatives to attend re-burials of exhumed bodies from the churchyard. There they were, many forgotten, entirely unknown Staffordshire and English Border names from over a century ago, from earlier times when only ironmasters worked the soft bituminous coal from mountain levels, the whole uprearing landscape of Daren pocked with these small, overgrown, caved-in holes, each with its hummocky mound-spill of debris turned green as the institute's front lawn.

"Green always comes back," Ellen said. "It's silly, all the shouting and screaming about coal-tips. Look at Daren, marked like an old man's face, and what's wrong with that? I hated coming home, but now we're living our own lives. It's good to live your own life."

"You hated circumstances," I said.

"I did ... this time I hope we get a boy," pausing from cutting sandwiches to thumb at her belly. "Brother for Lydia."

I said, "Beaut, you don't have to make my breakfast in the mornings. Stay in bed. I can fix things for myself."

"Hush up, I'm not helpless. Who had a bump yesterday? They were talking about him in the Co-op."

"Bloke from lower down. Eddie 'Lectric we call him. He was on extracting—extracting cogs; something hit him in the face."

"Will he lose his eye?"

"Left eye, aye, according to our ambulance man. I hope to Christ not, because Eddie's all right. His father went to prison for singing the *Red Flag* outside the manager's house. Years ago now, years and years. The bastards took him in for disturbing the peace."

"I worry about you sometimes, Reesy."

"Don't," I said. "The Caib isn't going to hurt me, not after what happened to Dai Stevens."

"Only you can learn to live with that, my love."

"I know."

Her sphinx smile glimmered. "It's always *I know*. Of course you do—often. Often. I fell for you straight away, didn't I? I mean it was one of the reasons, but, Rees, what I think is this: you don't care about ordinary things. Ordinary things annoy you. Yes, yes, let me finish!" She re-tied the sash cord around her bulging dressing-gown. Lovely, I thought, lovely Ellen.

"Remember this, boy?" she said, waving the foolscap sheets.

"Last year, the NCB competition, World Without War."

"Aye, World Without War," I said. "Their title."

"We should have sent it in, Rees."

"Doesn't matter, Ellen. Shove it back between your lovely …"

"Hush!" Her voice thickened:

55

" 'World Without War.
But first the premise: Could we inhabit it?
Braided hordes of eagled, star-pipped marchers
Seldom diagnosed as mad, our solid muscled
Swaddies desperately bored, the defiant erk,
Taut, as much concerned about his father's
DSO as girls, our honest, devious matlows
Shaped to blind obedience. We, then, ourselves
Inherit (query) peace, this earth's untruth,
Where fisted tables snowball further
Ultimatums?
   Many of us are television natives.
Or shall any racket, private row between any two
Be resolved in murder? Our cliques, claques,
Caballers, families their ample precedent.

Perhaps first a pre-premise, necessary discretion
In allegiance to Mr C. Darwin, perhaps,
Should be mooted, measured, weighed in wanting
Before that sequel Mount of Olives declaration
Echoes another gnat's-span moil of joy and chagrin.
The hypothesis might exclude sweet retribution.
We aren't blessed with mere multitudes below
—There are none below—but entire homo sapiens,
Nary one expendable to the next. Just one alone
Being the plague and glory of art, of everyman's
Inadequate faith, promise, his life's work moving
Via catastrophic norms yet ever aimed at clarity.
History plus, or divided by Mr Freud's exegesis
Will not let us (anyone at all now) claim *peace*
Requires martyrdom. Nor war neither, brother.

Nor *heaven* and *hell*—four judgement nouns,
Durable integers of survival's pristine order,
God-damned absolutes aptly tailored, fitting
Hindsight, reasonable griff, fate, genius itself
e.g. good old William Blake's soul prising,
Who saw us whole in terms of Was, Is and
Will-be, with sweetly pro-angelic floaters
Run off the sentient, self-same mould. Old W.B.,
He tenanted the howling wilderness of
Failure, too.

So again the given premise: World Without War,
For we who are bored by trick saints (sure, sure)
And daily sickened, festered by righteous edicts
From warring experts, from big specialists
Affined to Al Capone more so than Kristos maimed,
We who are (warranted like them, of course, proven)
Deprived, no, losers, no, encompassed by conflict,
By hope betrothed to love and hate, circlers,
Roundabout riders driven by nobody's silence,
Belly-aching at the still, small voices saying, This?
This isn't, not yet. Peaky, sensible voices saying,
Your peace my war is the world. Saying, Conscience?
Safe in your conscience, sibling, I fold, unfold
My arms.'"

I said, "Beaut, you make it sound stronger than it is."

Belly-proud, she lofted the bread knife like a priestess. "Only yesterday I read that strange piece you wrote when I was carrying Lydia. Dammo, you're not human sometimes. It isn't even a love poem!"

"I tried though, beaut."

57

"It's as if you were watching yourself having a baby!"

"I wasn't, though, beaut. Be fair."

"Rees, I love you differently from the way you love me. That's wonderful, don't you realize?"

"Fate, Ellen."

"Wonderful, supreme in a way—isn't it?"

"We pick the daftest times. Inside ten minutes I've got to climb the tump, change my clothes, collect my lamp and get down the pit. So long, beaut."

We hugged in the open doorway, pearled morning clouds high over the western sky, and I thought, rain or fine, next weekend I'll demolish Grancha's old pigeon loft. Bloody eyesore stuck there on the bank.

"What?" she said.

"We love each other differently, but it's good. Supreme, girl, supreme. You're the beautiful-est. That new baby in your belly's going to be supreme. Good morning, love."

"Bye-bye, Rees, watch out for yourself"—her doorstep manner composed, almost lyrical, waiting for the last glance as I shut the backyard gate.

From the top of the spring-green tump I saw the blind-staring oblongs of our bedroom window, and I thought, aye, mixing in marriage does make a man feel sorry for bachelors. Dead-enders like Percy Cynon. The nether dream which the poor cramped buggers pad out with loyalties. Straining the old platonic pus.

While changing into pit clothes I took on one of those precautionary moods: Hark at Reeso, Mrs Stevens's bingo-card philosopher, vaunting his lot. Five shifts a week until I'm sixty. See our kids educated all the way, see them head

58

out into the shrinking world, Stevens's blood helping to colonize the womb-boxed compass. But yourself, Rees, you'll spit coal dust long after your teeth drop from your gums. Spit up the old duff like Dai and Glyndwr Stevens.

Yuh.

Humming *Miss Otis regrets* as I entered Caib lamproom, spinning my brass check across the metal counter for lamp 967, the *Miss Otis* tune unconsciously reviving, finding its place inside my head as we crammed back, chest and ribsides in the cage, old Lewsin Lewis Whistler softly, thoughtlessly, trilling the *Riff Song*, and brazen-headed Charlie Page handing out Mintoes to everybody, Mintoe odour pervading the roadway as we walked in alongside Andrew Booth's boon, the trunk conveyor belt travelling back to pit-bottom. Andrew's final endowment to Caib—he retired before the institute daffodils withered. Andrew's two younger brothers were Coal Board men, white fingered and collared seven days a week, groomed sherangs in the regional office, both childlessly married to Aberystwyth University girls, young *Plaid Cymru* wives who canvassed Daren at local elections, enthusiastically futile against sanctioned fellow travellers on Daren's hundred per cent Labour borough council, utterly futile against a die-hard nucleus of Communist voters who abused the two Nationalists as if they were degenerate debs. Pairing themselves, B.A.Aber. below B.A.Aber., they sent a telling letter to the *Western Mail*, revealing their experiences in the Earl Haig Club where a cidery conclave of primitive Socialists educated the ladies, regaled them with coal-face adjectives, an old Arnhem paratrooper among these life-beaten veterans from Tredegar Bevan's Janus-faced idealism.

59

Still walking in, *Miss Otis*'s melody baritoning off-key inside my eardrums, tough little Charlie Page's Mintoe down to an apple pip under my tongue, reminding myself, vowing to break apart Grancha's pigeon loft, rake up and turf the steep backyard. Get it all done clean and tidy (rejecting the goldfish pond and the rockery schemes) before Ellen went to bed on our second child. A boy this time ...

Then Lewsin Whistler generated *When those saints go marching in* for a careless quartet, young Dicko Harding (scrounging tight-fist property-hogging dead-man Dicko's daughter's abandoned bastard—Hannah Harding ran away to Croydon, leaving Tal sole beneficiary) catarrhally croaking Louis Armstrong style as he did whenever called upon in *Waun Arms*, ending his joyous Saturday nights happier than his Uncle Tal boozing solitary in Regent Street Con. Club. The loneliest ex-husband in Daren. Scruffy Daren, I thought, marked like an old man's face. But old-timers die; Ellen forgot to mention dying. Not like John Vaughan nor Dai Stevens, old blokes slowly wearing out, fading away. A Grancha Stevens's death, leaving nothing except memories. Perishable memories, doomed, vanishing.

"Whassamatter?" Charlie said. "Talkin' to yourself? Thass a bad sign, *brawd.*"

I said, "We're short of Dowty posts and bars."

"Unless they come in through the supply road this morning, Reesy."

Fred Fransceska and a Ukrainian supervisor (the Germans brought their own nomenclature to Caib) turned off into the new Seven Feet roadway, Fred calling, "Shimai-ha, boys!" He'd quickly acquired a working store of idioms, catchpenny phrases direly harvested for peace of mind.

"How's Morfed then?" Charlie said.

"Lovely, mun!" Fred's eyes grinning inside the blue scarred anvils of his cheekbones.

"She ought to be an' all," groaned Charlie under his Mintoe-ed breath. "Been in practice a long time." Then, returning to banter, bawling over his shoulder, "Aye, she's one of the best, Freddie-boy,"—low-groaning again, "Duw, she'll spend money faster than that Aga Khan bloke. The man isn't born who'll keep up with Morfed Owen."

I said, "Charlie, share out the sweets."

"These bloody loshins are rationed, don't forget. Butties only, unless it's case of colic. Good Christ, I used to suffer colic when I started on the coal. Hey, Rees, whassis I hear about big Percy Cynon? Caught fiddlin' with some little girl over in Garden Terrace. School-kid she was, under age. Course he's got to manage it somehow, poor sod." Charlie gagged suddenly, dribbling Mintoe juice. "Just thought, Reesy, remember the time we queued up outside the hollow acorn tree in Daren woods? Big Percy last in the *gwt*, an' when his turn came Margie Miskin stopped shop like, remember? Old Percy, by the lovin' Christ, whatta state on him."

"Who was this girl from Garden Terrace?" I said.

"Not *from* the Terrace's far as I can make out. Why then, butty? Fancy somethin' in ankle socks now that your Ellen's in the club agen?"

"I'll belt you across the ear one day, Charlie," I said.

"Aye? You and whose army? For Christ's sake watch those nerves of yours, Reesy; anybody'd swear you'd been stuffed by a one-armed bandit. Where do you think you are, boy, chapel? Christ, there's no point in living if you can't take a joke. Look a'me last New Year's Eve. See, I goes home from work on afternoon shift, an' there's a bunch of kids playin' Strip Jack fuckin' Naked in our front room. Honest! That boy Hopkins from the butcher shop, he didn't have a rag on him. Kids these days, hair down their backs like bloody golliwogs. My missus reckons the sexes are changin' over. When some little fruit-cake comes down here in the old Caib an' clears my stent, that'll be the day for Charlie-boy to hang his tools on the bar." He spat out and fly-kicked his Mintoe, warbling happily, "Def'nitely, aye!"

6

Wrapped in herself, the strange glow not for sharing, Ellen bundled away the dinner dishes.

"Hiya, my love," I said.

"Selina Cynon came here this morning, after she'd been to the police station. They soon dropped the case. The girl was lying her head off."

"But who was she, Ellen?"

"Some new family moved into Lower Daren. Key man in the radio factory—um, Mr Wilson—they're living in one of the Board of Trade prefabs. Four children, according to Mrs Cynon. Vicky Wilson, she's their eldest, sixteen next month." Ellen slowly turned her head, jerkily like a pre-dawn songbird: "Apple tart or"—gazing upward, bemused—"cake, shop cake with a cup of tea?"

"Vicky Wilson?" I said.

"Yes,"—paused like a woman surrounded by, repudiating chaos.

"Did he—Percy, I mean?"

"Yes."

"I'll have a slice of each," I said.

She bent down. "No wonder you married me."

"Come again, love?"

"For sweetness!"—nose-rubbing like an Eskimo wife. "I'm putting words into your mouth," she said.

Serenely to and from the pantry, filling the kettle, slopping out the teapot, waiting again for the kettle to whistle, maidenly absorbed for all her plumping belly, kneading the nape of my neck with her finger-tips, murmuring, "I've been reading the notebooks, up to nineteen-thirty. Thelma Gibby probably did have an affair with Charlotte Cynon's husband. He's hinting at it like a small boy who can't keep secrets. Perhaps my dad was jealous. No, hardly, he was newly married to my mother. Thelma Gibby impressed him though, poor man."

"Nineteen-thirty," I said. "Year they had the first explosion in Caib. Seven men killed up in the Tylwth Teg district. Grancha Stevens used to talk about it."

The kettle whistled, and while eating Ellen's authentically tart apple tart and that mongrel-flavoured shop cake I fell powerfully in love with her. As many times before, many times, times all different, like exploration, a kind of inter-lifeline-fired geography. The caulking and rebirth of thinking.

It's damaged ideas that jabber above chill-deadened senses.

Pondering aloud, Ellen observed, "Selina Cynon has some holdover the police superintendent. They're about the same age. Is he a Daren man?"

"Born and bred, more or less," I said. "But listen, beaut ..."

"Finish your tea first, darling."

"Something else on my mind, not tea. Listen, beaut ..."

"I don't have to listen; you've been searching for the last ten minutes."

"Searching?"

"We mustn't wake Lydia," she said.

Lydia slept her afternoon constitutional, greyness dimming the bedroom window, Caib shaft-wheels motionless as totems raised to a foam-lipped Coal Board pharaoh.

"Where's the famous Account?" I said.

"In the drawer this side. Reach over, can you?" She tugged playfully milkmaid as I leaned to the table drawer, urging, "Rees, keep your voice down!"

"Here we go," I said, whispering, "Right: *That is the secret of life itself whether a man spends his three score & ten in Daren or whether he travels the whole wide world.*"

Ellen tugged impulsively. "Why don't you tell the story about today? About Daren and Caib and us as well. Every afternoon I'll light a fire in the back room. You won't be disturbed."

My stomach scrabbled away, jilted my body. "Rees Stevens's Account, you mean, Ellen?"

"I don't care what you call it."

"Documentaries are a menace, girl. Stinking, lousy, bloody menace. No, love, I can't write about us."

"Why not? My father was all muddled, almost a complete failure."

"We might fail."

"Grancha and Granny Stevens didn't fail."

"We might, Ellen, we might."

65

Lydia began crying; Ellen went downstairs to peel an apple for her—Lydia with my sandy hair and freckles, Ellen's square chin and wide dauntless mouth. Hazel eyes from old Granny Stevens.

"Don't you see how this could come between us?" I said. "I'd be like a two-headed man, one for living and working, the other for spying and listening. Worse than Saint Paul. Is that decent?"

"Decency doesn't come into it. We'll buy a typewriter,"— heedlessly scheming, palming Lydia out of the bedroom, giving a blasé hoist to her swollen under-belly, scorning the evidence in the dressing-table mirror, wedging herself back in bed, upright against the pillows, enthroned, positive as a daughter of Zeus. "I can type, Reesy, these two fingers and these two thumbs. Let me see, if I light the fire while you're having dinner, you can stay in there every evening until supper-time. Tea-time at least. Lock the door from inside."

"Beaut, be quiet a minute. *This* is what we wanted this afternoon. Understand, Ellen?"

"Of course. But after our fun and games you can lock yourself in the back room."

"Husht, Ellen! Ellen, listen; I'm not a cripple like your father. He had nothing else to do."

"Explain about the Germans and Poles coming to Daren," —blithely remorseless, one hand on her diaphragm, the other patting my mouth to keep me quiet— "and Fred Fransceska marrying Morfed Owen. She's having hers next September, by the way. She's huge, Morfed, like a mountain. You can also put down what the men think about the pits, or Will Paynter holding his place on the T.U.C. Committee. He's your union sec. And there's the new manager, Ike

Pomeroy. You miners, you usually exaggerate when you try to be witty. You don't like the simple truth. Exaggerate on paper instead of telling me lies—you do, Rees! Lies, but I love you, although I'm not beautiful like you say. My figure used to be all right, passable, and I don't want to grow old, I don't want to stop enjoying … ninety per cent of the women around here won't admit that." She smiled reflectively. "At least not until they're past feeling anything. Have you noticed?"—her mobile hand spider-running down my chest, down, flip-flip-flip, then she relaxed, fell deceptively calm, declaring cold as ice-lock, "Report it true about Caib tip-slide and all that wicked time."

By now it was evening gloom, every colour gone from the day.

Lydia appealed from the foot of the stairs. "Mam-my, mam-my!"

"What is it, *cariad*?"

"Mam-my!"

Ellen carried her upstairs again, our sober little toddler scrupulously gnawing the apple stump, dandled on Ellen's half-parted thighs in the grey-toned room.

"Well, you, matey,"—switching on the bedside table lamp —"shall I go now? The loving's over."

"I'll stay here, read the Account. Trumpet when tea's ready, my beaut."

She said, "Good-bye, darling."

Eventually they mastered the water problem & found the Four Feet seam, thus providing employment for well over 2,000 men in the days before mechanization except the war coming in 1939 deprived old Caib colliery in many ways, specially

67

manpower when France collapsed & the pits were forced to work three on & three off because we could not export coal abroad. Skilled colliers packed in to join the armed forces & naturally many did not come back to Caib or Daren or Wales for that matter. Often-times with my wife Kate I have discussed the families come & gone from Daren, large families disappearing forever without leaving a solitary trace, myself & daughter included in 1943. But I shall do my utmost to return once I am convinced that certain personal problems & tribulations are finished & done with. Life must be settled. It was fair shares & solid principle in Daren before the struggles came, private & money struggles during the bad Thirties period. From a village we grew into a fair sized town, Lower Daren brickworks producing fine bricks with fireclay from the Watkin Main Level. The accidental air raid at 11.40 p.m. on September the 9th 1942 left craters all along the quarry above Lower Daren, therefore the old Watkin Main will never be found again. Girls crowding the brickworks & a few more Irish & English newcomers among them so that is where Kate worked instead of going away to service until we got married. By then I had my own stall in Caib, comrade Twmws Cynon heading man who never put a foot wrong disregarding fresh starters rushing to enjoy big money in our pit. The best for wages in Wales without a shadow of doubt, a stall in the Four Feet worth twice the money you would earn anywhere barring one or two exceptional collieries over in Rhondda of course. Imagine a collier & his butty in the Caib averaging eight peggy trams a shift, he would be on quite a respectable living. All peggy trams in the beginning as were used in the house coal levels. Soon came those huge bomby trams. One day Pryssor Harding hurried out shocked from his weighbridge office to *look at a bomby with easily one foot six of RACING on top of the tram. RACING we called it in those days. Pryssor could not believe the one ton fourteen cwts measured on his weighbridge scales. He had to inspect the reality. Twmws Cynon RACED that bomby as an experiment but it was common practice on account of slow traffic underground as compared to modern standards. The more coal you RACED on your tram the heavier your pay packet, this caused a certain amount of wastage on the journey down to the screens but who worried? God knows there was coal galore in the Four Feet, more than enough to make Mr Joseph Gibby very pleased with his prospects. When he came to open Caib institute Twmws Cynon was on the stage right next to Mrs Thelma Gibby & the whisper went around the hall that he & she were due to catch up on old times. Nobody had concrete proof. She danced with him & him alone after we cleared the tables off the floor. Mr Gibby gave a very short speech, blunt & straight to the point. Stands to reason he wanted back the money he spent sinking Caib pit. She was the sociable one, Twmws spinning yarns & her laughing down at him in a black velvet frock guaranteed to put any man off his guard. As for Charlotte Cynon she smiled daggers in her eyes, you could see. Very nearly ready to give birth to Hayden Percival their second child, it was obvious Charlotte could not keep up with Twmws & Thelma Gibby traipsing around the dance floor, Twmws introducing her to everybody as if it was himself owned Caib not Joseph Gibby. What a character that man, taking him all in all. When he died from rapid consumption we missed him like losing a relative. All over in six months as God is my judge, leaving Charlotte still feeding Hayden Percival & the little girl Martha who managed to survive the*

T.B. clinging to her skirts as well. We took the cap around &
collected £72/9/0 for Charlotte in her distress. The very least
we could do as he was a man in a million.

"And yourself, old Sioni sick-man rambler Vaughan," I
said, Ellen simultaneously inquiring from the stair landing,
"What's that, Rees?"

"Your old man, him and his personal relationships. Why
did your mother leave him?"

She lit two cigarettes. "Finally you mean?"

"Finally—ta very much, love—or whatever. Why?"

"You've seen my mother, Mike Minty's only child. She's a
selfish woman. She can't help being what she is either; her
childhood was probably worse than yours."

"Sometimes I feel sorry for your father, other times he's
really spewy. Do you believe Thomas Cynon and Thelma
Gibby knocked it off a bit?"

"They might well have, Reesy. It seems to me Daren
people often do things out of desperation, a kind of bravado
to make themselves feel important. I'm sure it doesn't apply
to Thelma Gibby. There's something else about her—she's
like a bitch that belongs anywhere; but Twmws would take
the challenge if only to prove what others expected of him."

"You've got a bitchy streak, Ellen my love."

"Phu, matey, you don't know anything yet. Get dressed;
tea's on the table."

I climbed out of bed and back in with her.

"Randy!"—kicking and heaving the way we gambolled in
that yellow-tinted Horton caravan. "You ought to be a harem-
keeper! Desist, boy!"

"Gu-url," I said.

She panted excessively into my ear. "What a husband.

Dog, dog, dog. Doggy without a leash. I thought you were a philosopher, *cariad*."

"Not all the time, my lovely."

"I love you, too."

Worship the basic, mutual as Alpha and Omega, annihilating both.

At nine o'clock I called a pint and ten fags in *Waun Arms*. Five minutes later Percy Cynon arrived with a moon-faced bloke, bald as a cathode tube above shiny grey eyes, his false teeth slotted inside lips crimped from trying to please too many masters.

"Meet Rees Stevens," Percy said. "Rees, this is my cousin Howell Cynon. Pride of the family; he's a Coal Board draughtsman, aye, dropped some ballocks in his time, too, I dare say. How's the old Caib working?"

I said, "They're driving three shifts on that new main to the Seven Feet. Madmen—they make us Welsh colliers look like potchers. Sixty yards some weeks, and they're not short of a thing. Supplies? Perce, you wouldn't believe the half of it. What are you having, Howell?"

"Whisky, just a tickle of soda," he said.

"I meant, Howell, do you want bottled beer or a pint of four ex? This isn't Christmas-time." He carried his number plain, not so much cupidity as stupidity. No insight, no foresight. Hindsight scavenged bare.

"Two pints of Houghton's," Percy said, big Perce risen to eighteen stone since leaving Talygarn, strained veins webbing purply across his cheekbone flesh. He boozed every night, standing gigantic as a milk-stout advert against the bar counter, the straight handle of his alloy walking-stick jammed between the taut buttons of his waistcoat. My best man, the makings of a slyly shy, comfortable invert beginning to show.

Midway through his pint Howell said, "Oops, pardon me, gents," edging himself sideways through the bar crowd towards his call of nature.

I said, "Nice manners on your cousin, Perce. Say, *brawd*, what's she like, this kid Vicky Wilson?"

Percy's meaty face puffed injured righteousness, staggers hitting his breathing, chopping hyphens into his self-defence. "I doh-n't want to hear slah-nder from nobody, 'specially yuh-ew, Rh-eesy. I nev-her touched that girl, on my muh-other's life I didn't … didn't, didn't!"

"Smart girl is she, Perce?"

He steadied himself, grinding his teeth, poor crippled sod, whining like a typically hounded Silurian raper. "Wasn't my fault at all. Her fault, Rees, hers."

"Who mentioned fault?" I said. "It's your own business, strictly private. Why not bring Vicky to our house for tea next Sunday? Don't broadcast the news, just bring her along round about seven o'clock. We'll be expecting you both. You know my Ellen; she makes friends dead easy. True now, Perce. Stop worrying, man, there's damn all to worry about."

His grinding molars squeaked like honing a razor blade inside a wet tumbler. Howell Cynon came back to our table. The chat meandered, Percy drumming ratt-ta-ta-tatt on his artificial shinbone, cursing his job in a Remploy factory where they made cheap furniture for small wages. Defenceless as the sky, he harked back to that last shift when he rode the chain conveyor, his cousin Howell's mouth

72

plucking distaste; then clean off his own bat Howell said, "Of course it's a Class C colliery now," — whipping a fine Sheaffer pen from his inside pocket, opening out an envelope, his pudgy fist effortlessly sketching lines, crosses, arrows, and there it was: Waunwen mountain neatly hatched across the paper, X marking Caib pit-shaft, arrowed lines tracing the Four Feet seam northward under the course of Daren river, and Thyssen's new main roadway to the Seven Feet aimed due west, slanting beneath Waunwen.

"Over *here*," Howell Cynon said (off the envelope), confident as a priest in his vocational prime, the Sheaffer wiggling up on end like a de-ionized Shakespearian prickstand, "we have Brynywawr colliery." He smiled, nibbling the tip of his tongue. "Class A, do you see?"

"Aye, they're in the Seven Feet, been working it for years," Percy said.

"Exactly. And Brynywawr will rise the coal from Caib Seven Feet," — slitting open another envelope, butting them together, hatching the limit of Waunwen, fixing Brynywawr with the same strong black X and a circled Class A, the compact skilful fist sliding back to the first envelope, ringing Class C for Caib's X, then (skidding destiny) Howell Cynon streaked Thyssen's roadway beneath Waunwen to Brynywawr colliery. "Nineteen-sixty-three, Percy," he explained, cocking his bald head.

Percy brought in three more pints.

I asked him, "*By* nineteen-sixty-three, Howell?"

He gave the kind of down-up mouth to nasally hummed answer tendered as incontrovertible from expert to layman, and drew a meticulous arch near Brynywawr's circled Class A. "Drift outfall, do you see? The Cardiff mineral line here,"

—mapping British Railways from Brynywawr right off the second envelope. "Much shorter, much cheaper. And here," —careless now, his Sheaffer slashing haphazard, boxing an oblong around Brynywawr—"coke ovens, NCB labs, offices, car park. We shall be making a start on the Brynywawr development next spring."

"Howell," I said, "where do you work? I mean where's your office?"

"Cardiff, naturally, but I'm not really on Planning." He nudged Percy. "We have quite a pleasant flat in Cathedral Road, isn't that so?"

"Aye, nice place," guaranteed Percy. "Mind if I speak frank for a minute?"—his cousin's expression a tortured balm of obligatory kinship and amusement. "Burn those bloody scraps of paper and don't breathe a word about raising Caib coal in Brynywawr. There're lodge committee men in this bar."

"Birth, maturity and decay," almost chanted Howell Cynon, unconsciously signalling Infinity with his envelopes. "Well, gents, you'll have to excuse me. Long drive home tonight and my wife's a back-seat driver!" Balling the envelopes, he jig-laughed his brilliant teeth.

Percy wagged his alloy walking-stick. "So long then, Howell. You ought to pay us a visit more often."

"Keep up the good work," I said.

There was a bloke giving a slow, obsessed version of *Rock around the clock* out in the urinal, and a boxing match on the telly down the lower end of the bar. After the fight Tommy Farr ingratiated a few comments, knuckling his hambone hands, tentatively miming a punch or two, setting memories churning everywhere in the Principality. Memories travelling all the way from Clydach Vale, from Judge's Hall, Trealaw, to America, and back to Porth Skating Rink—Farr's beginning and end according to Granch Stevens. Old Granch did some sparring before the dust settled him for loving homers.

"My cousin's a bit of a tom pep," confided Percy. "You know how they are on the Coal Board, planning this, planning that. I wouldn't take Howell's word all the way, Rees."

"He had it off pat," I said. "He's *seen* the bloody drawings somewhere, but the point is the Germans are in on the development scheme and we haven't heard a word from the NUM. Our side doesn't know anything about it."

"You'll be all right if it comes off, Rees. Riding in on bogies instead of walking. They won't expect Caib men to walk through to Brynywawr."

"But all the money they've spent on Caib. Screens, bunkers at pit-bottom, washery, sidings, flocculation plant, new creeper for picking up the trams on top pit. Where's the logic?"

Percy said, "What the hell, mun, you'll still be rising coal from the Four Feet. Talk sense, Rees."

Walking home, I thought: Percy might make a steady go of it with that youngster. She's big-hearted, must be, taking him on with his one leg—innocently hoping for him, unaware that Vicky Wilson was lined up for approved school, in need of care and attention as they say. Who isn't, though—who bloody-well isn't? The job's too heavy for Jesus of Nazareth.

7

Dirty, king-coal-grained old Daren, gulleyed and humped like an old whore-master's carcass. We have about a dozen permissible semi-idiots and family skeletons by the breeding horde. Green skeletons. But Mrs Cynon's secret pull with Superintendent Seymour Lloyd remained inviolate as the unreafforested glacial bog from which Daren river sprang following the Ice Age, the Government fence skirting its hollow acres of rushes, moss and shivery cotton sedge. A few days after the Superintendent bore witness against Vicky Wilson big Percy disappeared. He and absconder Vicky lodged in a Swansea Town Hill back street for two months. Every Thursday he drove home to collect his NCB compo. We bumped into them (as it's said) in Swansea market, Vicky stiffly blonde as rafia, with Asiatic cheekbones and scatty blue eyes. Ellen steered Lydia in a collapsible two-wheeler pram. I carried some un-Daren buys (chrome coffee percolator, exotic samples of supermarket tinned foods) and

Ellen's shoes. Beautiful Ellen wore a new pair of Dolcis sandals. Our Lydia-child was swallowing purple grapes on top of crisps and a shilling Woolworth's trifle, conditioning herself to vomit on the 6.30 p.m. bus.

Haggard Percy, like a man living on stale air.

Ellen said, "Your mother's frantic."

"You haven't set eyes on us," he recommended, lowering a slow, thick grin at Lydia.

"Why don't you get married? Your father won't object will he, Vicky? Why on earth should he? Apply to the court if necessary," — Ellen warding off Percy, parrying her pregnant bulk between him and the girl. "What you're doing now is very stupid, *and,*" — scoring direct at Percy — "what kind of man do you call yourself, eh?"

"We haven't seen you, Perce," I said, taking Lydia's two-wheeler. "The Daren bus is due, so all the best for now. If you feel like it, call in our house next Thursday."

"Vicky, shall I speak to your father?" Ellen said, enjoying her abnormal do-goodness in the undefiled way that magistrates benevolently send a broken man to prison for committing his fiftieth petty offence.

The girl snickered revulsion.

I said, "Step lively, wife; we'll miss our bus."

Percy rocked on his heels. "It's all right, Ellen. Let it blow over first; that's our intention. Don't forget, you haven't seen us. I'm having my compo transferred to ..."

"Shut yer cake'ole," snapped Vicky.

Percy's breathing jerked soft snores in his throat, Vicky lurching him around a fruit stall, her blonde hair swishing like the docked tail of a fly-tormented horse.

I said, "Cheerio then!"

"How long is *that* going to last?"—Ellen musing, having to revolve her whole body to watch Percy and the girl.

"Madame Rees Stevens, marriage counsellor," I said, "Problems dealt with in strictest confidence. Please enclose stamped addressed envelope."

"I'm concerned about Selina Cynon, not those two,"—swooping the grapes off Lydia: "*Cariad*, your tummy!"

"And mummy's tummy. Come on, beaut, you look sexy in that fur hat,"—sale price, thirty bob in C.&A.'s.

Ellen revolved again, showing off a slow pirouette in the weekend hubbub of Swansea market, even her pink toenails sensuous in those size 3½ sandals. Imagination must be a volcanic part of loving. To see, just witness and leave be—fearlessly, I mean.

Lydia stopped in the middle of *Clap hands, clap hands till daddy comes home* to throw up into a plastic bag.

"*He shall have music and mammy have none*," prompted Ellen.

"*He shall have music and mammy have none*," parroted our freckled toddler, perfectly eluding Ellen's minor key. The men in the bus laughed and the women smirked approval.

Percy came home a couple of Saturdays later. I had the roof off Grancha's pigeon loft, another two swings with his Waun Level sledgehammer (this indestructible tool wrought by Thomas Ivor Cynon's grandfather, journeyman blacksmith in pastoral Daren, whose nickname patented forty years of steam coal-mining) and the door crashed inwards. I remember Granny Stevens screwing the birds in her soulburst grief, Grancha's daily devotion to them, and swung the sledgehammer like a nystagmatic miniature Thor until the four walls were knocked down. By God I wanted to weep, bleed tears, but Ellen came out from the house with a gallon can of paraffin.

"No, love, I'll chop it up for firewood," I said.

"Rees, what's the matter?"

"Nothing. Look, we can see Melyn brook our side of the tump now."

"There is *some*thing."

"Memories, Ellen, silly bloody memories."

"Write them down, boy."

"I'm not crippled," I said, Percy shouting from the backyard gate, "Crippled! Whass-this then, whass-this then ?"—rollicking refreshed as a freed dobbin horse up the slope.

Vicky Wilson had shot off to London with his wallet. He didn't have a penny. Neither was he worried, his mother being less dependent upon straight cash than any widow in Daren.

That night a young constable booked him in Daren Social Club car park. Later, under orders, he delivered Percy safely home, still dead drunk. Mrs Cynon advised the young copper regarding her personal friend, Mrs Seymour Lloyd, one-time eisteddfod contralto, chrysanthemum-grower, producer to Daren Dramatic Society, the full catalogue of blacks and whites, Mrs Lloyd's whims and fancies. Worth knowing beforehand to make life easier, especially on station duty, Mrs Lloyd's kitchen only two doors away from the charge room.

Next morning Ellen won with the paraffin, starting a bonfire that glowed all night. Best-man Percy allocated himself three Spartan afternoon shoeing the wood ash into the sloping yard. I raked it smooth, Ellen strewed the grass seed and the sparrows daily glutted themselves from dawn until I opened the back door. So we sowed again under the supervision of another Mrs Cynon connection, Llew Hopkins, ex-town crier, descendant of a line of butchers (his grandfather's the black bull ditched and shot-gunned when they sank Caib pit), slaughterers and butchers until Daren Health Department forbade the former. Llew maintained the gardens fronting Caib institute, again supervisory, caretaker of Caib institute his principal occupation, his word taken as law, irrefutable, free from chicanery and deceit because the crippling of his hip in the Four Feet seam designated Llew's avocation, clarified his authority as if ordained by the Almighty. From maimed, still unhealed young lamproom attendant he went directly to the institute when Joseph Gibby fleetingly came back to Daren, and thereafter Llew served the entire life of the hall, hobbling the long billiards room with his hooting vowels and black ebony walking-stick. He frightened collier boys until they learned to respect him. Few men admired him, none attempted to redeem his dreadful oral ignorance. Llew couldn't long-hand Llewellyn, simply LLEW HOPKINS ESQ CARETAKER CAIB INST. From Llew himself 'stute broke into Daren parlance. He had no friends, only primal connections, e.g. Mrs Selina Cynon.

"White cotton from that Welsh Embr'ideries shop. Milk-bottle tops," ordered Llew many days before he came to supervise the sowing. And, "*Diolch yn fawr*, Selina", gravely accepting one of Mrs Cynon's Gold Flake cigarettes, herself sole smoker of this time-past brand in Daren, obtainable only in Regent Street, next door to the Con Club where five generations of tobacconists (the Einons: Abe, Joshua, Victor,

Seaton, Reuben) had catered to four generations of Cynons, Percy's standing order one hundred and twenty Players a week, plus a screw of Plover chewing twist every shift until he lost his leg in Caib.

"Pavings?" inquired Llew, spavined like a Middle Ages grotesque over his black stick. "For why, Selina?"

"Ellen's pram, Llew. She won't have to bring it through the house every time, and with the second one coming soon, do you see, Llew, more convenient, isn't it?"

Alienated from prams, Llew hecked away a couple of paces, the threaded milk-bottle tops spinning, softly thrumming on the taut white cotton criss-crossed over short sticks pegged into the ground all the way up the yard. He reminded me of my grandmother, the same blind self-commitment. *"Dere 'ma,* Selina," he said gruffly, leaving us now, tracking out to the gate with the same bristling purpose as Granny Stevens. Syndrome of the indefatigable Celt, his intransigent attitude: *Watch out, I am on my way,* informing Mrs Cynon without raising his head, then standing like a withered tree for her to open the gate and limping away, his duty done.

Mrs Cynon repeated Llew's advice, saying, "He will speak to the Council foreman. It's up to us to pay transport from the Council yard. Lovely flagstones for you, from the pavements in Thelma Street."

Ellen said, "No, thanks, I don't want them, not from Thelma Street."

"I'll tell Llew, let him know the position," I said, running the unseeded pathway curve out to the gate. But he'd gone.

"Leave this to me," promised Mrs Cynon. "Vernon Price - Plasterer, he'll know what's best. I'll have a quiet little chat with him."

So we had a poured concrete path, the pale seedlings half an inch high, tightly sown, green for always when our Elizabeth was born.

The message came down the pit at 10 a.m., another sandy-haired baby girl, weight seven pounds. Mother and child doing well.

"On the piss tonight—celebrate," Charlie Page said, bending his elbow, taking the blade of his shovel up to his mouth. "Wait till you've knocked out eight like me; gets a bit abnoxious by then. I shan't forget the time my old gel dropped a miscarriage in the Gaiety—let's see, ten years come next September. Honest, my main thought was, thank the lovin' Jesus. I was playing cork pool over in the 'stute, six of us in the game an' I won the bloody pool.

She had our last baby the day those Russians sent up their first Sputnik, October the fourth it was, nineteen-fifty-seven. Now she can't have any more since they op'rated on her. Bad year that was for us, seven bob rise for wagemen and the following year the bastards asked us to work six shifts a week. Christ, our fathers must'a turned over up there in Daren cemetery. Us silly buggers, we fought an' fought for the five-day week."

I said, "What about if you had your time all over again, Charlie?"

"Nothing wrong with a man trying to dig his grave with his weapon," he said. "Nature, ent it?"

We didn't ease off throwing coal on the chains, welcome face slips from the front of the cut.

"Reesy, you heard the talk about the Germans drivin' through to Brynywawr?"

"Rumour?" I said.

"Aye, they were arguing in the Earl Haig last night. Morfed's big Pole reckons it's def'nite. He's a boy, he is; the guts of him taking on a piece like Morfed Owen."

I said, "Don't be a bloody *clec* all your life, Charlie."

"No but she's like one of those American maniacs you see in films who can't leave it there. Look, Christ, it isn't as if I begrudge Fred Fransceska or Morfed herself for that matter. S'life, ent it, natural, mun, natch-ur-al. My old lady had sixteen of us, seven boys an' nine girls. I got four brothers working over in Brynywawr, doin' as much for the country as Lord Alf in his little white aeroplane."

"We'll be in Brynywawr this time next year," I said.

"No doubt. Double bon cages over there an' all."

"Drift, Charlie," I said. "All the Seven Feet coal carried out on a main belt to this drift above Brynywawr washery."

Calculating his distance, he stepped back from a heaving spill of top coal, warning, "Watch it, Rees, it's workin' up towards you," reaching the bigger lumps first, throwing them on the chains. "Christ, mun," he said, "by the time a man shoves his feet under the table his fuckin' stent'll be down in Cardiff docks, way things are goin' on."

I said, "Progress, butty."

"My ring. See that new creeper machinery up on top pit? Five men workin' the bloody thing. Before now, *before*, old Sid Davies and his horse kept the whole pit goin' as regards full 'uns and empties. And lissen! The fuckin' nag was older than Sid hisself! As you know! Ask me, s'load of ballux. Those Germans'll work in the raw, the daft buggers. They'll be on sticks when me an' my old girl'll be watching concerts in Daren Social. I've seen plenty of slashers takin' the short-cut road up to Daren cemetery."

"My father was a slasher," I said, ending Charlie's talk.

"Too bloody true," he agreed.

We punched and shovelled coal until eleven o'clock, then from twenty past eleven until finishing time.

Outside the baths on top pit Tal Harding had his car ready to drive me home. There were two neighbour women in the house, Mrs Cynon in charge. Upstairs, the midwife was paying her second visit, offering the baby who looked inhuman, puggy, a reminder that I'd entirely forgotten Lydia as new-born.

"Sorry, Rees-love, we missed a boy again," Ellen said. She looked lovely, blanched pure.

"Are you feeling all right, beaut?" — small shucking squirms coming from the infant in my arms.

I heard the midwife sniggering discreetly, her and Mrs Cynon out on the stairs landing.

"I wasn't afraid this time, Rees. Shall we name her Elizabeth? It's a good name, Eliz-a-beth."

"Elizabeth Stevens," I said shakily, unable to put my grimed hands and blackened finger-nails near that fresh raw, wrinkled face, trembling at the stark gulf between us, man and six-hour-old infant, Ellen smiling her drained lips, but her violet eyes shone dark, dark, sombre, surrendering to trust.

"Love me?" she said calmly.

I said, "More than ever. More now than before we got married."

8

Charlie Page lost his place on the coal in April, a couple of weeks after Yuri Gagarin circled the earth, cheerful as a bus driver, in a hundred and eight minutes. In April a mobile X-ray unit spent three days in Caib ambulance centre; every man and boy had his frontal shot, medical science forward marching over dead bones. Twenty-six men were sent to Cardiff for NCB X-rays. Five of these were later taken to Llandough Pneumoconiosis Research Unit, real old-timers they were, too afraid, stubborn or ignorant to apply for X-rays in Daren hospital through their family doctors. Charlie had fifty per cent, the knowledge ageing him, lining animal despair in his leathery face. He stopped smoking, drank less and took to rambling the hillsides. Regular pathways through and around Daren woods, where other pneumo and silicotic cases eked out their careful days. Favourite open-air route, the old parish road over Waunwen. You'd see them on sunny afternoons (mornings were spent coughing, warming up blood and tissues, preparing heart and lungs), dotted groups and singles up to the Forestry Commission fence and no farther, slow moving as Klondike survivors against the broad green track.

Soon, true to his spirit, Charlie Page found himself a hobby: archaeology. He bought a pocket compass, magnifying-glass and trowel. His finds were carried in Franklyn's Mild tobacco tins. After the first tattling paragraph appeared in *Daren & District Clarion*, Charlie walked alone. He became unobtrusive, secretive as if taken over by the doppelganger of a Hunter and Fisher Folk shaman. Moreover, Charlie had another twenty years to cultivate this metamorphosis.

In late June he began sleeping out.

We were walking alongside Daren river, the path wide enough for Elizabeth's pram, Lydia trotting on her own between rides straddled across my shoulders. White-bibbed dippers whistled, panicking short flights upstream, pipits rose from the warm turf, jigging, trilling, caracoled down again like minuscule glides. Small dark trout hung in the sparkling shallows, inbred sensitives, flickering up into deep water blued by the sky. We were half a mile from home, winding below the new muck-tip, pressure already rippling the mountain slope, shearing the turf crosswise. Kneeling at the foot of the tip, Charlie Page in his faded pepper-and-salt tweed suit. He came down to us, abstracted, hands pressing and patting his pockets.

"*Shwmae* there, Charlie," I said. "Find anything?"

He said, "Howbe, Ellen. Nothin' much today, boy. See, it's better after rain, heavy rain, heavy, y'know,"—fumbling a tobacco tin from his pocket: "Last week I found these"—

86

his stiff fingers peeling cotton wool off a clutch of small, fossilized mussels.

"Good gracious," applauded Ellen—my ever cordial wife —Charlie watching her as if she might suddenly become dangerous.

"I'm not sure yet, two hundred million years old, more p'rhaps," he said. "Must call in the library agen. Find out, see? Hey, just think, salt water everywhere over Daren. No mountains, no woods, no coal. *Duw, Duw*, there's changes, ah, Rees?"—scrupulously tucking his finds in the cotton wool and *snick-snick*, the elastic band off his wrist twice snapped around the tin.

"We're on a picnic," Ellen said. "Would you like some sandwiches, Charlie?"

"Not between meals, thanks all the same,"—vagueness widening his sunken, light grey eyes. He rolled his head. "You'll see my *cwtch* up by there. Spring lock on the door. Very handy in bad weather like we get so often."

Charmingly inoffensive, Ellen strolled away, wheeling the pram, her and Lydia singing *Old Macdonald had a farm*.

"Man," I said, "you're enjoying life since leaving the Caib. How are the wife and family?"

"Truth to tell, Reesy, I stay out of their way. Thirty-four years underground, me; now I'm making up for lost time like the old Chinks do when they retire from activity."

"But you're keeping busy, searching the tips up there, tramping the forestry roads over the top. Aye, word gets around, Charlie. You've been seen; people are on the watch-out since that article in the *Clarion*."

Serious, pucker-faced, he said, "We all make mistakes. I was fuckin' daft when that youngster came to our house.

Look, some other clever bugger told him,"—glancing after Ellen—"about my stuff in the museum. *Duw*, mun, I'm nothin' when you consider those experts. Professors and doctors they are." Then abruptly, "So long, Rees, I'm away now. Don't mention down in the Caib about my little *cwtch*."

His *cwtch* was a patchwork of slag-stone walling, old tram-planks and mildewed timbers once carefully notched, hatcheted by men who were probably dead. Discarded pieces of corrugated sheeting made up the forward-sloping roof, the sheets camouflaged with turf and rubble. Housed into the hillside, Charlie's *cwtch* looked like a mountain fighter's derelict observation post. A damp, unhealthy den. All the materials came from Caib tip.

Ellen said, stating, "Isn't it ridiculous. He's uneducated, lived happy as a *mochyn* all his life, and now he spends his days searching for Stone Age relics. It's quite mad."

The sandwiches were all eaten and we'd finished off a flagon of home-brewed ginger pop. Lydia slept on a rug. The baby was beginning to lose her temper.

"Snobbish attitude, beaut," I said. "Old Charlie has found flint scrapers and arrow-heads up on the forestry roads. He's proving that Hunter and Fisher Folk travelled this far inland from the coast. What have we proved? Nothing. Nothing yesterday, nothing today, nothing tomorrow."

"You clever man," she said, winking affected admiration. The baby howled.

"Throw out thy marvellous left tit and feed the child," I said.

"Write it all down about Charlie Page,"—deliberately squirting a fine spray at my face, her rebuffing elbow swinging swiftly at my throat: "Stop it, that's enough, Reesy!"

We dozed in the sunshine, Elizabeth sprawled replete, wailing lapwings and bleating sheep on the other side of Daren river, rough pastureland and peat bogs rolling away to the horizon. Between waking and sleeping I felt like a dwarf waiting to become gargantuan. Then came a vivid, sliding dream of pre-industrial Daren, two five-mile-apart feudal mansions, clusters of white-washed cottages, wolves prowling Daren woods (wolves were extinct, but dreams dislocate chronology), hump-backed salmon running the river aggressive as dingo dogs, packhorse trains and cattle drovers travelling down the parish road, feuds and fraternizing between the serfs of Daren and Brynywawr, pitchforks and arson, true hurt-love and hate-rape. A bastard-sourced dream, remnants of oral heritage and mish-mashed education. Then the dream dissolved, intensified again: a white-maned, nanny-goat-bearded patriach stood alone on the green tump above our house. Some Iberian chieftain, Celtic gauleiter, Brythonic jugular slitter, Romanized arse-hole scraper, court favourite, poet ... John Vaughan chanting in Cymraeg! He shrank visibly, collapsing to one knee, pleading, stiffening into the death mask he wore when borne neck deep in slurry out through the back door of 9 Thelma Street.

"Rees," she said, "wake up; you're grunting!"

I dunked my head in the cold river water, wriggling nymphs instantly cutting out, lying doggo, speckle-disguised, or slithering under pebbles. Hunkered over the pool, I watched a pair of magpies plummet down the new tip, then swoop off laterally like wire-operated pantomime artifacts, landing on Charlie Page's hide-out. Ellen blew a piercing whistle, two fingers vee-ed in her mouth, but we were too far away from the birds. They planed down off the roof, squawking conversationally.

"Where did you learn that trick?" I said.

"Winchester. A boy named Jack Fleming. He used to kiss me after school."

"Anything else?"

"Tickled, once. Feeling better now, matey?"

"Jack Fleming? What else could he do besides whistle?"

She screeched viraginous, "Fancy you! Jealous! Rees *gwenwynllyd! Dere 'ma, ŵr bach.*"

"I don't know so much about your private life, Ellen," I said.

She lay outstretched with the baby draped across her belly.

Lydia amused herself beneath the pram. Fine kiddies, I thought. Perfectly normal. No trouble whatsoever. I'm, we, Ellen and I, we're lucky. Twelve tons on the chains tomorrow, but we're blooming. Ours is a great marriage. Sound as the rock of ages.

"Selina Cynon teaching you Welsh?" I said. "Next thing you'll be joining *Plaid Cymru*. What's your ticket, Mrs Stevens, a poop-stirring bureaucracy in Cardiff like the one in Whitehall?"

Ellen stroked up and down the baby's back. "This *is* Wales. It's Welsh coal. If you had any pride you'd speak Welsh. I'm going to vote for the National Party next election."

I said, "Can you prove it's superior to be born Welsh than, say, Spanish, or Greek, or Hindu? Where's the goodness in being Welsh? Have we got double navels or bigger brains? Wouldn't you like to be a Russian for a couple of years? Or an oriental Jewess? Think how nice it would be if the American Kennedys had a negress great-granny."

"Shut your mouth. Stop ranting at me," she said.

"You lush Irish mongrel," I said, dripping over her. "Put Lizzie in the pram, my beauty."

"We can't, darling, not here. Somebody might see us."

"Who? They're in the clubs or sleeping or watching the Sunday film on telly."

"Love me, Rees?"—fatalism darkened her eyes again, dark, dark eyes to make a saint feel caged in flux.

"Of course I love you."

"You never say it unless you want something."

"For Jesus' sake, we're real mates!" I said.

"I love you, too, matey,"—tremulously fervent like a young girl, lifting up the baby, comforting her in the pram, murmuring, "There-there, Lizzie fach, we mustn't keep your father waiting."

But our Lydia-child clambered over us.

"Soppy knicks! Never mind, *cariad*, never mind, accident, accident!" sang Ellen, patiently soothing as if the living universe bobbled placidly in a safe ocean of toddler's piddle.

After tea I went into the back room with John Vaughan's Account. The window overlooks a low mortar-crumbled wall between ours and the house next door. We each have a few square yards of unglazed cobbles and lavatories squatting back to back, with a crack in the door of ours through which you can see Melyn brook. Way down the street, above sixteen crumbling parting walls, stands Ike Pomeroy's nine-roomed house, built for Caib colliery managers in 1928, while Number One Lodge members were docked tuppences every Friday to pay for the institute. Ike Pomeroy succeeded Andrew Booth. Tall, slender Ike, thinly moustached, fast-witted, humourless, efficient, executing NCB directives perfect as a bladder blown by the wind. It was impossible to fault him. He delegated authority according to the book, Ike himself happily governed by mining economics like a truant officer is ruled by the miching boys who justify his job. Ike Pomeroy neutralized Self. His rather bow-legged schoolmistress wife somehow dropped into Upper Daren secondary modern school—a traditional backstage tactic, the local educational authority offering salaam sahib to the NCB area manager. A dozen Daren-born teachers are on the waiting list to come home from the black, tan and off-white zones of London and Birmingham. Consequently, what I'm saying is you have to know someone on Daren Borough Council to get a decent berth under the local authority. Hoary Wales, aye, learned in guile. Dry-runs are alien to our body politique.

We couldn't imagine it then, summer of 1961, Ike Pomeroy coming to effect the last coal raised from Caib Four Feet seam. Prompt into action, slender Ike obediently organized a new pit-bottom junction, the main conveyor belt feeding two 200-ton concrete bunkers, the system working precise as a Smith's watch until the Germans knocked through to Brynywawr. And afterwards no more coal from the Four Feet came up Caib pit-shaft. Only men and supplies went down. Utilitarian Ike, necessary as a lavatory chain between sterile hygiene and fertile corruption.

Ike, I thought, his bow-legged wife mowing the lawn in a

halter-neck polka-dotted summer frock, if Twmws Ivor Cynon was alive he'd curse you black. You pox-true functionary.

Ellen called, "Rees, what are you doing in there!"

"Your old man's Account, I'm back on it!"

She said, "Huh."

Aye, I thought, Shon crap-gatherer Vaughan, cont:

There is no replacing a man like Twmws Cynon. Pray God his name will stand for as long as coal is lifted from the cruel bowels of this earth of ours. One hundred & ninety workmates sang the wonderful O FRYNIA CAERSALEM over his grave, little suspecting eight hundred of us would be singing it for the seven men burnt to death in Caib before the leaves fell off the trees in 1930, smoke pouring down Caib tip coming from Waun Level the old airway return. As I say it made people wonder about Christianity despite sermons to make your hair stand up on end. Sermons, what a famous time for sermons. The hwyl came every Sunday night from Baptists, Methodists, Wesleyans & Pentecostals singing & shouting & nobody about anywhere on the streets till the chapels emptied. Card schools in the dingles & in Daren woods of course, playing Nap & Brag with a lookout for any policeman. Police had nothing better to do. Men such as Seymour Lloyd making names for themselves. Devil's cards. What a mockery. All gone now. Two wholesale wars saw to that, killed off religion better than any spear in His holy side. Often I wished to possess religious faith. Frankly it never came. Any kind of faith I used to beg for in later years without success, so it must be the way I was made in the first instance. From strict Catholic to easy-come-easy-go Pentecostal after we moved into Thelma Street, that was Kate's progress until eventually her true nature found outlet as it was bound to, starting when I broke my

93

instep bones up in the Tylwth Teg district where the explosion look place. She said she wanted to visit her relations in Ireland. Being her husband I naturally contended, "Let me start back in work first to save some money." She said, "Sell our Pearl Insurance Premiums to Dicko Harding." "Not those please, Kate," I said. As if that would stop her. Ireland? She never did go to Ireland, it was Queen Street, Portsmouth, leaving me grass widower for two years. Two years torture with no one in the world to turn to excepting Charlotte Cynon for a cooked dinner on my way home from Caib pit. No fire warming the house & how can a man wash his own back in a wooden tub? Dicko Harding made fifty pounds clear profit on those Premiums which were intended as savings for our old age. A man without genuine conscience for all his charity & tangerine oranges for children on New Year's Eve & various backhanders to the parish council. Money his god that Dicko Harding. Money, money. If there is a heaven he belongs to that parable about the camel passing through the eye of a needle. When elected treasurer of Caib institute my proposal was to stop Dicko Harding from entering the building unless he paid non-affiliate contributions as certain shopkeepers were obliged to if they wished to enjoy our facilities. Instead they made him vice-president of Daren Bowls Club & therefore he bought membership in a roundabout way although Lodge Number One & a Welfare grant actually kept the rink going. Bowls did not appeal to me in the slightest. Things such as games take up time that deserves to be better occupied. Our main concern was to get organized to counteract low wages & bad conditions. The basic evils. We provided billiards, bowls, football equipment, dominoes & draughts in the library with Llew Hopkins institute caretaker, us committee-men taking

94

turns in the library itself until Dai Stevens left school. But he was too wild in many ways. Pity he was killed however as he had a good head on him as regards selecting books. Matter of fact he put his own Left Book Club books on our shelves to make members realize we were being robbed right, left & centre by the coal-owners, Joseph Gibby & Sons included. To think young Dai was still under 21, but he knew the rough road we were on. He knew. The committee wanted to send him to Ruskin Labour College only he preferred courting. Dai preferred galivanting over to Brynywawr every whipstich, always missing from the Library, Llew Hopkins threatening to hand his notice in unless one of us took charge of the books. Only stamp the date and watch out for SILENCE he had to, nothing more. Ned Tremain was appointed librarian eventually, doing his best of course but badly handicapped by nystagmus. Those safety oil-lamps gave Ned nystagmus & cruel blinding headaches to the extent he did not know where to put himself. He signed on the panel permanent just before Kate came home to Daren. We were together in Doctor Stanton's surgery when she marched in as if it was merely a case of jaunting back from Lower Daren. 'The key,' she said. 'How do you expect me to get in the house?' God in heaven I must have drunk hundreds of bottles of medicine for my bronchitis & chest complaints. Actually it was myself that had the first X Ray when we bought the machine for Daren Cottage Hospital & Doctor Claude Stanton said, "Clear as a bell, John. Climb Waunwen every Sunday, fill you lungs with fresh air." To my mind it is not so much conditions as worry, worry. Fuming & fretting damages human health. My chest felt better disregarding hard times to come until 1940. The beauty of it was Kate seemed to settle down again which is *what a wage slave wants most when he is doing his level best to provide food, shelter & clothing for his dependants. But she interfered concerning my responsibilities as treasurer. There was no persuading Kate in the light of reasonable argument, craving for more whist drives in the institute for instance. Always whist, her & one of the Miskin girls off night after night. Luckily for safe keeping I placed my treasurer's account books with Charlotte Cynon. You could trust your life's blood with Charlotte. I have seen her facing up to trials guaranteed to burn human feelings to a coke. For example lodgers. Lodgers on the dole during slack time & never a bad word spoken against her. Lodgers coming home drunk while she was rearing Hayden Percival & the girl Martha. Also anti-aircraft soldiers when they brought two pom-pom guns to protect Caib in 1941, one of these soldier lodgers trying to take advantage of young Martha, a ginger headed scally-wag from Newcastle who got exactly and precisely what he deserved in the end, him & Chris Jones standing toe to toe behind the institute boiler house for ninety-seven minutes on a Sunday morning. Everything arranged to legal rules. But still there it was, young Chris could beat any man in Daren before the overhead rope caught him in Caib. It had to be Cefn Coed Asylum for his own self protection after that. His sense of responsibility went scattered beyond control. Chrisy's father & mother decided to live in Sketty to be near him. To all intents & purposes they were deprived of their only son. Chris lost control as many men do for lesser reasons. To my mind a true account of coal-mining is impossible to relate without foul language & red raging temper coming in their proper places. Same applies to cowboys I should imagine although never an eff appears in all the western books that I have read to kill boredom. Romance. It must be all romance. When you see a man out of his wits so that he does not care what he says, weeping & cursing as many, many times I have witnessed colliers, firemen, labourers, conveyor shifters & on one occasion a haulier praying to his horse when the horse failed coming up the deep from Number 3 district, praying on his bended knees until madness overpowered him & he punched the horse down with his bare fists. I am referring to Billo Cassam. Where is Billo now? Six feet under as a consequence of double rupture. Billo Cassam from Saerbren Street. Savage behaviour. Spain has got nothing on coalmining. With regard to poverty as shown in adverts begging for charity, we have seen pot bellied kiddies in Daren without shoes to wear on their feet & it is no use saying the past is dead, let bygones be bygones. Not when you consider how a sincere man like Ramsey Macdonald stabbed Labour in the back. They have all done their share of stabbing the working class quite apart from victimization by employers. Prime outstanding example re miners: Arthur Horner. Some of the finest Federation fighters left Daren forever after being victimized. Men beyond blame. They had to earn a living. The minutes of Caib Lodge and Brynywawr Lodge would make modern trade union shop stewards believe we were fighting a lost CAUSE. Untrue. There are no lost causes only different ones.*

Lydia came into the back room for her good-night kiss, Ellen following her. "Listen to this," I said. "There are no lost causes only different ones."

Ellen remarked, "He learned the hard way—say *nos da* to daddy, *cariad*."

"*Nos da*"—Lydia piping obediently, and my heart crowded

pure sensation, a leaping crackle of the blood, seeing wild, sandy-haired Dai Stevens in Lydia, and myself triangulating both, her pappy lips innocent as Horlick's flavoured petals.

"There, *dere nawr*," Ellen said. My wife Ellen, Mrs Selina Cynon's willing pupil for every *Shwmae* and familiarizing idiom that binds tight the work-, bread-, bed- and pavement-bonded people of this bloody Wales of ours.

9

Private contractors dismantled the flocculation plant, stripped the interior machinery, the empty building echoing rat squeaks, downpouring rain and the melancholic sibilance of draughts whistling in through broken windows. The long, empty stables, stenched pulse of the Caib before my time, echoed loose sheets creaking and flapping on the roof. Hundreds of red-rusted horseshoes, bent nails still clenching ragged strips and shrunken fragments of chitin hung over man-high rails along the mildewed, whitewashed flaked walls, and dozens of red-rusted "shafts" and "guns" lay bogged in weeds and rushes behind the stables like the shucks of armoured reptiles. Not a house door in Daren carries a *lucky* horseshoe. That trustful rustic past is destroyed, forgotten, buried.

Caib colliery dam was blown down and back-filled with muck from the Seven Feet, and when the neglected smoke stack collapsed one gale-storm September night it obliterated a stray sheep-killer dog almost over the spot where they shot the black runaway bull in 1924. Again pilferers scrounged the soot-grimed ochre bricks to build garden walls, lean-to scullery extensions, garages. The colliery watchman (ex-professional wrestler, exile recently come home to a cushy number on the strength of his reputation) made deals in Daren Social and Welfare Club, even borrowing a Coal Board lorry to make deliveries. History rebounds on the NCB. Looting from collieries carries the hallmark of principle, privilege of the underprivileged. Exploitation by faceless coal-owners matched by equally faceless, certainly depersonalized, NCB top-dogs making decisions affecting rent, food and pleasure. Ultimately, historically sanctioned to boot, the Board executives will brainwash, maim, harass and kill more colliery workers than all the private coal-owners combined. The times deliver men indifferently as tides leave wrack, jetsam and trove, debouching a Kosygin there, a George and Harold here, a Sukarno elsewhere, and always wherever needed, or even wastefully, *people*, men like my father, John Vaughan, the Miskins and Howards, Fred Fransceska, the Tremains and Pages, Llew Hopkins, men like 'Caib' Cynon, whose grave has disappeared from the cemetery—Daren's ten 6 in 1 gradient hillside acres brought from Joseph Gibby's father (his ownership not to be investigated) for £17 an acre, the business arranged and settled fifty years before Mike Minty tramped over Waunwen parish road with a pocketful of golden sovereigns. Seventy-nine redeployed day wage-men and surface workers travelled twenty-eight miles a shift to long-life pits outside Daren. Caib old tip was ringed around the carved, flattened base with sapling silver birch trees, the new tip finally abandoned in June 1964, when all the waste muck went out through Brynywawr Drift, trammed from there conveniently downhill to marshland, where merely frogs, newts, beetles, sticklebacks and winter feed for infrequent flights of mallard were destroyed.

Now we worked the Seven Feet seam, Caib colliers adjusting themselves to Meco cutter loaders roaring, snarling, whining up and down the faces. A new agreement gave us three shillings a day dust allowance and goggles to wear in the face. We lost the three shillings a shift after they rigged water sprays on the Meco loaders, but the dust still rained: *... particles of less than 5 microns (1 micron= 1/1000 of a millimetre) have the greater pathological significance. The relative pathological significance of various dust components is not fully established, but it is known that particles of free silica have an important influence on the causation of fibrosis of the lungs.*

Aye, sure. Black-mouthry, for the use of. Aye indeed.

Science coming in, craft and brute strength petering out.

Better fitted to adjustment than most, Ike Pomeroy flourished under the new regime, swanning along the new roadway in a mine-car like a bogus emperor to his office on Brynywawr pit-head.

Conscientious Ike, assiduous at all times, innocuously macabre, the writing gradually appearing on the wall: the Seven Feet was losing money. Absenteeism, accused the Coal Board—gob you, jack, you're not grafting in the face, half-thought the men without saying it outright, their wives and daughters travelling besides, forty, fifty, sixty miles a day for easier money than working in coal dust that smothered your cap lamp every half-hour. Caib belonged to Brynywawr

101

and we were in the red. We had to produce more coal to pay for the new machinery and pit-head development on Brynywawr. Pay for the losses in Caib, too, and the only currency is coal.

The German firm's men lived in caravans behind the concrete and glass administration block on Brynywawr, thirty-seven identical caravans plugged in to the colliery generator. They were driving another roadway, opening up the Seven Feet for development: press-button mining by 1967. By 1967 the furnacite plant would be ready, processed coal avalanching on the market. All we had to do was make the pit pay until the machines took over. We were notified accordingly, copy-signed handbills quoting out-put required per man-shift stapled to every employee's wage packet.

"Propaganda, it's like Russia," Ellen said. "If the worst comes to the worst, I'll get a job in the television factory. You can look after the nippers," — a snigger of ridicule metaphorically offering kiss my behind to the future, sufficient unto the day is the evil. Perhaps she was a better, truer miner's wife than myself a miner.

"If they close Brynywawr we'll have to move from Daren," I said.

"Why should they, after spending millions on this advanced mining scheme?"

"They closed the Four Feet seam, brand-new bunkers at pit-bottom scarcely used. Practically new washery, screens, flocculation plant. We don't know how these people think," I said. "Young colliers on the coal faces, we're losing confidence in the industry."

"People never know what other people think," Ellen said.

"Clues then," I said. "Clues for the men who are doing the graft."

She said, "Planners can't be doers. You'll have to wait until you're told."

More centralized plan-thinking closed Daren railway tunnel; we were cut off, *Western Welsh* buses slashed to run every two hours from Harding's Square, and Caib N.U.M. lodge muffled because we were now amalgamated with Brynywawr lodge under a different regional area. A deputation from Lower Daren radio and television factory met our M.P. in the Commons. He piped up in the House, was duly recorded in Hansard and committed to limbo.

"Let's buy a second-hand car," Ellen said—second-hand from necessity, as we were paying for the old Coal Board house where my grandparents lived and died.

I said, "What for? We don't bloody well go anywhere."

"All right, mate, all right, we won't buy a car. You're working too hard. Take a shift off tomorrow."

"It's faster work," I said. "Three cuts a shift and you can't see straight for the racket. Know old Lewsin Whistler? They brought him out yesterday, lump of coal broke his ankle. Lewsin's gone past it for face work; he should be on a button job out on the gate road. Five of us, Ellen, and it's all we can do to keep ahead of the machine, just fixing up props and bars. Ah Christ, it's getting crazier every week. Minutes, love, seconds, minutes, they panic over minutes like prima donnas. Minutes, lost minutes. Spending millions of pounds and panicking over minutes. If my father was alive he wouldn't have time to leave the face for a piss let alone the other thing."

103

"I don't mind, Rees. It's better to talk about it." She said.

"Bloody *Coal News*, the daft, glamorizing bastards. Anyone who writes for *Coal News* deserves a pill of powder rammed down his gullet. They must think we're stupid—maybe we are, most of us. It's like cheering on a football team for these propaganda merchants. Sporty, see? All muck in together, boys, heads down, arses up and out with the coal. Never mind a fuck about my grandfather, my old man, all the compo cases standing like ghosts on the street corners. Space age, by the loving Christ. When we're not heroes we're out-and-out wasters. Carrion-headed bastards blah-blahing about absenteeism in the newspapers, they can only see miners in terms of black and white. I'd like to watch those Fleet Street tigers, watch 'em in action with a twenty-four-pound puncher, that's all, simply breaking up big stuff to keep the chains moving. Five shifts a week, fifty weeks a year, on the puncher and dust coming back so thick you can feel it clogging in your teeth. We're all wearing goggles in Brynywawr Seven Feet. Some of our blokes are attending the outpatients for eye treatment. Rash around the eyes. Sweat rash. Aye. The bloody ventilation blows through like the wrong end of a Hoover; if it didn't, the fucking pit would go up like a volcano. And our union, it's gone to pieces since we've been under the Brynywawr area. Old Watt Howard packed in altogether when Number One finished. Lodge sec. for ten years; now he's labouring on the council house estate. He threw away about three hundred quid redundancy pay. Why, Ellen? Because there's no guts left in the men to fight. Jesus Christ, they're working all kinds of shifts over in Brynywawr. Men who don't know the meaning of trade unionism, silly-born bastards they are. They come up top pit after a shift, they bath, eat a dinner in the canteen, load their tommy boxes and go straight back down for another shift. They're sleeping over their meals in the canteen. If my grandfather saw this carry-on, he'd spit blood. Honest to God, there's no principle left."

Ellen laid Elizabeth in her cot. "Reesy, you mustn't feel sorry for yourself," she said.

"I'm not! Take it easy, girl! All I'm doing is counting the odds."

She said, "I saw Eddie 'Lectric in the post office the other morning. He hasn't worked since he lost his eye. Tal Harding slipped him five checks for Daren Social Club. Why don't we go to the Social Club on Saturday nights? Charlie Page and his wife are there almost every night of the week."

"Charlie in the telly room and his wife playing bingo. You want to play bingo, Ellen?"

"We could go to a dance. You haven't taken me dancing since Lizzie was born. Selina will sit in for us."

"Old English or Pop?" I said.

"Pop! C'mon, brute," —lolloping into action before our transistor radio heated in to the BBC's 'Newly Pressed'.

"*Duw-Duw*, you're pretty good," I said. "Sweet jungle hips, you haven't lost your lovely rhythm."

"On your feet," she said, "or I'll lash out with the well-known Ellen Stevens's karate where it hurts."

"Irish Ellen. How're we doing, beaut?"

"Nicely, boy."

"Psychological gravy, my love. Long time no gravy. Hey, what's that for?"

Airy-fairy as that Dame Fonteyn, she choreographed another moth-fluttery slap to my face. "Stop fantasying, Rees. You'll spoil us."

105

"Right... comfort me with dumplings and carved sweetbreads, luncheon meat and lemon meringue pudd, trotters and mulled wine, sperm-whale cutlets and whipped cream. How we doin', gel?"

"Very nicely," — by now indifferent, gone on her own, dancing lost, lost without hope, negligent.

"Love me?" I said. "I know I'm awkward sometimes."

"You don't knock me around, Rees, only that one time."

"I was drunk though, beaut."

"Forget about it, matey."

"*You* haven't forgotten."

She said, "I suppose people can't love without hating."

"That's it, Ellen."

She laughed, dancing, laughed carelessly, unwinding to ecstasy, a wonderful total howl gurgling downwards, bending her over. "Reesy, Reesy, you stupid guilty fool! Guilty as sin. Look at you! Oh God, oh Jesus bless us, if we can't *talk* about your parents they'll never die, don't you see?"

"But I was drunk, Ellen."

"That's the best time! I haven't been drunk since Selina Cynon fed me gas and air on Elizabeth. My grandfather was a drunken navvy, my mother chased her fancy, my father..." She pealed joy, pagan, ringing: "But I feel perfect! I feel perfect. I'm your wife. *Iesu mawr*, isn't that enough?"

"We'll burn up the town next week-end," I said.

"And start another baby before Lizzie's off the breast! Steady, matey, take it steady, hm!"

Someone next door jammed on the volume of their television, a neutered trio effetely ragtiming Heinz 57 varieties, and the baby whimpered awake. We cuddled over her cot. "There, there, *cariad*," Ellen whispered.

I said, "Ask Mrs Cynon to sit in for us tomorrow night."

"Are you taking a shift off?"

"We can't afford it, Ellen."

"Honestly, boy, some mornings you come downstairs dragging your feet like an old man."

"I'm all right, beaut. Faster work in the face, but I'll get used to it."

"Please stay home tomorrow, Rees. It's Friday, the last shift."

"We can't afford..."

"Afford!" She picked up the baby. "Reesy, do you think I enjoy seeing you become a work-horse? Night after night, too tired to lift your head off the pillow."

"Not too tired, Ellen."

"I don't mean what you're hinting at. We live for the weekends," she said.

"Since when, for Christ's sake?"

"All the time, matey. Here, hold this one. Lydia's very quiet out in the backyard; she might be wandering off."

"I can't afford to lose work," I said. "We're paying for the house, the furniture, the telly, every-bloody-thing's on tick!"

"What about me?" she snapped, leaving her lips spread, teeth showing.

I said, "Ellen, love, don't ask me to jib."

Stepping out of the cage, I joined the queue behind the mine-car barrier, Jesse Morgans in command like a neurotic sergeant-major. Jesse hated his job, resented bullying youngsters who made a carnival act of riding in on the mine-cars. Purring along at twelve miles an hour, Jesse's brother Islwyn told us about Lewsin Whistler in hospital. He

107

demanded a jam-jar; his wife took one in for him. Where else could he spit 'bacco juice?

"Dirty old habit on the man," — this censorial grunt from Seward Tremain — cousin to nystagmatic Ned Tremain, long since dead from cerebral meningitis. Seward was lay preacher in a Baptist shanty chapel scheduled for demolition under a road-widening project behind Daren Council offices.

"I bet you've got a few dirty habits," Islwyn said.

"None at all against the ten commandments, lslwyn *bach*."

"Don't you fuckin' *bach* me, Seward. I was filling coal when you was still on the pot," lslwyn said.

Seward sat hunched, implacable over his cap lamp dangling from its flex between his knees. "Foul language won't get you anywhere, butty, except in trouble on the judgement day. "

"Up your *twti* pipe" — Islwyn drawling like a tele-screen ponce.

Dicko Harding shouted, "Ah-one, ah-two, ah-three! *Mine eyes have seen the glory of the coming of the Lord; He is trampling out the vintage where the grapes of wrath are stored; He hath loosed the fateful lightning of His terrible swift sword. His truth is marching on,*"

"*Glory, glory hallelujah,*" sang Islwyn, young Dicko standing crouched, beating the time, a dozen tribal throats bawling, "*Glory, glory what a helluva way to go, Glory, glory what a helluva way to go*" — *John Brown's body* shanghaid to close the chorus: "*And his soul goes marching on!*" with Seward Tremain's sluggish basso hooting like pentecost descended upon spiritual stasis. Alone then, faithful Seward continued: "*He hath sounded forth the trumpet that shall never call retreat,"* but Dicko Harding (old tight-fist Dicko's illegitimate grand-nephew) began and broke off *When the roll is called up yonder* for lack of support, our entirely sanguine travelling mood ending on friendly insults and bickering as we dismounted at the gate road.

Islwyn flashed his cap lamp. "Hey, men, look at this. You'd never see the likes over in the old Caib Four Feet."

It was a set of repairer's tools locked on a toolbar, the shovel blade chalked with capital letters: KEEP YOUR HANDS OFF THESE, YOU BASTARD.

Borrowing chalk off Seward Tremain, Dicko spelt out: SMILE WHEN YOU SAY THAT, STRANGER.

Islwyn said, "By the Jesus, there's been big changes since I started working underground as a boy."

"More to come," Seward Tremain said. "More to come for sure."

We stripped off in the gate road before going up into the face. It was quiet, the Meco cutter loader in the stable at the end of the run, two men changing the picks. The ventilation blew steady as Atlantic wind, wisping curls of dust right up the length of the face. The night-shift fireman came down under the white prop line chalked on the roof. "Boys, be careful about fifty yards up the face," he said cordially. "There's a break running on to the coal from where we crashed the gob last night. Shove a couple of flats across it. Righto, lads, straight face, ah! Don't hold up the Meco when she's ready to come down. What's the weather like up top this morning?"

I said, "Friday weather over in Daren. Christ knows what it's like this side of the mountain. Some of your Brynywawr blokes don't know the days of the week; they'd live underground if the NCB brought down a few old bags and a fish and chips shop at pit-bottom."

"Rees," he said, "you're making good money on this Meco team. *Iesu*, when I was a kid we'd be holing over the stank all day to fill two trams."

"Aye, we've heard all about hand-cut coal," I said. "Do you see any old colliers working on the coal these days? The poor buggers can't take it. Another few years and you'll be downgraded; they'll put you in charge of whitewashing manholes or some bloody thing."

"Mechanization," he said. "You can't expect old men to operate these modern machines."

"Is there a war on?" I said. "Shove us youngsters up in the front line, is that the idea? You and the bastards who invented Meco loaders, you'll kill us off yet."

He couldn't understand, and I don't blame him.

"Rees, what the fuckin' hell's the matter with you? Anyhow, I got no time to fuckin' argue. My shift's finished. Do your best."

We were driving the gate-road stable on, cutting in, shovelling the coal back, posting and flatting the roof ready for the Meco after she made her first cut down the 180-yard face. When she started roaring Dicko Harding and Reg Page (one of Charlie Page's four Brynywawr brothers) went up to the break. Dicko soon came back to the gate-road stable.

"Give us a hand, Rees," he said. "Dowty post out of line, tight against the bloody coal. We'll have to double up on the back row, shove a few more bars on before we can extract. Won't be safe otherwise."

"He kept his mouth shut about that Dowty," I said.

The oldest man in our team raised his goggles to his forehead and landed another of his morning phlegms on the conveyor chains. "Officials, I've shit better," he said.

Star-bright far away up the face, cap lamps were shining and we could hear the Meco above the racket of the chains.

"First things first," I suggested. "We'll have to make it safe. They'll be down here ready to turn the machine by half-past nine, fresh picks an' all."

We went up to the break in the roof, our forty-nine-year-old stable-man collier steadily effing the night-shift fireman. The Dowty post was inside the conveyor, eighteen inches from the coal. Rushing the job, we doubled up on the last line of posts, sending steel flats across the roof break and free-end bars forward to the coal.

"Ent safe yet," said the old bloke, "not if you was to ask me."

We were squatting like aborigines stuck in ritual, the Meco growling fifty yeards away up the face.

"What else can we do?" asked Dicko.

I said, "We'll tell the fireman. The Meco boys can stand clear and let the machine plough through. Any muck that comes down she'll load it on the chains. Shouldn't be too much."

"Me, I'll be down in the gate-road stable," said the old bloke.

So the Meco came through the bad spot, all clean coal swimming along the conveyor and while they were turning the machine in the lower stable we fixed a new line of Dowtys and bars up the face.

"That ent bloody safe at all," warned the old bloke.

It wasn't either. The fall came before the second cut

reached the break in the roof, soft coal mostly, trapping the electrician for a couple of minutes, but we dragged him clear. He had bruises on his left thigh, that's all. Shock, too. His jaw shivered and he couldn't talk much.

It wasn't a big fall, but the Meco cable and water pipe were under it. Careful work, mole scrabbling. We threw the muck back over the chains. The overman came, him and our old bloke chatting mining principles polite as two Q.C.s in chambers. Once we had the conveyor running again the electrician rode out to the gate road and went home. Cup of tea and a fag, that's what he wanted, just like any temporarily beaten infantry man. We were down ninety minutes on cutting, so the overman stayed in the face, him and the fireman helping out with the Meco loader. No doubt for morale as much as anything. They weren't like us, on tonnage.

We were posting the top-end stable when the big fall came, *behind* the Meco. Nobody there to cop it, thank God. The chains stopped running.

"There now, like I said," pointed out the old bloke, old merely because at forty-nine he was the eldest.

"Right, men, let's have you," the overman said. "I want this face ready for cutting by the time the afternoon shift comes in."

At two o'clock I changed places with Reg Page, working the coal inside the fall, soft coal, mashed soft, like a bag. We spragged as we cut in, but not enough. Not enough sprags. Neither was it the coal that did the damage. I rolled, elbowing inside the fallen coal—soft coal—rolled over on to my back for another squirm to get away, safe, clear, with nothing worse than shaken breath. Like the electrician. So when the stone came down off the inner lip of broken ground, I was flat on my back.

Thank the Jesus Christ for morphia.

Up in the ambulance centre I saw Ellen surrounded by black fog, standing naked, smiling, the blackness blotting over her silent as the shape of a scream.

10

Daren Cottage Hospital overlooks the park where it skimps out to a clay lane. Directly below the park, Upper Daren secondary modern school, built on two levels in 1913, stone Gothic arches carrying the second storey. The playground was asphalted in 1949. Stretched mummy-flat on boards, I used to listen to the eleven and three-o'clock playtimes: yells, squeals, skipping chants and twin sounds of a football booted and smacking against the playground wall. Late October kept the park quiet. It was merely a patch of grass, some copper beeches, one raggle-taggle flower-bed, and the clay lane a dumping-site for builders' rubble. Rough nights the leaves rattled in a row of orange-blossom trees riding parallel with the ward windows.

My bladder and bowels were fibrous, layered dormant as winter moss.

Ellen said, "Reesy, have patience; it isn't for always," — coming with her pale face and burdened eyes every evening.

Books, cigarettes and Ellen's terrifying stoicism. Mrs Cynon would dangle Lydia and Elizabeth over the bed. They all visited in turn, young Dicko witlessly bringing sexy magazines, pulch girls throwing it at you on every page, and Reg Page came from Brynywawr, our old bloke, too, and Fred Fransceska brought Welsh cakes baked by Morfed. Charlie Page gave me a small tin of toffees, presenting his gift like a courtier. "Put the tin by for me, Rees. It will come in handy, see?" Percy Cynon came twice a week, unpleasantly morbid, inarticulate, aligning his crippling to mine. At Christmas, Tal Harding loaned Ellen fifty pounds to clear debts and affirm the Christmas spirit without feeling Scrooge-minded about spending money. When Tal sat beside the bed we had little to say to each other. "If you're short of anything, Rees, let me know." He only meant money.

"I'm short of balls at the moment. They're gone dead," I said.

He smirked respectfully, fatly boyish.

"Tal, you're looking at the thirty-eighth case of busted pelvis since the Number One lodge paid for this hospital. I'm useless right across the groins."

"Give the bones chance to mend, Rees."

I said, "Time will tell, aye, sure."

"Can I bring you anything?"

"I've got to wait for what I want, Tal."

They brought Yuletide into the ward, struggled it in beyond earshot of a youngster dying from peritonitis in a bed hidden behind screens. He died between the turkey dinner and tea-time, screeching like an hysterical schoolgirl, cursing words he'd learned secretively, his elderly mother hooped like a rag doll, alone on a chair outside the screens.

115

Next day the boy's father shook hands with every man in the ward. Guilt. He wanted to share out his guilt.

True to Daren, heavy snow disrupted everything for a few days in January. The road up to the hospital was impassable. At the bitter end of the month an ambulance brought in a ninety-three-year-old skeleton-man. He'd spent ten years in some old folk's hospital. They laid him in a bed opposite mine and overnight he curled up under the sheets, dying without a whimper.

I wanted to go home. I could use the lavatory, but there was scant control in the business. No vibrations either. Just nullity.

"Of course you will," Ellen said. "I know how you feel, Reesy."

"You don't," I said

In February I stood outside my own front door, looking at the siding below Caib screens. Five men like black imps were dismantling the lattice girder-work of the pylons carrying the aerial ropeway. Two small rivulets were frozen white in the unnaturally fresh-tinted, huge shallow scooped hollow where Caib old tip once lifted its black pyramids up the breast of Waunwen. "No more muck-buckets," I said. "The new tip will be green in about seventy years."

Ellen called, "What?" coming out from the kitchen. "Matey, you'll perish. I'll bring your overcoat."

"It's quieter these days," I said. "Screens idle, washery idle, only a few trucks fetching up pit supplies."

She rode my left arm around her shoulders, snuggling in close and I winced at the warmth of her, warm as prayer made physical. "Cleaner as well, Rees. Did you mention seventy years? In seventy years time Caib tip-slide will be forgotten. Those silver birch trees will mark the edge of the forestry. They're going to plant trees right around Daren. My father says there were trees here before, long before he was born. They were cut down during the First World War, and much earlier, the time of the Corn Laws. France and Britain were at war, remember? See across there, the hillside above Daren woods—that was cultivated long, long ago. On sunny evenings you can see the shadows of the plough marks. Tal showed me how to look for them, from this side, off the mountain road when the sun is setting."

I felt colder than the day.

"Have you seen them, Ellen?"

She hooked my weight over her shoulders. "Hm?"

"Those bloody plough ridges?"

"Darling, I'm not interested. It's in the Account. We were talking about my father one morning in the post office. Tal said his great-grandfather kept a shebeen where they brewed beer illegally for the navvies who were building the railway."

"I'm cold," I said.

"And jealous! Oh, marvellous, marvellous, you stupid man!"

"I can't help it, Ellen. Not now, not the way I feel."

"It will come back, *cariad*, eventually. The doctor told us it would come back. You've only been out of hospital a week."

"We can't be mates the way we used to be."

She said, "We must wait together. It will come back. Come indoors, Rees, please. I've lit a fire in the back room."

Through the back-room window, above sixteen mortar crumbling parting walls, I saw Ike Pomeroy's wife wrapped ball furry as a Lap woman, pacing to and fro across the lawn.

"She's pregnant at last," explained Ellen. "Lie here on the couch, Rees. I'll put a blanket over you."

"Thanks," I said, as if we were strangers hoping to become neighbours, and while the short February afternoon chilled to twilight, I slept, dreaming the reality of her return...

THEN, between the heyday and ultimate dissolution of Caib colliery, Ellen came.

From then to now, taking a double broken pelvis and spoiled husbandhood, taking these—pelvis and fulcrum—as warrant black enough to spell out Ichabod and triumph. Spell out in terms of ruffian jest and thankless document the social misery, fragmentation, the powerless jackalese of Daren decay.

11

Big Percy protesting false righteously, "Bloody hermit, worse
than old Charlie Page. It's time he pulled his finger out, tell
him from me! A man's got to, *got* to show willing. Fetch him
from in there, Ellen."

This I overheard, then her saying, "I'm sorry, Percy, he's
busy. If you'd care to wait — would you? Perhaps you'd like
to help me. I think it's one of our children's socks stuck in
the washing-machine. We'll have to turn it upside down.
Unscrew the bottom panel. Come here."

"What do I know about washing-machines, Ellen?" —
their voices blurring away into the kitchen.

At five o'clock I set out on my more or less habitual daily
mile: Daren library, across to Caib institute, through the
maroon-painted side gate, circle the bowling-green and Tal
Harding's bungalow (bought by one of the bank managers
for £3,800) and into the woods, free-footed, mindless, a
zigzag meander. Deliberate hermit, hair grey-lined at twenty-

seven, frail in the mind as a man handicapped from birth, uncontrollable pisser, loving Ellen like torment refined by the upsurge and dissipation of smaller hurts, nervous day-worn abrasions. Lobo Stevens on a fag-end death wish, superior to it by the same token.

The bank manager's wife said, "Nice afternoon, Mr Stevens. How are you keeping?"

She loomed peasant limbed, harmonious among shafts of budding gladioli, a stainless steel trowel held crucifix high to her over-ripe breasts.

Waste, I thought uncharitably, relishing the adjective. A bake-house woman like that wasted on a man burnt out in the oven.

I said, "Aren't your gladioli early, Mrs Thorpe?"

"Very early indeed! I took a risk with them, oh yes!" She giggled, jiggling the bright trowel. "Sometimes I love taking risks, experimenting with life. D'you know, Mr Thorpe promised me a row of cloches for that border against the fence. Promises, Mr Stevens, my husband is a king on his own regarding promises. So, I decided, pot on you, and look! My little sweetpeas survived the snowstorm we had in April."

Reading approval from obliquity, she said, "They're on strike again in the television factory. Disgusting, I think. As I was remarking to Mr Thorpe, those people should be slogging in the colliery. Every week accidents, terrible, terrible accidents sometimes, and we hear ignorant so and so's complaining about the price of coal. Dig it for themselves, that's what I say."

"Aye, right idea," I said, benignly confirming the inhumane.

"It's nice to see you getting better, Mr Stevens."

"Takes a bit of time," I said, wondering to myself, how connect with Mrs Thorpe? Socially connect. I couldn't let her know, even encourage her to experience *me*. Experience my splintered ego. For her sake I didn't want her anywhere close to my thinking. We were objects one to the other, incommutable as cabbage and fish. Wifely Mrs Thorpe, tolerably déclasséd by her husband's severe urbanity, the vulture-shouldered shape and aura of him, pared by commerce down to a grey-roaned core. She wasn't unhappy. Fringing on quaintness. Shockable as a rainbowed bubble, pink globous bum filling her blue frock, baby blue eyes comforting her engulfed mind. Connect, I thought, make it simple, easy. Appease. Surrender my broken I for thee. For thee, for thee fraternally—my tongue locked on anguish.

"Ellen and I enjoy a chat every Tuesday evening in the Women's Guild. Ever such a lovely person, your wife," said Mrs Thorpe. She dropped her trowel, forearmed her cleavage as she slowly bent over, plumply awkward as a man-shamed Venus, her wavy brown hair falling in two trim-edged sheafs from the whiteness of her centre parting.

I went on into the bursting woods, a flighting May-time cuckoo idiot—calling overhead. The trees heaved ceaseless sap, leaves, knots, chlorophyll alchemy, the ancient trees were vast pulsing islands breeding and feeding and bleeding a criss-crossed married myriad. Insects, birds, lice, viruses, fungi, mammals. Down below, hermit Stevens creaking along on his thickened girdle, doubling my more or less habitual distance, emerging out on the rolling hillside. I crawled upwards, feeling for the plough marks: they were there, inclining a bare inch in every yard of cropped turf.

Her father put this into his Account, but I was jealous of her, not John Vaughan the curdled old moaner. Green for jealousy. White for purity. White for leprosy, my helpless heatless piddler glassing the grass blades. "You're no good," I said, like warning a clip-winged hooded angel. "No good to me," — remembering Ellen's uncomplaining chime: "We'll wait together", and feeling our patient waiting transferring over to indifference. She always said, "It's probably psychological. We can wait." Her father perished psychologically before Caib tip-slide killed him. Perished estranged from womb, Kate Minty's miasmic vortex. Poor old moaner.

But, I thought, campaigning hopefully, it isn't, cannot wholly be this sexual business. When the fire douts you light another. Fire after fire, fire from fire, spark to spark flickering, flaring, fusing, arcing the living breath. Foundering death.

Beaten to hell, I thought. I'm beaten, almost, I'm almost beaten.

I sat tree-top high on the hillside, wracked as a glutted infant, two cuckoos crochet-braining the alien day, the blind sun carnal as a bedbug, bandit warblers drilling the greenery, thrushes greased on snail-meat carolling treadmill rape, carnivorous wrens wafer-boned from incest, rawed hover-flies shagging the atmosphere, south breezes fanning the young leaves like hire-purchased eunuchs, a blast-barked oak tree false as Moses, vulcanite dung beetles trundling sheep-shit, Mrs Thorpe tickling herself sick, singeing the gladioli spikes, larks exploding skywards like crystallized shards of Frankensteinian afterbirth, prurient wood-pigeons honing their glands on cooes, and twilight, a reddened band of twilight garrotting the summer evening like a cannibal's wreath.

Despair muttered, roused from nowhere: "Rees, go home. Try again."

Trying again in the day-warmed bedroom, and stranded between her breasts. Desolated. Sweating the same nullity. Arid. Weeping our waiting together.

"Do something... this," she wept. "You'll have to now, Reesy, you must now."

"My lovely beaut," I said, wrecked the same as ever.

She shivered, shivered, curling away, flinching under the pillow.

In the morning a letter came advising rehabilitation, approximately twelve weeks followed by a suitable course of occupational training.

"Interfering bastards," I said.

Ellen said, "Of course, this will interfere with everything. You can't leave home; it isn't fair. I don't mind living on the dole, if you don't. Pretty soon Mrs Cynon will be able to look after the nippers while I go out to work. Hundreds of young wives are working in Daren."

"Sorry about last night," I said, beginning to endure my sorries to her.

"I'm not, if you're not. What do they mean rehabilitation? How can they rehabilitate people who've already been robbed?"

I said, "Ellen, we've been living in debt since I refused to go to Talygarn."

"Phu, we're the big Welsh spenders, I suppose! At least the house is paid for, but look what it cost us. *Iesu*, a roof over our heads for the price of your busted pelvis."

"We still owe Tal Harding that fifty quid," I said.

"Let me worry about Tal Harding, and the butcher and the baker. You'll have to go out more, Rees. Find company, make friends, I mean. Have you heard about the contractors washing Caib new tip? It's going to take three years. That's something fantastic! Why didn't they wash the old tip, for God's sake?"

"Aye," I said, "bloody fantastic."

"Imagine, Reesy, first the old tip from Waun Level and Caib pit, then after the slide they dump it around Waunwen, and now they're going to wash the same old muck and cart it away. All of it."

"Money talks, beaut. Sometimes I feel I'd be better off tending pigeons like my grandfather."

"You can't avoid what you're doing. It's in you. Now, love, tobacco from the Co-op this morning?"

Distant from her, I said, "I wish we were real mates like we used to be."

"Oh, God alive, we are—of course we are. Tobacco?"

"And two packets of papers," I said. "Ta, beaut."

"Huh, beaut. I don't seem to have time to keep my hair tidy. When the milkman calls tell him to leave three pints. We owe him a couple of quid, but he has the biggest round in Daren, and besides, I detest his wife. Every Guild night there she is, snip-snapping like a spoilt poodle. Any husband worth his salt would chain her to the bedpost."

"Mrs Cynon teach you that kind of talk?" I said.

"Selina knows a thing or two about what goes on around here. A councillor went to her house yesterday, asking her to join the Ratepayer's Association. It's being overrun by Communists from the Earl Haig, those poor devils who live on pipe dreams, not a sparkle of joy in them from one year

124

to the next. Selina could tell this councillor bloke about the Chairman of the Watch Committee who sold twenty-four houses in Lower Daren three months before they came under slum clearance. Imagine! The damn old crook."

I said, "Where's your sheriff's badge, Mrs Beaut?"

"Cheerio, love!" she yipped, Lydia and Elizabeth dumped in the pram and off to the Co-op, dauntless, ten times the woman my mad grandmother ever was.

Corruption, I thought. Corruption by every swilling corpuscle in Wales. Daren corruption in £1 notes. What could she do if Tal demanded his money? Offer in lieu? Once or fifty times? We didn't have fifty ha-pennies in cash. The Co-op had to be paid up every quarter, grand slam at the expense of the breadman, milk-man, butcher, clubs, Electricity Board, Gas Board, furniture company. We diddled fundamentals like ace economists: new broom, dustpan or bucket, shoes, lino, bedclothes, crockery, paint for the door on the lav, firewood, light bulbs, ink instead of one-life ballpoints, Ringer's A1 redeeming the loss of Senior Service, all-rounder soap for babies, adults and washdays, jam instead of cakes at sevenpence apiece, hot toast camouflaging margarine, the recurrent problem of finding Ellen's non-committed half-crown every month, when we bought biscuits they were shop-softened mixtures, we rushed the telly up into the attic when a rumoured detector van toured the streets, we schemed every day to stretch the pennies. And every plan from Ellen mastered NOW. She rode todays like a fresh-mounted pony express rider, yesterdays sank behind her like utilized, finished and done with, grounded nags.

I was down to one presentable collared shirt, Ellen to her specially preserved frock, knicks and vest when I *had* to attend the nearest rehabilitation centre. Attend or else. Thirty-eight miles each day by slow train from Daren Halt.

The nurse said, "It isn't uncommon, nothing to worry about. Didn't you know you were partially colour blind?"—slotting the spotted test cards back in her folder.

"Will it get worse?" I asked.

"Possibly, as your eyesight deteriorates with age. Through here, Mr Stevens, the doctor will see you now."

He was middle-aged, heave-ho hearty, kneading and finger prodding back and front around the damaged zone. "Pass water all right?"

I said, "Water is all I can pass. Mind if I get dressed? I don't like being pawed over."

"Bowels all right?"

"So long as I'm careful."

"Why the resentment, Mr um-Stevens?"

"I used to be a miner; now you're treating me like a bloody cog."

"We're all cogs in different ways. Righto, put your clothes on." He watched me dressing. "How tall are you?"

"It's on that report sheet," I said. "The nurse measured me a few minutes ago. All I need now is a price label stuck on my forehead."

"Five feet nine?" he suggested.

"Five feet nine for the last eight years."

"You've lost an inch or so," he said.

I said, "Put it down to grafting in low seams before they invented Meco loaders. Where do I go next?"

"It's dinner time, um-Rees,"—grinning safely dispassionate as a monastery barber. "Follow the other chaps

126

into the canteen. One of the instructors will take care of you." He barked sharply as I opened the door, "Mr Stevens, why don't you stand upright?"

"Joke, mate," I said. "That's a real gem of a joke."

"All right, take it easy,"—his untouchable grin tiding across his schoolboy face.

Underground you eat your grub-time sandwiches in small-knit groups, identities anchored, sharing thought-ponds as much from necessity as comfort. The talk might range from feeding a sick dog M & B tablets, sensational orgasms and classical footballing to the contingencies of politics anywhere around the newspaper and telly world. You're a blackened man eating whitened bread under artificial light in a manufactured airstream. Unlike travelling on the London Underground, you hear earth grumbling its own language.

A bloke in the canteen queue wanted to know where I come from. I told him; he was from Cardiff—Kérdiff, he said, addressing me as *Taff*, him being worldy, Kérdiff sophisticate. We were all crocks and cripples. Leg irons, walking-sticks, club feet, jarred psyches, neurotics, scarred hearts, ulcerated stomachs, passenger limbs, flayed minds, diverted I.Q.s, dammed imaginations, the white-coated instructors coming down the line, selfishly self-assured as classified robots. We were alphabeted off to specific tables. Mr Oliver was looking after esses to zeds—we had a Cockney-Jew rehabilitee named Zangwill who suffered a breakdown while serving in the Army. Married to a Maesteg wife, Zangwill had a nose thicker than simply hooked from tribal chromosomes; a ponderous, bluish beat knee of a nose. He wanted to become a postman. No more than that. Bottom echelon Civil Servant, Zangwill the Post from Aldgate to somewhere in Glam., South Wales, with his Humpty physique, heron legs and desperation to serve. Life had ransacked Zangwill of his Hebrew inheritance.

As we (rehabilitees) drifted out from the canteen, trainee chippies, brickies, fitters, capstan setters, draughtsmen, toolmakers, radio and television mechanics crowded in from the workshops. Mr Oliver gave us toning-up tests to measure our productive aptitudes, dismantling and reassembling old telephones, clocks (if you had the innocent nerve), old radio sets, bits of engineering, carburettors, degutted magnetos. Dandruff had reached Mr Oliver's eyebrows and he wore five pens and a pressure gauge in the pockets of his artificial suede waistcoat. Every half-hour or so his desk phone rang for the next man to visit the psychologist. Industrial psychologist, presumably one of those as opposed to any other sort.

My turn came on the third morning, but while journeying home on that first evening I pissed between stations. Had to, compelled without mercy, gale draught blowing through the open compartment door and four tidy commuters squinting a mixture of disgust and awe, as if I'd thrown an epileptic fit.

"Can't hold it in," I blabbed. "Accident to my pelvis; lost control ever since."

We discussed our defects, all of us pretending we were birds of a feather, but I felt like a traitor. Wednesday morning the psycho (as ex-servicemen rehabilitees called him) made me feel criminally traitorous. He was youngish, unwrinkled, pale as lard, with trained eyes, ears and voice, and the lips he was born with spread like pupae beneath the perfect ovals of his nostrils. His immobility teased colourless pictures inside my head, doggy-spectrummed images of him buried to the neck in running slurry like Ellen's father, but Mr Harcourt surfaced fiercely on gleaming skis, riding the tip-slide with Olympic verve, precision, his face deadpan as if it didn't belong to his body.

Mr Harcourt's smallest movements were magnetic, like rapier flicks.

"Have you thought about learning a new trade?" he said, G.T.C. time ticking my lifetime in that scrupulously chared, polish-smelling office. The man was doing his job; had to do it efficiently, otherwise he wouldn't be sitting on his side of the desk.

"I'm writing these days," I said.

There was something strangled, gone dead in him. "Well, they say there's one good book in all of us. What's yours called?"

Then Mr Harcourt exposed himself, emptily jolly as the middle pea in a pod of five: "Ah, another *Rape of the Fair Country!* Splendid. Don't misunderstand me, it's an exciting project; I'm with you all the way; I admire creative people, but surely you have to think about earning a living. You can see the problem; I mean your wife and children. By the way, how does she feel about this writing? Does she find it unusual?"

I said, "Let's be honest. If I told you, it wouldn't make any difference."

"Are you happily married?"

"It comes and goes," I said.

"Happiness comes and goes?"

"And marriage."

He scribbled on his note-pad and signalled a query with his silver-plated Biro. "Explain what you mean."

I said, "My wife and I are happily married."

"You don't want to talk about it?"

"No."

"Why not?"

"Because you're only concerned with me making a living. You wouldn't bother a monkey's fuck if I was half-batchy so long as I made a living."

"Er, that isn't a very original metaphor."

"It wouldn't do for the men who come in here to be original."

Genial as PLJ in a heatwave, he remarked, "At least you're the most offensive."

"That's all right," I said, suffering my own bluntness. "Now we're discussing you as well as me."

"Mr Stevens, I'm here to help you, despite what you seem to think…"

"And help yourself," I said.

"Perhaps a clerical training course. Will you…"

I said, "Mr Harcourt…"

"…write two thousand words for me? Any subject you like. Hand it in to Mr Oliver."

Desperately point-blank, I said, "Every fucker wants to be a literary giant. Teach a bloke to read and he's the bloody Lord Muck of the holy word."

"You seem to have the old four-letter verb on the brain this morning," he said, bland as Vick in a sore throat. "I'll speak to Mr Oliver. You'll want some privacy to write the essay. We'll call it an essay. Write anything you wish."

I said, "You're on the look-out for material. I've stopped being a man in your eyes."

"Good morning, Mr Stevens," he said.

The dandruffed instructor cleared elbow-room on a bench littered with broken light switches. "This will do fine," he said, checking on his wristwatch. "You're being allowed two hours. Let's see, four sheets of foolscap, pen—here, borrow this one. Anything else you want? No. Right. What about tea-break? Wait, bring it over to my desk. Right?"

"If you say so, Mr Oliver."

"Beg pardon?"

"Pardon?" I said.

"This is Mr Harcourt's responsibility. Education always begins upstairs after the second week, but you're a special case; yes, for the next two hours,"—urgency brightening his light brown eyes as he strode away to Zangwill, who had jabbed a screwdriver into his chest, the small puncture blossoming a ragged red rosette on his white shirt.

I used a couple of pages to show off, conjuring up twisty titles: PERSIFLAGE VIA JAY VAWN, MAMGU (grandmother) DAYS AND NIGHTS, FLOWERING DUFF, REQUIEM FOR MISS WILSON, CYNONS BY RANK AND DEFILE, THE GOB-WALL SHEIK, SILICOTIC FANCIER, THE ELLENITE TOW, CHAMT OF THE STALLED MECO, HERE-UNDER DAI HIMSELF, SYMPOSIUM ON CARBON, MOTION FOR SEVEN HAULIERS, CUTTING PWCINS UNDER MOUNT SION, MONOGRAPH ON CLOD, DUMP-END BLUES, ON THE TAMPER, THE ELLENIC CONCORDANCE, SOIREE BELOW THE AERIALS, GUMMING MASTER, OUVADE FOR GWALIA, THE MANAGERIAL TIC, SONGS FOR THE BARONESS, WEIGHBRIDGE TO DIGNITY, NINERS IN MY GROTTO.

Here I stopped and went out to the breeze-block-built lavatory, a cadaverous long-shanks bloke named Tony Webber squatting like a coolie against the wall, cruel clockwork motions jerking him as he retched blood. I fetched Mr Oliver. Somebody else ran for the Centre doctor. Five minutes later they slid Tony Webber into an ambulance; that was the last we saw of him. I went back to showing off, cooking titles until tea-break.

The instructor was standing behind me. "Making progress?" he said.

I gave him the foolscap sheets. "Nothing special, Mr Oliver, but if I can stay the pace for the next hour something should come." He was reading worriedly, wriggling his specked eyebrows. "Crystalline stuff," I said, "like the Flying Roll crossed with the millennium's diagnosis of tumult."

"Be careful, fella. We've seen some queer cases coming to this Centre. Now, take my advice; start all over again. I'll scrap this lot. You can't play silly-bees with Mr Harcourt. We're here to find out what you can do, and then you'll get the best training available over in the workshops. Don't you want to be independent?"

"Not if you are. So long, god, see you after tea-break," I said.

He stuttered, "Fella, hey-there-hey," but I kept on walking.

Mr Harcourt shot his cuffs and machine-gunned his Biro. "I recognize some of the mining jargon," — his smile hanging like two minutes' silence on Poppy Day. "But I'm afraid you have me at a disadvantage most of the time. What does this mean: *The Ellenic concordance*? Ellenic and Ellenite. Explain the significance."

I said, "Am I on the couch now?"

"Well, obviously, unless writers express themselves clearly they fail to communicate. This isn't my language, nobody's but your own I suspect, and I should say it promises very little for your success as a writer. It's-um, clever-clever,

132

copied from some style or other. Have you done any work for newspapers or magazines?"

Scant raindrops began to peck at the window-panes, waxing to fat, slippery purrs that brought silvery-green tones into the room.

"Aye, it's clever-clever" I said

"Ellenite, Ellenic, presumably Ellen. Is she..."

"My wife."

"Do you want to be an office worker?"

"No, thanks," I said.

"You're going to have a lonely time, my friend. Journalism?"—glancing up from his busy ball-point.

"No, thanks."

"Do you want to be lonely?"

"Is there any alternative?" I said.

"You are suffering,"—the intonation of Egypt lost behind veils and muffled gong-beating in his voice. "Because you're suffering you've created a barrier between yourself and society."

I said, "Against this place in particular."

"Yes, all right, as you say, *against*. And what happens if you fail to communicate? Does your wife have faith in you?"

The rainstorm spun swiftly away and his eyes glinted flat as beads in a ju-ju above he held stillness of his body.

I said, "Are you married?"

"Answer my question. Drop the barrier for a moment."

"Faith?"

"Does she have faith to prevent you from destroying your marriage? That's what I mean."

I tried to declare myself truthfully, like salt disappearing

133

in water. "I'm living with a kind of dying. When I win I'll be reborn."

"Ha, death, rebirth! Most of us cannot afford to worry about dying and rebirth. Perhaps it's easier for you to mystify the circumstances of your injury instead of facing up to reality. Are you, Mr Stevens?"

I said, "Let's define reality."

"Now you're being facetious. This Government rehabilitation centre is real, yet you reject all it stands for after only two days. You'll think differently after twelve weeks, plus a further six months' vocational training."

He was becoming slightly bored, irritated, pushing his notepad out of alignment with his right hand, his ball-point clicking under his thumb. I waited on him, more *against* than bored, sullen with dread, the pen suddenly winnowing across the pad again. Sunshine starred the wet window-panes. Heavy machinery hummed down on the ground floor, marrying the dulled resonance of a trainee singing at the top of his voice.

"Is there anything else you wish to tell me?" he said.

"Regarding what?"

"Yourself, man, the kind of work you feel capable of doing."

I said, "No, but listen; when you're on the way out you might wonder what the hell you've been doing. Are we finished?"

"For now, certainly. You aren't prepared to co-operate. We shall be having another chat in a couple of weeks."

"So long, then," I said.

Early in July, on a thundery morning, the Centre manager cracked down with a ranty, Oscar-winning pep talk, Brigade of Guards or its near equivalent barking out of him, and then the Government wrote me off. Personally worse off than when I started in the Centre, physically and morally — if these are divisible. I'd lost more than a stone in weight, I found it difficult to speak to men unless they were colliers or colliery workers, Lydia and Elizabeth were futureless shadows, and Ellen, dauntless Ellen, a great sad neutrality weighed between us. We forgot, changed, we confluenced on stale daily habits, the dribs and drabs of loss.

12

They (the invariably outer they) braced the high-pitched chapel roof with steel columns and cross-beams before demolishing the blue pennant stone frontage of Calvaria. Then they built the supermarket entrance, fashionably off-set, skewed inwards from the pavement, all-glass double doors swinging under two-toned pebble dashing. Mrs Cynon looked after the children while Ellen shopped for bargains on opening day. We quarrelled at breakfast, continuing over lunch, a money nag qualified by not having any. She borrowed two quid off Selina Cynon for this shopping festival.

"We'll have to pay it back next Friday when I get my dole," I said.

"I'll pay it back when I start work. Selina happens to be my friend. Have you finished? I want to clear the table."

I said, "We still owe Tal Harding that fifty quid."

"Oh, hush up, misery. The back room's waiting, although

you should get some fresh air. You were stuck in there again all last night."

"Following your old man's Account. He was madder than I am. As for Kate, selfish, sexy Kate, she really creased his guts the time she carried the baton in Daren Darkies jazz band. Aye, before you were born."

"Reesy, you're not mad, just cranky like your cranky grandmother."

Front-line Ellen Stevens, wearing her best dress, necklace, earrings, lipstick, and we had a full pantry of cut-price food. Our Lydia gabbled little mother sentiments to a doll coaxed out of Percy; Elizabeth sat in a high chair delivered after dark by a member of the Women's Guild at the behest of Mrs Cynon. We were poor, but nowhere near the prewar standard of poverty in Daren. Poverty succoured by Sunday pie-in-the-sky in Calvaria Chapel. Ten thronged chapels and one church in Daren during the Hungry Thirties.

"When you've finished," she insisted impatiently, posed with her fist on her hip like Pilate's wife watching him make a mutt of himself.

I went into the back room, my *cwtch* of rebirth where I tried not to shrivel, John Vaughan's number seven exercise-book still unopened on the couch, and in number six, his auto-comments on marriage and poverty:

Times have altered beyond. Beyond dreams. Us men who have seen two wars have also seen many inventions, motor cars, aeroplanes, atomic bombs, cinemas, wireless & television & even plastic shoes. Once we all ate the same food. Not any more. Once a man & wife lived on £21/1/6 per week. Without option we were limited to table, chairs, bed, wooden settle, chest of drawers, candles, the Bible, 6d a pint beer & 4d for ten Cinderellas. *Never again. Warm woollen clothes are not a God-send any more. Good leather boots to last five years & Melton serge a lifetime. Large loaf 3½d.*

Bread tasting delicious after a week but not any more. I could go on & on but only fools deny progress. We ourselves were making steady progress for all our poverty. When there were only two wirelesses in Daren we had the third. Kate brought it home in a pram belonging to one of the Miskin girls. "Where did you get that article from, Kate?" I said. She replied, "Only 2/6 a week, we'll go without pictures on Saturday nights." As if we went every weekend to Daren Gaiety when the basics of food, rent & clothes swallowed every penny of our finances. I was not even on piece-work in Caib at the time, being repairing by night after chronic ill health made me give up my stall in the Four Feet. For years & years this bad chest of mine. Night shift often meant low health & poverty. Mostly strong men worked days regular year in & year out. Either strong or well-in with officials & this went against the grain with me in my position of Lodge treasurer. Night shift suited all right as our committee meetings finished by nine o'clock. Therefore I could be down the pit without rushing by half-past ten. "Where is your cheque book?" she used to persist whenever we were at rock bottom. "It is not MINE, woman, as you know full well. Do you expect me to rob my fellow workers?" but principle shed off Kate like water off a duck's back. In a way I was glad when she went to Queen's Street, Portsmouth, as then I did not have to carry the double responsibility of Lodge funds & her temptation. Regarding Daren Cottage Hospital cheque book it never left Councillor Dewi Benjamin's possession during the eleven years he was Hospital Committee Hon Sec till he died in the back lane behind Regent Street. I was forced to resign, no alternative the way he utilized public funds. Sheer greediness. Gambling & drinking together with my wife's so-called friend brought about the man's downfall, Miss Edna Miskin herself with Dewi Ben in the lane when his heart collapsed. My wife's personal friend, that girl Edna, I am sorry to confess. We all live in ignorance at some time or other, whether working class or middle or high class or royal blood. For instance I felt proud we were doing good work with Caib Inst. bringing concerts, dance bands & putting on social occasions for everybody's benefit. Of little interest to me personally speaking but seeing your fellow men & their families enjoying themselves gave us cause for pride. Genuine pride. The community spirit. Marvellous in those days although I myself followed old Twm Cynon's proverb, WHERE IGNORANCE IS BLISS 'TIS FOLLY TO BE WISE. We lived, from hand to mouth, my wife Kate robbing Peter to pay Paul every Friday. Why did she do it? Lack of principle. Nothing would stop her galivanting, growing younger instead of older & there was I cutting pwcins in Caib, happy in my ignorance I swear while the house belonging to Joseph Gibby on whist drive nights no better than a red lamp. Llew Hopkins included. Even a hippety-hop like him. Girls would not look twice at Llew due to his legs. "What are you going to do about it?" says Kate on the morning I came home at 3 a.m. when Mog Mason broke his ribs. Mog passed unconscious in a pocket of gas while ripping top standing on a full tram of muck. Fell across the rails, poor old Mog, night shift for 23 years. I rode with him in the ambulance, wiping blood from his mouth. Home by the short cut afterwards, longing for a cup of tea & expecting welcome from Kate, company for sleeping with on a bitter January night. Ignorance

& innocence must be closely related. My ignorance on this cold crucial morning, her mystery man skelping his get-away out through the front door while I was untying my bootlaces in the kitchen. The gall, sheer gall. "What are you going to do about it?" she wanted to know, standing there in a mauve pais brand new to me & unpaid for as I discovered later. "Go on, raise your fist! Let me tell you, John Vaughan, it will be the sorriest thing you have ever done in all your born days!" She reminded me of her father Mike Minty coming out from WAUN ARMS with a load on. Dangerous as a mad dog. I slapped her bare neck with my muffler all soaked from Mog's haemorrhage. It was the blood frightened her, nothing else. She used up two buckets of hot water. I had to rebuild the fire & wait another hour & a half before bathing myself, her drying careless as a cat in front of the fire. It took me three years to learn his name, Mansel Rimmer whose father Jake lived tally with Mansel's mother Mari Samuels until they both passed away from smallpox in 1927. Previous to this Jake Rimmer lodged with my mother while they were sinking Caib. Although wanting to kill Mansel I realized it would not cure Kate. She scrubbed my back in front of the fire as if her conscience was perfectly clear. Also cooked my rasher & fried bread. Around 6 a.m. we went to bed, Kate first to warm the blankets. She was like that. Few men on nights would have their beds warmed ready for them unless the wife was too lazy to get up & make breakfast. How do you contend with a woman who cannot cry? I never once saw Kate weeping tears. One winter she had a bout of 'flu very bad. Myself I sat under a towel sniffing Friar's Balsam, bronchitis as usual. She fell right downstairs, banged her head, boiled some water & condensed milk & climbed back upstairs. Nothing else in the house but *tinned milk & water. All without saying a word or begging for help. Brass, a woman of brass. Her father Mike had it in him as well. The same kind of attitude impossible to touch this side of the grave. Hard as brass itself. Fearing nothing alive on two legs. To my mind she joined the Pentecostals for fun, which is the same as saying religion is made for those who are deprived of fun. Personally I had Lodge business to keep me fully occupied & when jazz bands became popular I seconded the motion to allow Daren Darkies to train upstairs in the institute during wet weather. We won first prize in Swansea carnival, the shout going up on Singleton Park as DAREN DARKIES competed in their black & white outfits, bazookas & drums all paid for by raffles & street collections, my own wife leading the parade like a trotting pony. She threw the baton highest, old Soldier Perkins her great trainer who himself lost his kneecap with the South Wales Borders on the Western Front. Late that night fireworks spouted all over the sky, then Kate suggested sharing a bottle of White Horse with her under some evergreen bushes. Celebrate success in private. A warm summer night as I well recall, everybody happy whether losers or winners, children asleep on the grass. "Who bought this, the Darkies committee?" me asking in all innocence. "Pub in town," she said. "Pinched from behind the counter when his back was turned. Pass it over, I'm dry as a bone. How do I look as a darky girl?" It takes a lifetime to learn that confession is best, only I cannot remember my answer. Kate! Kate! Kate! Why? Why? Why? Deserting me when all I wanted was to make her contented. I felt prouder of Kate than of myself.*

"You marvel, you breathless wonder, you Daren flame-thrower," I said, the smell of Singleton Park evergreens in my nostrils, whisky tingling my throat, fireworks coruscating against the summer stars, the customary gymnast toppling round and round on high goalposts, and Kate Vaughan recumbent under the bushes, violet-eyed Eve, charcoaled Ethiopian from Thelma Street offering Sioni-boy her bounty.

Glancing up, I saw Ike Pomeroy leaning out of a bedroom window, directly above his wife almost edibly sun-suited in cherry red, bow-legged Atlanta supine on a white rubber airbed on the lawn. It was Saturday afternoon, every television set in the street showing the gritty-eyed heroes and heroines of Wimbledon.

We're all different, I thought. Different humans all over the place. It's bloody agony.

Mrs Thorpe was in the garden behind the bungalow, sunny mistress of her ethos plot, her arms, legs and centre parting tanned olive brown. The gladioli spired and flagged like standstill coloured flames, bees tippling amongst the sweetpeas, the moist black earth fading to dark, crimpy grey where she had hoed between rows of lettuces, dwarf beans, radishes, carrots.

"How nice to see you again! Feeling poorly, Mr Stevens? Lost weight, too, I should think. What you want is a good long holiday in the country. Nourishing food, rest, change of atmosphere, that kind of thing. I know when I was awfully ill some years ago our doctor warned Mr Thorpe and by golly it made him sit up and take notice. I stayed with my sister in Devon, grand month, came home feeling like a new woman."

Somehow she gathered inquiry from the sort of grunted affability one is obliged to sound off against toothless fate.

142

"Nerves, the doctor said. Me suffering nerves, when to all intents and purposes I never knew the meaning of nerves!"

I said, "Tal Harding tried to cultivate this garden. He made a poor job of it."

"Yes, we heard, but Mr Harding had trouble at the time." She coughed superbly beneath her fingertips. "You know, one doesn't like to be nosy, pry into other people's affairs."

The worry began again, the same fretful anxiety to make connection. Make friends with homely Mrs Thorpe. Simply connect. And then it came so *simply*, thinly vacuous as sand complaining against gravity, drawn only towards friendship while *Grandstand* and Eamon Andrews wound up with cricket scores all over the summer-afternoon island, my senses crawling troubled from insufficient sleep the night before, Saturday silence on Caib colliery, NUM and NCB ignoring the curse of Genesis, and that uncanny effluvium from Daren woods, August malevolence, traceless, anti-human. Anti-consciousness.

"Ellen and I seem to be at cross-purposes these days," I said. "Nothing works right for us any more. As you say, perhaps I should pull up my roots for a few weeks. But it isn't nerves; more likely sheer boredom. Boredom and failure."

"Come now, Mr Stevens, failure, *no*," —pleading softly, herself immunized, sweetly plump, warm, comforting.

I said, "Something's missing, gone, lost," —banalizing the truth, covertly pleased to charge embarrassment upon Mrs Thorpe, her girlish shuffling lifting a fine, hissily fine uproar off the crushed gravel path, compassion lapping her round blue eyes, the gentle distress of a never-tempted earth

143

goddess. Lower firmament eidolon softly foot shuffling in the pebbly gravel. "Never mind; most things have to get worse before they become better," I said.

She broke a husky protest, turning as Mr Thorpe came out to wave from the back door: "Bye-bye, Emily—hullo Mr Stevens, hullo there!" He canted sideways from a leather satchel in his right hand, a tight white linen jacket profiling his humped shoulders like uncooked chicken meat.

"Bowls tournament," she said. "They're playing somewhere over in Brynywawr."

We watched him driving past Caib institute, under the railway bridge and out to the main road.

"Good luck, George," she called softly, placidly loyal. "My husband is skip this season. You wouldn't call him a brilliant player, but he's terrifically reliable. Do you play bowls, Mr Stevens?"

"Old Sir Francis Drake's pastime. No, Mrs Thorpe, the game doesn't interest me." Nor old John Vaughan, I thought; you're getting to be like him, Reeso. Whited ghoul, shellacked in the guts, de-knackered, stoned in the gonads, killed in the pills, lonely. We're all lonely, waiting for the trap-door loneliness that finished off Granny Stevens—hold on, Rees, connect, if you fail, fail trying.

She came over to the garden gate. "D'you know, Mr Stevens, every Saturday throughout the summer,"—squeezing jubilance from her contentedly slack-pursed, fretless mouth—"he's off playing bowls! It's like a vice to him, truly, Mr Stevens!"

I said, "What's yours?"

"Yours first!"—gamin delight trembling her evenly swathed brown hair.

"If I told you my vice, you wouldn't invite me into the house for a cup of tea," I said. Fail? Fail in trying.

She resisted contact at teacup level, blurting, "You'll never believe! I love smashing glass, bottles, jars, all colours, then you make pictures and designs in cement. Lay them in quick, quick, you have to be ever so quick. My experimental shed, it's over there behind the hydrangeas." She spun limber as an athlete unable to stand still, heels spurting the gravel.

Iesu, I thought, echoing Ellen's echoes of Mrs Cynon, this great way-out Madame Thorpe. She's on her own, travelling solo like old Charlie Page the Hunter and Fisher throw-back. None but the pure in heart shall inherit.

She flurried around inside the shed, inch-thin slabs of decorated cement propped against the walls, crude cockerels, stiff-winged doves, a seaweedy crocodile in the dark green shards of a Houghton pale-ale bottle, stereotyped church steeples, fairy-tale-designed houses, arabesques, curliques, elongated diamond shapes. Beneath the shed window her glass smashing barrel, into which she drove a ball hammer time after time like an absorbed rampaging child. When I touched her shoulder she glanced shyly aside, offering a squat vino bottle plus the hammer to go with it. Conversation waned to exclamations, the blind intimacy that crows out from loneliness.

We mixed a bucketful of cement, stirring it on a flagstone outside the shed. She shovelled it into a shallow plywood-based mould no bigger than a tea-tray, concentrating, teeth bared as she floated a smooth wet surface.

"Ready?" she whispered. "Will you, or shall I?"

"You, Emily, please," I said.

"Shall I?"

145

"Yes, you, it's your…"

"Next time, then!"—her suntanned arm swooping, scratching out a huge sunflower head with a spoon handle in the wet cement. Watching her, I fell into the kind of reverent shock which ends childhood. The sunflower blossom was a ludicrous thing, setting hard, symmetrically shattered and setting shattered hard, painstaking Emily bent over the workbench in the early evening sunlight, shards clashing, her breathing faintly audible, happily, quietly demoniac.

We mixed another squashy dumpling of cement and while she went indoors to brew some tea I scrawled a Cerne Abbas giant figure, decked his storming phallus with hydrangea petals, then outlined his loutish hulk and rib-cage with peaty-brown fragments from a large Nescafé jar. I felt the search was on, had to be signified, displayed. Failure meant nothing, not a damn thing. I saw myself male to plump Emily's female. Begun at last, this bid, challenge, sweet hazard between every good and mutual evil.

"We'll have to break it before my husband comes home," she whispered. "He wouldn't understand."

"You understand, Emily?"

"Not really. I don't like flirting, can't very well in any case," —lowering her head. "Flirting makes me feel ashamed."

"I've been ashamed of myself for a long time," I said.

"Don't you love Ellen?"

"This is different,"—the truth of the difference beyond reach of reason.

"I couldn't face my husband," she pleaded.

"Emily, sometimes I can't face living. We'll give ourselves a week, shall we? Can't you see, I'm more afraid than you are?"

"Good-bye," she said, braving trembles that shook her flared skirt. "Wait, I've made tea. Come inside for a cup of tea first, before you leave."

13

Every afternoon I walked around the sprawl of Caib colliery. Six hundred men on three shifts and I knew them all by their Christian names. Knew many of their parents, wives, their skills and paucities. Most of them knew me, learned our leaked-out secret founded upon the workaday settling of history: *Rees Stevens? Him? Poor bugger can't make any more kids since he had his bump. See Rees in and out of Daren library? Bloody ghost of a man gone, no push left in him, be on the dole till his pension comes through. Reesy's had his lot.*

And Ellen's place, her designated role and character: *Now there's a smart young filly running to seed. Longer it goes on, worse she's going to get. No argument, stands to reason. What's good for the gander don't have to be good for the goose. Not that it's Reesy's fault, s'just the sort of fuck-up on the home front that leads to what you read about every Monday in the old Dee and Dee Clarion.*

Thirty men down at a time in the cages. Men only. Stacked tram-rails, steel roofing-rings, lagging timber, track sleepers heaped around the pit-head. Local workmen's buses pitched on Harding's Square. Two old steam locos shunting up and down the siding. Green Waunwen stretching steeply, bulking north and west. All that week I watched the day shift rising and the afternoon shift going down. Two-way streams of men from the pit-shaft to the baths.

On Friday afternoon Charlie Page came straight downhill from Waun Level, his face weather dried, faunishly reticent.

"Bit of foresight and they could'a saved Thelma Street," he said. "That water comin' out from the old Waun, see, Rees?"

"It was trenched to run into Nant Melyn," I said.

"When? I'll tell you when. The time Gibby built Thelma Street. That's when. Only they filled the ditch with muck when they extended the aerials."

I said, "Aye, true enough. The stupid bastards."

"Rees, who was area manager in nineteen-forty-nine?"

"No idea, Charlie. I was still in school."

"He's the one who extended the aerials. So long, see you around, boy."

He skirted Caib top pit, a neat, leathery little man, lean growing, his gait rather flat-footed, the *pad-pad* of a long-distance rover. Pneumo caking fifty per cent of his lungs.

The last afternoon shift bon went down. I saw a lad standing on a wheel-less tram, another lad kneeling up on his shoulders. Sparrows' nests, I thought, under the caves of the old stables. The ex-wrestler colliery watchman shouted at them from the lamproom doorway. They ignored him until he began walking, then they ran around the long, derelict building. He returned to the lamproom.

It was clouding over, gusts bringing the grinding clank of Rollo's tip-washing plant way up the river gulley side of Waunwen. Rollo & Sons; they blackened Daren river every time it rained, their silt beds flooding over. Tomorrow, I thought, tomorrow at five o'clock, I hope—my own pale Ellen an idle stage prop, expediently off-stage as I headed for home.

The watchman came out. "Hey, mate, you're trespassing. Gerroff the colliery premises."

I said, "Shwmae, butty. I'm Joseph Gibby's grandson. Who are you?"

"Take no notice, Rees,"—the lamproom man sniggering like a prisoner released from solitary. Traditional cripple as in every pit-head lamproom, he said, "How's it going with you these days, Rees?"

"Not too bad, Erfyl. I'm not wetting all over the place any more."

"Compo run out yet?"

"Christ, aye; we blew the lump sum on our house. Now I'm on twenty-five per cent disability."

"Same as me, Rees. Factory job in Lower Daren would suit you, boy."

"I'd have to change my sex first. *Dabbo [Da bo' chi]*, Erfyl."

"Cheerio, mate," said the watchman.

I agreed, "All the best, butty"—thinking, all the best, Emily, all, for us tomorrow afternoon.

She insisted mildly, "Impossible in the house, no, no, I'll follow you later, soon, please hurry."

We walked deep into the woods, dampness subsiding, smudging floppy scurryings in the upper foliage.

"Might it thunder?" she asked.

"We'll be struck dead by forked lightning, lovers burnt to a single cinder in the very act."

"Shh, Rees, no."

Emily's noes were the yesses of her docile heart, herself a lax, warm pasture of femality, and I had no touchstone, no measure, nothing to rouse, upraise, bear passion. Gentle Emily. Gentle Rees. Gently with myself, exposed Rees, like an outcast accomplishing breathing though scourged throughout his nerves. Scrupulously persistent, careful. Bearable. The hewn tender way of slaves honoured to eliminate any pain. Thrill purified, marrow-spitting thrill projected as goodwill, a sooth service because every alternative carried suffering. Our quiet riot, my own pale, humbly defenceless riot, and by the Jesus God I felt grateful, gentle Emily Thorpe's quaintness flowering wondrous, becalming the arrogance of triumph.

Man again, I thought, man *alive*. I've conquered the senseless host rattling my lifeline-dauntless Ellen still blurred, off-stage, a contingency, a past happening.

Like ordinary lovers we were seated on my raincoat, mutually affectionate, Emily sharing a punnet of strawberries from her garden.

"Ah-well, dear, feeling better now?"

Necessary as faith, as breath, I said, "This has been the trouble between Ellen and myself."

"I'm sure, Rees, yes, surely. Do you know, for a while I believed you were George. Mr Thorpe was much the same at first." Her large blue eyes blazed incongruously ferocious;

"But once is enough, understand? I'm afraid of scandal. I'm terribly afraid. It wouldn't be fair to George and Ellen. I think it's shameful, really I do. We mustn't get involved any more."

"You're a good woman, Emily."

"I'm weak, awfully weak. My husband, I dread to think, I mean..."

"You and I, we're two of a kind," I said, mountain fog lowering down, chilling the skin-prickling summer drizzle. Blanching browns and greens, the white fog filed in between the trees, enforcing primeval stillness, throttling coil pressed upon cold coil, driving life from the woods. The warm drizzle stopped, quenched by the fog.

"Really speaking, no harm's been done so far," she said, worriedly crushing the empty punnet in her lap. Levering off one elbow, she funnelled her arm through a jungle of cow-parsley stalks, brought me a sudden, glorious close-up smile, and thrust the punnet away out of sight. "Time for us to go, Rees."

The following Saturday afternoon I watched George Thorpe playing bowls on the rink near his bungalow. Before the teams changed ends, I met Emily in her garden shed.

This time panic helped, Emily's inevasive urge to get the business over and done with, the shed window slatting a flat, glass-waxy apron of sunlight across her thrown-back throat. I felt impulsive as a street dog, without his limited, wise aggression. The hit and run, slash and snarl and whirling scamper of a street dog, Emily finally composed, marginally distressed, clutching, hitching at her clothes, her olive tawny legs nimbly co-ordinated as she slewed down off the work-bench.

"There, now you don't have to come again," — patting her ovoid tummy, utter blandishment dousing the panic. "You're all right now, dear, aren't you?"

Too much of a canine, lacking his scruff-necked resilience, his guaranteed guts for survival. My hackles were gossamer shreds and the pit of my stomach moaned leaden. I felt I couldn't walk out through the shed door, meet Saturday afternoon. I felt scragged, Venus diseased, the old numbness returned, ego threatened by rigor, icicled spine swording through to my crying brain-pan. Brain mixture crying down upon castaway flesh and bones clotted around by sludge.

Impotency leaves potent hurt inside the corpus.

She whispered a frightened politeness, sidling out through the door, skimming straight-kneed along the gravel path to the bungalow.

A small collapse of shards clinked in the glass-smashing barrel.

Smoke I thought. Take it easy. Roll one of your A.1 burners. She can't do any more for you now. Emily's good, she's been good to you. Aye, Rees, you've brought this on yourself. Take five. Greedy waster, count your blessings. Once in twelve bankrupt months, then second time you dive at it like a bloody Guy Fawkes with a dose of uncivilized napalm inside his trousers. Some Cerne Abbas fertility giant you are, mate. Guh, matey. Hey, you're a Daren ha-penny sparklight. One of the NCB's forsaken Foreskin Fusiliers. Ex-thigh rider from the Caib. Take it steady, Rees. As you were. All right now. Coming along nicely. Carry on, boyo. You're a bloody pantaloon. Aye, one of them. Old John Vaughan, old Shon moaner, he didn't have a donkey's laugh in him.

I day-dreamed about Ellen. Her and our two girl kiddies. Two little Stevens's squabs. Ellen had it all planned out for Monday morning. Mrs Cynon would collect the nippers at eight-thirty. She'd take and bring Lydia home from school. All I had to do was cook the dinner by half-past five, when Ellen came from the factory. Lovely Ellen, my Winchester beaut come home to Daren, dragged home by her old man.

"Here," panted Emily. "You look dreadful,"—peering closer, head shaking, whiffling the matching downfalls of her thick brown hair. "Has it passed over? Back to normal now, Rees? You really did look awful. Here, drop of Mr Thorpe's Sanatogen wine. He drinks it when he feels off-colour, mostly during the winter. Exercise, I tell him, take more exercise."

I nagged stupidly. "You're a good woman, Emily. Shall we make—ah, break some more glass next Saturday? They're playing away next week-end."

"Go on home," she said. "Rees, you must go. It's bad, bad. I feel disgusted."

Saturdays my only living prospect, Emily Thorpe Saturdays: "Next Saturday, please?"—hoping to mend myself, thoroughly mend, uniquely as before, cherishable, ready for Ellen, but not even confronting the real Ellen, only stranded Rees between her breasts.

She reached into the barrel for the small ball hammer. "I shan't be your weekend habit! Go home, off home!"— hammering the bench, a frantic tantrum. "I'll tell your wife about you, so there!"

"I'm sorry, Emily, I'm sorry."

"Good-bye, Rees,"—whimpers trembling her girl's mouth. "I don't like it very much. You men never realize, never, never. Go to Ellen; she's your wife."

Down to the blighted pith again, stuttering, offering for the last time. "You're a guh-ood woman, Emily, good... good woman. Suh-so long then, love."

"It is best," she said.

The bowls players, ingrained champions one and all, were coming away from the changing-room, and out in front of the institute. Llew Hopkins leaned over the low, iron-spiked fence, snapped off a yellow carnation and skewered it in his button-hole.

"Who won the match?" I said.

"Us, bach, our side did. Been moochin' agen, have you, in them old woods? Not much like the other Stevenses, you're not. Moochin' about day after day. *Myn jawch*, you wouldn't ketch Dai or Glyn Stevens idlin' about the place as if they didn't know what to do with theirselves."

"Evening paper come yet?" I said. "Is it in the reading-room?"

"Reesy, lissen, I got certain orders from the committee, orders that don't apply to yourself special, true; but you can't go inside there agen till you clear up. Look now, compo, shurance an' dole cases s'only thruppence. Thruppence, mun —who'd miss thruppence a week? See Watt Howard's son, that boy of his Luther. Get a card off of Luther, pay your dues and from then on you're a member same as if you was still in the lodge."

"You'd stop me reading the newspapers, Llew?" I said.

"Makes no odds. Orders is orders."

I said, "Llew, only a fool would argue with the 'stute committee."

"See that Luther Howard!" his town-crier's eruption drumming echoes under the railway bridge.

155

Llew Hopkins, I thought, when we bury him in Daren cemetery Caib institute will fall down, on members only. Old screw-shanks Llewelyn, short-timing nights with Ellen's mother while her mandrel and shovel Sioni cut *pwcins* down in the Four Feet. Pair of three-yard rails and two bomby trams of muck every shift, as per the bloody price list agreement.

14

She swore, "Damn it all," swankily feline in black Bri-nylon tights: "For God's sake be reasonable. Pull yourself together."

"Ellen, shut up," I said, Tal Harding conscientiously launching another cigarette to his lower lip, alcohol hunger fazing out of his system, our shrewd little Lydia wrestling too vindictively with Elizabeth on the hearth-rug (cost-price rug, de-luxe, exotic, from Daren Co-op warehouse), some clock-face slogging out the news on BBC Wales as if trilling NCB canary mutants were adapting themselves to methane gas around the perimeter of his soul, Mrs Cynon sitting statuesque, arms folded like a tribal ikon, flat planes of age starking the bones of her temple and jaw, my swanking Ellen cat-savage in tight black tights and frilled white blouse with black shiny buttons—her working-wife rig.

"Lydia," she warned, "you'll get a tanning, my girl."

Tal fish-gawped his tireless G.P.O. face at Mrs Cynon,

who flickered glances at all of us before readjusting herself to the Welsh news.

"Are you coming?" insisted Ellen.

Another hair-greying year gone by, other changes, hopeful changes presumed inevitable to ameliorate the flinty gamble of profitless accumulation. Changes equated to what the Joneses have or what they want to secure. Any kind of Everyman Jones, included the endless rash of Joneses registered, classified, scaled, categorised, pruned and awed, pimped upon and pulverized, blown up and taxidermized, glamorized and catechized, spangled, finagled, derided and lauded non-stop for ever until receiver Joneses and transmitter Joneses click *Blip-beep*, *beep-blip*, associating on every level except chasing back with Holy Writ haunted from some eternal Jawa.

"Can't, Ellen, not tonight," I said.

"Huh, sunshine Joe. Will you look after the children?"

"I'll sit in if Rees wants to go out later on," advised Mrs Cynon, her and Ellen exchanging sagacities with eyescrews and ties of the mouth.

Ellen and Tal were carrying-on, as we say. It's a needling point of inductive reasoning whether or not I fitted the cuckold index. A man cannot lose what he doesn't want. In my case not have, the wanting futile, become wasteful on that score. Or perhaps tolerable, better defines any condition both up and down from dying. Death itself we haven't learned to bear except transmogrified, transcendentalised, transmuted, muted anyhow in dubious-cum-worthless trances, in trances exposé full-stopping at limbo. Dark trances lit by being allowed to thank the Christ one doesn't worship that we're still *here*, breathing, eating and all the rest; as much of the rest as necessary being crucially necessary.

Feline Ellen, side-stepping our marriage cul-de-sac, was carrying-on with Tal. A sorry arrangement. But again, still, sorrow does make the next best thing concretely desirable, *carrying-on* a vital slap at *not* carrying-on. Jealousy, too, becomes tolerable, like a dirty handkerchief for ever in the same pocket.

They went to a Daren-posh dinner and cabaret in the television-factory canteen, proceeds in aid of the widows and children of two Caib men, Seven Feet face packers on day shift, killed when a misfired night-shift shot crashed roof on top of them. Misfires are never listed in the NCB's Ref. No. S.F.2 records, although each record sheet has a column for misfires. Two packers killed outright. Killed outright—clean meant off the tongues of colliers since long, long before Welsh coal steamed Blue Riband liners across the Atlantic. Our enhancing verdict: killed outright.

I bathed and Mrs Cynon towelled the children, the brave old suffragette favouring Lydia, who bore sweetly pink cherubim innocence to its flesh and bones penultimate, curled on Mrs Cynon's lap, drowsing into the old lady's murmurous croon: "*Myfi sy'n magu'r baban, Myfi sy'n siglo'r crud, Myfi sy'n hwyan hwyan, Ac yn hwyan hŵy o hyd.*"

Elizabeth also fast asleep.

Mrs Cynon said, "You'll meet Percy and Howell my nephew in Daren Social."

"I'm going along to share a couple of pints with Charlie Page," I said.

"Charlie's more normal now," she approved. "It's a bad sign when a man drops his family to go roaming the mountains."

159

"Four of his children are married, the others are working except for the youngest boy. They're off his hands," I said.

"Rees Stevens, you can't say such a thing about families. Families are families, blood is thicker than water."

Charlie was in the small upstairs lounge, patiently alone, orientally spruce, his jacket pockets stretched square from carrying tobacco tins. Every Thursday he walked to Lower Daren Central Library, chasing up some archaeological item, some clinching niche in the tell-tale matrix of man and matter. He seemed dedicated, peaceful pursuit of the Hunter and Fisher Folk his charm against pneumoconiosis. On him was the grave, unflappable absorption of a boy scholar. Having won through his little purgatory, now he was green-finger planted to last a long time. We yarned about earlier days in Caib Four Feet when Andrew Booth managed the pit. Broken colliers, like damaged soldiers, have to reason out experience, justify it in talk. Sanguine behind his pint, the interlocked tips of his fingers across his chest, Charlie said, "We'll see the end of it all, *brawd*, you and me."

"They've finished spending money on Caib," I said, "but the coal's coming out like a sea from Brynywawr."

"Now then, Reesy, in point of fact I was over the other side this morning..."

"Looking for the start back on the coal, no doubt?"

"Pull the other one," — grinning spry as a faun. "No, see, according to my information they're in the shit as regards the Seven Feet; temporary perhaps, I'm not saying it isn't temporary.

Remember down the Four Feet? We'd have a run lastin' a coupla years, then she'd knock out to sixteen feet of bloody rashing, dirty old *mum-glo* stuff and no matter what we couldn't hold the top up. Am I right or am I wrong?"

"Right, Charlie; we came across a few jumps in the old Four Feet," I said.

"Same trouble in the Seven Feet. Two conveyor faces buggered at the moment. Take my word for it, boy; I was making inquiries over there only this morning. I'm not saying they won't drive on inside the jump like we used to in the Four Feet. Only, fact is, they got to keep other things going over in Brynywawr: coke ovens and that, lotsa dead-men in the offices, little fillies an' all."

I said, "Aye."

"But they don't count. It's the likes of you and me that know full well how the big shouts on the Coal Board operate when a face starts losing money. No messing—agreed? They say, right, look, here's a new cutter, here's a new system, phones and loud speakers all over the pit, walking cogs or some fuckin' new method of working out your pay docket. Or they'll build us a new washery like that white elephant on Caib—agreed? But the fuckin' coal still isn't coming up top pit, is it? Not till they're through the jump? Course not. Bloody impossible. Right. Close the face. Bring in contractors, drive new headings, fetch in the foreigners, aye and when was it—nineteen-fifty-five?—we put our fourteen days' notice in 'cause the Coal Board tried to bring Italian labour into the pits. Psychology, Rees-boy, they got us taped as 'gards ways and means. We fight for shillings, they talk in millions. Christ, you must give 'em credit. I mean, Christ, look at what's happening to pits all over the bloody country. They got us taped." He pulled a Chinese-uncle smile, patting his chest, "Not Charlie Page, though."

161

"Me neither," I said, wishing I had the stomach to work underground again. Return, go back anywhere for Ellen. For Rees, her bought-and-paid-for ex-man, 7s. 6d., stuck in our back room, Johnnie Vaughaning my days and nights on pensioner goolies.

"Let's find Percy," I suggested. "He's with his cousin, a bloke from the NCB offices in Cardiff."

Charlie's lips firmed together like praying. "Go ahead you, Rees, but don't include me in a big booze-up. Another glass an' I'll be on my way."

I brought them up from the bingo hall, Howell Cynon's baldness mooning above a huge black beard. He began blinding us with production figures and the future of coal until old Charlie said to him, "You're on about this progress, boy, but when you come to look at it sort of from the very beginning, see, you get a different idea. Understand, Howell, I'm not disputin', only it's a question of shoving such things in their proper respect... perspective, I mean to say. Take a dekko at it this way. Once we were babies, then we were boys, then youngsters huntin' for a bit of oats, then married men, then fathers rearing kids of our own, then old granchas, so on, on and on I mean. Agreed?"

"The seven ages of man," Howell said.

"Rubbish, butty, if you'll excuse the comment. Thass the main trouble, after short cuts all the fuckin' time."

"Analogies do not prove cases," — Howell sparring cleverly, up-zooming his brilliancy, ready to expertise, whip out Sheaffer and paper.

"In my opinion, honest opinion now, I'd say we were still in the baby stage as 'gards progress," explained Charlie, switching his intimate leathery faun grin at Percy: "Big un,

I'll swop my pneumo for your swinger. Throw my missis in as well to make up the bargain."

Percy hit his artificial shin with his alloy stick. Topping eighteen stone, losing his eyes inside rolls of malt fat, he was gaining esteem, the block-ended relish shared amongst untried, womanless men. "Come on down to Remploy with me, Charlie," he said. "Coal Board compo on top of earnings, you'll do all right."

"I've done my whack, Perce."

"Ker-iste, mun, there's ten years' work in you yet, easy."

"Me too, thirty years," I said.

Percy banged around with his stick, rejecting controversy. "Trouble is, Rees, you're not a fit man: can't be, mun, else they'd have put you on to something in that training-centre place. I'd go back down under tomorrow, no hesitation. Short hours, machines to do all the graft—Christ, aye, I'd be there."

Announcing pure Admin. Exce. solace, foolproof as a Band-Aid on rabies, Howell Cynon said, "Personally I don't think it would be wise to consider Brynywawr Seven Feet. We're meeting geological snags, but, of course, you chaps know more about it than I do. You've actually experienced deterioration; you have had to deal with these problems. Serious reports are coming in from Brynywawr particularly. Indeed, I shouldn't be at all surprised if the colliery comes under reclassification, possibly closure, unless, you see, *unless* the OMS improves. Naturally, the Board's policy is to grant a reprieve period, three months, six months, even a year if the colliery can be made economically viable."

"Well, I'm off. Goodnight now," Charlie said.

"Hang on, mun, I'll give you a lift home. What's the

rush?"—big Percy playfully scything his stick at Charlie's legs.

Charlie hooked two thumbs in his waistcoat pockets. "We'll see the end of it all in Daren," he said.

"Every fit man will be offered alternative employment in one of our long-life collieries,"—fashionably bearded Howell assuring three crocks as if changing pits was like changing a pair of socks. As if miners were migratory Americans hitched to romance, to LIFE not quite over the next horizon. Mobile Americans too empty to seethe outwards from stillness.

I remembered Ellen and Tal. Some fourth-rate cabaret team was smarming the crap out of the guinea-a-head diners, Ike Pomeroy and the Brynywawr manager scheduled for notice in *Daren & District Clarion*, another smell of grief for the two widows. Pan shots around the fancy-balled-up canteen. Ageless Taliesin Harding (finer boned in the nose inherited from old miser Dicko) under disciplined weaning from the booze, and Mrs Ellen Stevens, popular supervisor on 4B shop floor. Two esteemed Darenites. Yuh. Rees Stevens's wife flogging fifty quid's worth of marriage property to the man who lost her seven years ago. Probably trading the deal in his car, parked on the bend of the mountain road from where you can see traces of ancient cultivation shadowing the hillside above Daren woods. The carrying-on contract aided and abetted by Mrs Selina Cynon, fix-it queen of the good life rounded and whole—this huge slob's mother.

"There's a bloke who's changed," argued Percy, false surcharge quivering his exiled male hulk. "Charlie there, hardest little bugger in the Four Feet one time."

I thought, Percy, old fork-tongued talking mirror, you're bogged in some sort of mammy-dream and I'm neutered, useless for Emily Thorpe, let alone my black-haired, pale-faced mate. Baldy Howell's no good for anything, never has been, he's one of the dregged Cynons, Welsh parrot squeezing the purulence of profit and loss.

"Ker-iste, I could show you scores of men in this club with the dust," Percy said. "Doesn't stop them from being sociable in company. What's he on now, Rees, still searching for remains up around Waunwen?"

"Good, fascinating," approved Howell. "Quite remarkable in a place like Daren, especially Upper Daren. It's such a poky dead-end hole really, since they closed the railway tunnel. My wife has always loathed coming here; she feels she can't breathe, but, of course, she is rather sensitive — isn't she, Percy?"

He said, "You can say that agen. Me, though, I wouldn't shift from Daren, not for two bloody legs. Come on, knock it back; plenty of time for another round."

Howell Cynon jibbed politely, forefingering some straggly hairs from his crimped upper lip. His Castro beard gleamed like Brylcreamed swarf.

"Bring your wife along next time, Howell," I said.

A few parties were cross-bawling old ballad choruses, the lounge acoustics self-charming as a bathroom, the night wearing on towards stop tap. Outside the club I bulled Percy into driving us to Lower Daren.

The factory car park was full, five long rows extending to the railway fence. Man to man, Percy complained seriously, "Listen, Rees, it's none of my business. My old lady, she'll be wondering where the hell I've got to, won't she? Course I've heard the talk about Ellen and Tal, but it's none of my business. What time are they due out?"

"Ten minutes, Perce. Sit tight. I'm not using you as a witness or anything. Remember the time we didn't see you and Vicky Wilson in Swansea market? Your old lady's taking care of our kiddies. Just sit tight; whichever way the ball tamps, you won't get involved."

"None of my business, this," he said.

As she climbed into Tal's car, I crabbed out from the dark and held the door handle. "Much obliged, Tal", I said.

"Come with me, Ellen; we're walking home."

"Have you gone mad? In these shoes?" My wolverine wife, Tal on a fresh cigarette, dithering with the choke, headlights fanning and cutting out all around the car park, factory girls suavely rooted as Buckingham Palace garden-party dames, boyfriends and collier husbands laughing, confident as gunboat commanders. The chosen, the hop, step and jumping social van of Daren, heeding for whom the bell tolls.

Percy muttered, "Hullo there, Ellen. Shwmae, Tal." Tal duffed his brand-new fag and perfect blandness came out of him. "I don't understand your attitude, Rees," he said.

She wrenched violently. "Stupid, let me go! Rees, if you make a scene..."

"Come on, Kate Minty," I said.

"Let go of my arm!"

"G'night," Percy said, plunging away on his stick.

Tal smiled like a Russian offering peaceful co-existence, leaning across her, tipping small taps under my wrist with his knuckles. "Jump in, Rees. We'll be home in a few minutes."

"Don't do that, Tal," I said, the only possible threat, as integral to neurotically archaic miners as to any hidebound gallant from Boston, Mass.

Ellen slipped off her right shoe. I slammed the door on the blow, then jerked it open again. "He's enjoying this," I said."Move, girl, *out*."

"Waster—you rotten, filthy, dirty waster!"

"Get out, beaut."

"I'm sick of you!"

"*Out*," I said.

She laughed, barging her black head at my stomach, abrupt rabid laughter and white teeth. I saw him closing the door, fastidious, the engine humming quietly.

"Now what, matey?"

"Don't sneer," I said. "Say good night to him. We're walking home."

He passed us at the factory entrance, sedate as a hearse driver.

"I thought you wanted to rush me into a dark corner somewhere," — the pavement width between us and I could hear the reedy whisper of her stockings at every stride.

"Beaut, you're slightly knock-kneed," I said.

"What's it all about? What are you going to do?"

"Be quiet, Ellen; for Christ's sake shut it. I've listened to you getting back at me long enough, so *shut up*. That's the message. We're starting it this way. Stop bitching. Shut up."

"I'm not supposed to have any normal social life, just work, work and wait for *you* to become normal. Calling me by my mother's name... what about your own mother? She was a slut, cheap Brynywawr slut! It's coming out more and more, her evil nature. Sometimes I feel like killing you. Two years, Rees, *two* whole years! You must think I'm made of stone."

The streets were deserted, hay-smell wafting from a smallholding below the bomb craters left by Goering's hit-

and-run raiders in 1942. The craters were fern-sided down to stagnant pools, the tadpole ponds of boyhood. A wet quarter-moon, up-tilted to hang your shirt on the lower horn, couched the matt-black remainder as if protecting it from becoming a Patrick Moore space junction. Pigeon senseless, I aligned the North Star to the Plough, a sky-filling dark cloud sheeting over, flatly sombre, its profiled leading edge sucking out stars, layer after layer until misty rain began to fall.

She tied a yellow chiffon scarf around her head, marching stride for stride, our shoes pressing dry sole prints on the faintly damp pavement.

"Ellen," I said, "sometimes I feel like killing you, too."

Her tish ended adamantly, grunting scorn.

"More than wanting to kill Tal Harding," I said. "He's hollow, like a cup."

"Tal's a better friend than you're a husband," she said, the rubbery swish-swish from her stockings lost inside a night rustle that spumed the fine rain into a razzled maze around the street lights.

"Don't wait for me," I said, turning off towards Caib institute. "Good night, Ellen."

"What? Rees, come back, wait! Rees ... you swine."

The maroon side-gate was locked. I climbed over the low, spiked fence, Llew Hopkins's wallflowers sickly sweet, then hurried around the bowling-green and Thorpe's bungalow.

"Rees!" she called. "Rees, wait!"

I waited inside the edge of the woods, seeing her paused in along splay of light escaping from the bungalow.

"Reesy!"

Reacting for the first time, I felt stupidly murderous, mere intent severed from the doing. Killing Ellen would be like destroying the rest of myself. Annihilation, end of the end. A man can't hate himself that far, not unless he's entirely lost, stone mad. Gone lunatic at past midnight in Daren woods, twenty spits and a câm from my deprived wife, a further ten câms to Emily earth goddess, dear Emily, puppeteered by goodness devoid of passion. Affectionate Emily, pansy tender Emily, warm brown across my half-blackened life.

"Where are you, Rees?"

"Here," I said.

She kept jabbering about the children and Mrs Cynon, and I kept telling her to shut up, blundering along in the wet-grassed darkness, tension sweating, stricken desperate as a wounded rat, my imagination (affliction's only holy) centred, pledged like the seed that made the Cross. No man escapes his cross.

Waist-deep in dripping cow parsley, I said, "Take your clothes off," squawking scrapy-throated like a Garden of Eden rogue. "You hear me, girl, clothes off!"

"Oh, my God," she said, and she humphed surprise matter-of-factly as a broody bird.

It wasn't paradise regained, but thrown-out pairs make their own particular oases on wasteland. Have to, at whine's end. Shaky, small enough victory, strolling home hand in hand, drenched as Rio Grande wet-backs. I told her about Emily Thorpe, had to tell her, driven to by resentment, by the fear of feeling inferior. She said, "Only six or seven times with Tal, because, Reesy, it was better that way than with half a dozen. Wasn't it better? Like you and Emily, wasn't it?"

169

"Something similar, Ellen," I said.

"Two years, my love!"—thumping her hip at me, gay, two years sloughed, discarded like wrapping-paper.

"Be quiet, beaut, I'm not right yet."

"You ah-are!"

"We'll see," I said.

"I love you more than ever now, Reesy."

Around the blacked-out bungalow, down alongside the bowling-green, over the low fence, seven red carnation heads crammed inside Ellen's brassiere (gesture of redemption, gospelly sensual), Llew Hopkin's 'stute front lawn patch reeking of metaldehyde slug killer, and we hiked the gradient to our house, where Mrs Cynon slept bolt upright in my grandfather's kitchen armchair, a classical portrait of matriarchal rectitude, of imperishable she-Cymru dignity.

"Percy's been here," she murmured, "and Taliesin Harding called in for half a minute. Not a sound from Lydia and Lizzie-fach. I'll sleep on the couch in the back room. Don't mind, do you?"

Ellen blanketed her warmly on the couch, whispering, her and the old lady whispering together like excited chambermaids.

Two o'clock next afternoon I waited outside the office on top pit for Ike Pomeroy.

15

Luther Howard, more persuasive than his father Watt, heeled slowly around like a witch-doctor inside a circle of clean-faced colliers.

"Now, men, let's have it perfectly clear, shall we? We're all agreed our original price list became null and void when we ran into this jump. Since then we've been on allowance, working just as hard, harder some of us in really bad conditions. My contention is this, *due* to conditions in the Seven Feet, *due* to Ike Pomeroy sticking by the old price list, it's time we had a new working agreement. In other words it's time for us to have a share of the cream. We've sent deputations, we've tried reason, but so far we're up against a stone wall." Luther's chopping right hand stood quite still on the open palm of his left hand.

One of the men said, "Put it to the vote."

Luther said, "Either thirty bob on top of present wages or a chance at the coal in another face, either that or arbitration. It's up to us to make Pomeroy see things our way. Most of the blokes are married. I'm single, but as you know when it comes to victimisation by circumstances beyond our control, then by Christ it's enough to put any man's back up. This jump could go on for six months. We might still be on the muck next Christmas."

"Put it to the vote," they said.

Luther counted hands, plus his own, declaring, "Unanimous. Right, men, we're as a body, so they can't touch us. I'll see Ike Pomeroy. Listen, here are the three alternatives: thirty bob extra, a chance at the coal, or arbitration. Any questions?"

There weren't any. They were all victims in their own eyes. All identical.

Ten minutes later forty afternoon shift men returned to the baths for their day clothes.

Then I went in to ask Ike for a job, his healthily bony face moustached for caballero extravagance. Maybe he could prove it with his slightly bow-legged wife.

"Rees Stevens! Where have you been keeping yourself? Sure we can fix you up,"—his bright utility eyes glinting the vacuity of concentrating two ways. "It's our pleasure to do what we can for a collier with your record under the NCB. Pumps-man by night. Look at those silly sods going home. Luther Howard, that fella would cut off his nose to spite his face. Start Monday night, Rees. Monday night. See old Seward Tremain at pit-bottom, he's over-man by night. What's your disability, Rees, what percentage?"

"Twenty-five," I said.

"Have you been down-graded since the accident?"

I said, "Not since I had my first Board medical."

172

"It wouldn't do for me to sign you on if you couldn't cope with the job; common sense, Rees, you understand. You'll have to walk about four miles a shift."

"Nights regular?" I said.

"Nothing else available for a compo case like yourself. Ted Mayhew is on days, Ianto Pugh by afternoon. They're both compo cases." Ike grinned, gay spirited in devised chaos. "Old Ianto's on his last legs; he might ask for his cards any day, then you'll take his place on afternoons. Seniority rule; you know the principle, Rees."

"Yeh, seniority," I said, feeling trapped the way her beaten father moaned out his Winchester years.

Seward Tremain was a back-slider. He lost his Baptist shanty chapel where he 'saw the light', his eldest son went to Borstal for breaking and entering, and Mrs Tremain took to her bed with angina. Seward back-slid negatively, his sobersides *hwyling* and hymning succumbed to durable moroseness. He belonged to the second generation of firemen officials in Caib Four Feet, resigning to work a coal stent again when production was concentrated in Brynywawr Seven Feet. Then, after losing his chapel, his son and virtually his wife, Seward rejoined the official's union, off-shift fireman graduating to overman because he was loyal, responsible, no man's fool underground, despite the humdrum shambles of his faith and fatherhood.

"Reesy," he said, "I remember the very day you had your bump. Haven't seen much of you since either. See your missis now and again, wheeling the kids down Regent Street. There's Dai Stevens stamped on your kids all right, no mistaking."

We were at pit-bottom, Seward booking in the last of the night-shift men as they stepped forward to the mine-car.

"What's it like on the faces?" I said. "The other afternoon I heard Luther Howard charming his mouth off about this big jump in the Seven Feet. Are they driving through it, Seward?"

"S'all we can do, and hope for the best. Anyhow, Luther's happy now."

"How much allowance are they getting?" I said.

Seward grunted satisfaction as the mine-car pulled away. "Twenty-three bob a shift. If the contract foreigners were still here, they'd have knocked through to clean coal weeks ago."

"You've changed your mind about them since you were on piece-work," I said.

"Rees, you been out a couple of years; you've lost touch. There's too much niggling among our boys. They're too fussy, always picking on the wrongs before the rights. C'mon, let's look at the pumps."

I said, "Maybe our Daren men are after their tanner's worth of justice today instead of waiting for it to come with their pensions or dust compo. From what I saw of the German contract blokes they had no bloody tradition at all. They didn't know good conditions from bad. Only the unprincipled sods from our union ever went to work for that firm."

"Everything's changing, butty. These days it's number one comes first. I got fifteen per cent dust myself. Doesn't bother me much."

I said, "My wife wanted me to take a shift off the time I copped my lot."

Seward's face mellowed beneath his helmet. "Mentioning that, Rees, there was my old lady. She had a touch of the second sight. Good old woman she was, aye indeed, heart as big as heaven. Truth now, she never let us kids want for anything if she could afford it."

"You know what my mother was like," I said.

"Aye, poor gel."

I thought, gone, gone, dead and gone. Thank God I found Ellen. Thank Jesus we found each other.

There were three water pumps working non-stop around the clock. One at Caib pit-bottom, the second along Caib's original main airway return road linking to the steep upcast to Waun Level, the third pump at pit-bottom in Brynywawr. I had to round the pumps twice a shift, oiling and packing grease boxes, travelling the old main airway return on a pump-handle bogie, with a mine-car lift back from Brynywawr at the end of each shift. A girl wearing boots, boilersuit and gloves could do the job. Any twig-limbed slip of a girl.

Pacing the route, I usually reached one of the supply or gate roads for company at snack-time. Middle-aged repairers working in couples—Lewsin Whistler had fallen back nights, repairing with another one-time face collier, Jenkin Howard, brother to Watt, uncle to Luther. Jenkin (Shink Patch, on account of his one eye) was sixty-three, bowed to shellback from fifty years pick and shovelling. He nurtured homers, like my grandfather. After Watt quit the industry there were still seventeen Howards working underground, all grades from labourers to craftsmen. At weddings and funerals the whole tribe foregathered, men, women and children tied by blood and marriage, filling the huge barrack-bare room above

175

the Earl of Haig Club. Daren primaries, these Howards, older than the Cynons, with a relish for argument, quarrelling, banter, vituperation in dialect Welsh. Daughters who bore occasional bastards held their offspring in warrant, irreducible from, committed to the clan, the family name. These indestructible Howards, never a one of them seceding, exiles arriving home on holidays from London, Slough, Coventry, Birmingham or wherever, and the family pattern extended wholesale, as if they were not prodigals, rejecting even news letters, but maybe a trifle late home from pub, club, shopping spree or seaside outing. Great Howard people, to make Coal Board executives appear transiently homuncular, which they must be, in truth, estimating themselves superior to the base of the pyramid upon which they shrewdly totter, directing and obligatorily throat-cutting without wit or passion. As if faultless SUCCESS runs the grain of human hearts tighter than the reach of grass to sun-fire.

As if Rees Stevens, twenty-five per cent compo pumps-man, was predestined to obedience until the doomsday of clocking in and out.

At the end of my first shift I walked down the tump, Ellen standing outside our backyard door the way my grandmother used to stump out to look for my grandfather. Half past seven, quietness over Upper Daren, the day shift gone down, two local buses standing on Harding's Square, waiting for stragglers to come off night shift. Nant Melyn bounced white foam and vinegar-coloured flood water. Too early yet for Rollo & Sons grinding into Caib new tip way up the river gulley.

"Hush," she said, "I don't want the children to wake until eight o'clock."

"Aren't you going to work this morning, Ellen?"

"I might, later. Your breakfast is ready. How was it last night? You look good, Reesy."

"The job can last till I'm ninety, beaut, unless I electrocute myself."

"But we can't sleep together for five nights a week. Say when, love."

"When," I said, grieving minutely, Ellen dexterously spread-eagling herself, ladling milk over my porridge, replacing the saucepan on the cooker and reaching spoons from the cutlery box. Watching her, and a puling grief inside my stomach: John Vaughan's burden.

"Pork sausages, beans and fried tomatoes ready for you in the oven", she said.

I said, "At least you won't hang a red lamp outside the door while I'm tending the pumps."

Her mouth tightened, came smiling rigidly tight, movement fiercely stopped from her whole body. "Better stay at home, matey, look after the fire, dress the children, cook dinner, better for you to stay at home, be my time-keeper."

"I wanted a man's job, Ellen. Any schoolkid can do what I'm doing."

"Shall I work nights for you in the Caib? Aren't you afraid they'll be queueing up for me in the pit-head baths?"

I threw the porridge at her and then we rolled from wrestling to angry heat, someone murmuring a weather forecast on the radio, prating softly apologetic as a sensitive humbled by lifelong prejudice, Ellen smearing her porridgy chin at my throat, sucking small love-bite begs, our clock-trained daughters scampering around the bedroom-brain-splitting the moment, the boon suddenly loosed, set free

177

like scorched earth from no met. man ever. And when the children came downstairs we were squatting shoulder to shoulder on the hearth rug in front of the fire, post-tranced as two neophytes.

Lydia preached exultantly, sing-songing, "Daddy-is-workin', daddy-is-workin'. Down-the-Caa-haib, down-the-Caa-haib."

Elizabeth waddled over our legs, bleating bewilderment, wriggling close to Ellen, Ellen whipping off her blouse to wipe the sticky mess from her chin, cuddling the toddler down to her bare breasts.

"Where is Nana Cynon?" demanded Lydia, wilful as Lot's wife, standing straddle-legged in her red pyjamas.

"She'll be here soon, *cariad*. Did Lizzie-fach pee the bed last night?"

"No, mam, it's dry all over."

Flatly far-off as a harvesting machine, our cute, chrome ribbed transistor on its shelf next to the Skyline utensils rack, hummed news about eighteen thousand BMC workers on strike, followed by the Metropolitan Police Commissioner's report of two hundred and fifty-four thousand, two hundred and eleven indictable offences in his area, an increase of eleven per cent over the previous year. Estimated deaths in the Los Angeles race riots, thirty-four. Nothing fresh from Vietnam.

I said, "Your titties are glory-doves."

"Hush, mind your tongue."

"I could swing on them like Jack the Giant-killer."

"My God," Ellen said.

"Not Him, girl, but I love you. We clicked together like two comets that time."

"I love you too, Reesy. Do you want more porridge? I

can't eat now. I feel all gooey inside." She mouthed above Elizabeth's head, "I'm coming upstairs later on, to be near you, only to be near you. Okay?"

"Shift off from the factory, beaut?"

"Everything stops for love," she whispered.

"*Ach y fi*," accused Lydia, scratching dried porridge out of my throat hollow.

At the end of August Mrs Cynon decided to sleep five nights a week in our house. She designed and enjoyed this contingency, the youngsters making endless demands upon her, Lydia reading primer-book fairy stories with the bounded lightness, bell-singing articulacy of an actress everywhere beautiful except in her emotions, the old lady listening like the dame in charge of the Last Supper. Lydia had discovered penmanship. She scrawled on all the walls. Each side of the lavatory chain in black crayon and Bic: LYDIA STEVENS. On Elizabeth's thighs: LIZY STEVENS. Mrs Cynon wore NANA CYNON across her forearm for three days.

Ellen plumped out like an hour-glass, while I became stringy lean from spending solitary hours tramping my round, foregoing the mine-car ride back to Caib pit-bottom, the extra mileage helping towards a full day's sleep. Stringy lean, fluid, sloping the roadways to and from Brynywawr underneath the Ice Age hulk of Waunwen like a reliable, decent-quality man-animal.

In September the Seven Feet fault knocked out another coalface, leaving two conveyors in full production. We heard rumours as in the days before Caib Four Feet closed down. Brynywawr coke ovens were part fed on coal hauled by road from an open-cast site, a scientific Hobson's choice fiddle, mixing Seven Feet coal with the softer open-cast coal. Then the hammer fell in December. We had three months to 'live'. The jump worsened, killing Caib and Brynywawr. Caib first, thus Daren first at the same stroke.

But in December surface labourers began demolishing Caib's stone-built powder magazine, this familiar landmark tucked into the base of Waunwen, and a contractor's concrete gang laid footings for a new magazine.

"Now it's time to go," Mrs Cynon said. "Enjoy Christmas at home and sell the house. There'll be empty houses and shops in Daren. We've seen it before, but never so bad as this."

I asked her, "Who'll want to buy a house just a couple of spits away from a dead colliery?"

"The Coal Board, *bachgen*."

"Aye, if I'm transferred to another pit."

Elbows on the table, she smiled defeatless enigma. "I was chatting with Alderman Griff Thomas, him from Lower Daren, not to be trusted with his own mother once upon a time. Griff says the Board of Trade refused the council's application for an extension to Remploy, where my Percy does his bit, as you know. We don't read such items in the *Clarion*. Another thing, ever since Caib finished rising coal the council's been trying to find a factory site, advanced factory for turning out washing-machines. Work for hundred and twenty men, reckoned Griff Thomas, but they can't find a site after three years, so we'd best forget about it for another three. What's a hundred and twenty men, I ask you! Plain as daylight to me: they don't want people to stay here in Daren. Only work for girls in that wireless factory down there, and they're on short time January, February and March every year."

"We're still building the council house estate," I said. "New houses, new industry; it's obvious, isn't it?"

"Reesy, pack your traps and leave after Christmas, otherwise you won't be able to forgive yourself in years to come."

"I can't go away, Mrs Cynon."

"Forget about the back room for the time being," she said. "I know you've been busy in there, but there's such a thing as common sense. I myself would love to come with you and Ellen, only I've gone past it now."

"Percy won't leave Daren," I said.

"Him? Duw, boy, you don't realize. Go to bed, or you'll be like a stick when Ellen comes home this afternoon. Remember, have a good heart-to-heart talk with her. She'll do whatever you say, it's up to you *then*, see, Rees?"

We hedged a few pros and cons on Christmas Eve while laying out the kiddies' toys. Twenty quid's worth of toys— if the working class cannot supply their children with riding ponies and four-course meals, they'll infest hire-purchase systems to give them Christmas and birthday presents, humanising commerce, crime and silver-spooned womb-throwing. Expendable people versus dependables, all wobbling the brotherhood circle, with any Chancellor of the Exchequer doing a Simeon Stylites bowel and bladder act in the centre. Hail the brotherhood! The day of the square peg is at hand, he's studying form in the betting shop and his help-mate is chewing Black Magic with a *Coronation Street* saga-piece unfolding in front of her. Meantime the round pegs are sapiently planning painless assassination, foraging into enlightenment, measuring alter-egos, double-crossing schizophrenia, brain-washing apprentice tycoons and cosmonauts, hurting without hating, working nights in Lyon's Corner House and inventing disc shearers for the Gellideg seam in *Peyton Place*.

All hail, all blessings. Well-aye.

"That's for Elizabeth, give it to me," Ellen said, carefully snatching the walking, talking, make-water, five-guinea human-haired rosebud plastic doll. "Honestly, Rees, there's no reason why we should be bothered. The NCB can't promise you a job because of your disability, so where do we go?"

"It isn't settled yet," I said. "We'll be allocated after they've fixed up the colliers, packers, craftsmen, officials, all the men they can't afford to lose. When it comes to our turn they'll work the seniority rule. Unfortunately I broke my contract when I refused to go to Talygarn. We paid for this old house instead. Christ, beaut, I wish I didn't have to go to work tonight."

"Are you sorry, Rees."

"I don't regret much, Ellen, not much."

"Then neither do I. See this, from the girls in the factory. Like it?" She hung the nightdress in front of herself.

I said, "Have you told them about our two years, the time I dried up?"

"Reesy!"

"It's almost invisible," I said. "What's the matter, are they short of men in your factory?"

"Women are always short of the right men; that's why the chapels are empty and the pits are closing and we swop governments like cushion covers. Every time something goes wrong it's due to women living with the wrong men. *Iesu*, six storybooks for Lydia, three from Selina Cynon. Our daughter's going to be a scholar. Your pick-pick-picky old brains, Rees Stevens."

"She'll probably marry a collier if he's the right man."

"My God, it's a long way off."

"You can't blame men, Ellen."

She said, "The right loving must come from the right man. Please fetch Lydia's tricycle. Percy hid it up in the attic. Mind you don't fall, Rees-love. I shan't wear my new nightie if you break your whatchewmaycallit."

"Are we getting the right loving?" I said.

"Don't you know?"

"Is it as perfect as it used to be, Ellen?"

"Now see what you're doing! Separating it from everything else. Listen, matey, are you some kind of Welsh mountain pony, only good for eating, sleeping and huh-huhing?"

"You're a pretty lush mare, beaut, especially since you've grown more curvy these last few months."

Two piles of Christmas toys between us, carol singers rolling up the street from *Waun Arms*, duty calling by the minute—I had to be down Caib pit by eleven o'clock, just four safety men: two officials, electrician and pumps-man Stevens.

"I have always loved you, Rees," she said, coolly absolute as faith, faith scoured of dross by the war and peace of day by day by day. The living welter.

We climbed the frost-bound tump together, a bright round of moon knobbed above Waunwen, then she fled back to the house in case the children awoke.

Seward Tremain and the banksman were alone on top pit, the second fireman and electrician already down below, every other Caib miner at home for Christmas. We rode the

183

windy cage in silence, a can of grease between my boots and Seward's Davy oil-lamp hanging from his belt.

"I'll be in West 12 gate road around grub-time," he said. "See you, Rees."

The shift wore out, passed like a broken promise. On Christmas morning three safety men and two electricians went down. After washing I collected my firewood block from outside the pit-head baths, a torch beam hitting me full in the face, the ex-wrestler watchman grunting, "Whassis, ah? Tisn't block day, you know that?"

"Allowances in kind," I said. "Read all about it on page so and so of the annual Coal Board report in Lower Daren central library."

"I'm booking you, Rees."

"Fuck off," I said.

"Hey, watch it, careful now, careful..."

"You're practically on the dole, butty, and you haven't done a day's honest graft in your life. Less than three months to go now, then you'll be signing the dotted line every Friday. Caib smoke stack can't fall down a second time either, and the Germans won't be coming back to Daren. If I were you I'd make for home; your missis and Santa Claus might be working a flanker."

"All right, all right, we'll see how chopsy you are to Mr Pomeroy. What's your lamp number?"

"Three 'o three, dum-dum special right between your bloody pimpers. Listen, butt, if you'd like to make Ike Pomeroy really happy, remind him about your customers in Daren Social Club. Sand, cement and chippings delivered right to their back doors when the Germans were building those underground bunkers for the Four Feet. And tell him you'd like to hear the story about Mrs Pomeroy, the time she gave a talk on local government to the Women's Guild. That's the idea, butty, put the torch away; it makes you look like a queer statue of liberty."

"Righto, shut it, now shut it, you big-mouthed bastard."

"Happy Christmas," I said. "Stay frightened. You're in the shit right up to your eyeballs."

He skulked across to the lamproom where he slept most of the hours he should have been patrolling the sidings and around the pit-head. I came down the tump, expecting to see all the lights on in our house. They were, Ellen wearing my sportiest sweater over the gift nightdress, red Chunky four ply flopping to her thighs. She'd had about four hour's sleep, her black hair pillow-coiled against her left ear—I sleep high-headed on my right side. We seldom breathe at each other, Saturday and Sunday nights. The kiddies had abandoned breakfast. Under licence derived from Calvary, they were glutting themselves with nuts and chocolates, sitting back to back surrounded by toys and monkey-nut shells.

"We shan't be moving away from Daren," I said.

"You've finally decided. Good." She drooped over the table, blinking, the kiddies squealing liberties in the next room. I loved her like life.

"They'll have to bring factories here, jobs for men," I said.

"Hm. Are you working tonight, Rees?"

"Doubler tomorrow night, beaut. Ianto Pugh's doing my turn tonight."

"Good," she sighed, lolling her head.

I remembered my grandfather snoozing over his breakfast,

pink bacon-greased lips across his coal-black face, hands washed to his hairy wrists, *Daily Herald* propped against the loaf and the pot of strawberry jam, bucket of water simmering on the hob, my grandmother knuckling his nape, ordering him not to waste good food, bath himself, go to bed out of the way. He, too, finished up working night shift in the Four Feet, before his last seven years' full-time devotion to racing pigeons. Ellen's white nape, black whisps springing tight as an airedale's curls, reminded me of my black-faced grandfather jarred awake by the old lady's great ugly knuckles—the same strong hands that scrammed Andrew Booth's face from eyebrows to jowls during the stay-in strike: Maggie May Stevens, one of a housewife gang who attacked Caib officials when they refused to allow food to be sent down the pit. You could hear the strikers singing *Calon lân* and *Bread of Heaven* from the mouth of the shaft. They held competitions, solos, monologues, played Tip-it, hunted rats and sent up the old men and the sickly ones... before my time.

John Vaughan's time. His Account rides my head like a burr.

16

Success comes to those who refuse to be overcome. Therefore when reading about improvements as affecting coal mining I am inclined to take the view that we fought the good fight. Like the Salvation Army song namely Fight The Good Fight With All Your Might. After fourteen year here in Winchester where these sloppy college boys are not one jot better civilized than we were in Daren, as I say after fourteen years any item of news re coal mining is guaranteed to pluck a chord from those olden days when the miner was considered the lowest of the low. To some ignorant minds he is still Taffy Jones dressed in a muffler & cap with a couple of whippets behind his heels. As if this man Jones would never breed horses for the St Leger or Grand National or Derby if he could afford anything other than those dainty little whippets. Smart young men fishing in the Itchen with keepers behind their backs are no different from collier lads groping for trout in Daren river. Sunday mornings you would see youngsters

*setting out with lurchers & terriers, the sporting instinct used
to run in families from father to son. Foxing, fishing, hares.
You had to walk miles from Daren for rabbits. The vital thing
is to have an interest in life instead of stagnating body & soul
as you would witness all ages of men on our street corners
during bad times & good times. Nothing on their minds. No
interests except backing horses, football, women, coal & the
Great War. We brought some of the finest political brains in
Wales to Caib institute, these educated men from all walks of
life including Quakers who came for the sake of conscience
but it was like feeding pearls to swine apart from a handful
who appreciated that there was more to this life than six shifts
ending with a booze-up. In my opinion the Sunday foxers &
fishermen were superior to those street corner loungers. In all
fairness you have to respect a man's interest even if he does
not respect yours. Many of us gave years to Federation
business expecting nothing but decent respect for our
endeavours which is as it must be because no committee in
the world can function without goodwill. When goodwill
relapses other committees are elected. Lodge Number One
both suffered & triumphed in 1936. Firstly there was friction,
two viewpoints clashing when 43 day shift colliers threatened
stay-in strike. God alone knows we had plenty of wages
grievances to bring us all out on 14 days notice. The man
who invented stay-in strikes was definitely a genius. He
opened up public ignorance like a surgeon, I mean the way
we won sympathy for stay-in strikes although these strikes
were trifles compared to slow starvation. When Ross Butler
came as under manager he tried too many new broom tactics.
As if good & bad do not exist. But he was neither big enough
nor strong minded enough. Better men than Ross Butler have*

fallen by the wayside when it comes to fighting for principles. Sometimes they look to be winning but in the end they either bend with the wind or fade out altogether. Our case was open & shut. Unfortunately men on the off-shifts failed to rally round, causing friction amongst ourselves up until the actual moment of action. Ross Butler victimized Cled Howard, accusing Cled of filling out dirty coal & failing to keep his face posted according to mining regulations, whereas the crux of the matter was that Cled spoke his mind & had no regard for the consequences. When the management put Cled sponging by afternoon it was then his day shift butties instigated the stay-in. 43 men under for seven days, 32 men for thirteen days & we won hands down. I personally disagreed with certain elements who smashed windows in Ross Butler's house as it brought out the police against us. Butler had a bad name. It was bound to stick as circumstances built up against the man. In, robbing many, many colliers on yardage he saved pounds for Joseph Gibby & sowed bad feeling for himself, ending in the kick in the privates from Cled's cousin Mervyn Howard. Our Lodge arranged for Mervyn's solicitor. The plea self-defence. Actually Mervyn's wife Dilys gave him the black eye to prove his case but someone unknown carried the word across Daren to Ross Butler. At the trial in Swansea Assizes Butler brought in false witnesses who swore on oath that they had seen Mervyn kicking him on the pavement outside Vic Einon's tobacconist shop. Mervyn served his six months & went away to Dagenham. Ross Butler was transferred to another colliery. A deputation pressed Cled's case to Joseph Gibby's agent & Cled Howard won his place back on the coal. Fight, fight, it was always a fight for the strict necessities of life. Up to a point we could rely upon support from the chapels.

How pathetic to see the way they were torn between fighting for a living wage & religious teaching such as loving your neighbours & the meek shall inherit the earth. Joseph Gibby & his father before him owned the best earth in Daren. We had three deacons on the Lodge committee, our guilty three from Calvaria & Bethany because none other than Joseph Gibby himself held the deeds on their places of worship. No wonder Karl Marx said religion was the opium of the masses. No wonder it takes ages & ages for justice to come about. Justice indeed! For instance Mr Gibby's agent looking down the mouth of Caib pit, our men singing hymns for his benefit to show they were in high morale & he said with a sneer "They won't be singing by the end of the week." The truth is he was a lucky man. Once the news spread that neither food nor jugs of tea would be sent down to our comrades hundreds of women came screaming up from Daren, Andrew Booth & his day shift firemen taking the brunt while clever Mr Agent & Ross Butler stayed locked inside the colliery office until the police arrived. There would have been court cases for assault only Joseph Gibby sent a telegram stopping all legal action. Wise man. The woman would never have forgiven him. Mrs Glyndwr Stevens left marks on Andrew Booth which he carried to his grave although Glyndwr himself was at that time hard heading man up in Waun Level, out in sympathy strike of course because we had learned the principle of unity: UNITED WE STAND, DIVIDED WE FALL. My own wife Kate brought sheer luxury foodstuffs up to top Pit, where from God alone knows. The stay-in offered her free rein to get anything she could from any source whatsoever. Sometimes we have to admit that women like Kate make a mockery out of authority & law & order. Big lumps of ham, full jars of Lovell's toffees, tins of salmon, slabs of loaf cake, best butter, chocolate truffles, bottles of pop, there was no end. The Lodge refused to send down beer, best Houghton dark stout she had to bring home but I was too ashamed to take a sup of it. I did not like the way she was enjoying herself. Anyone who came to the door had a bottle of stout slipped into his pocket. I said to Kate, "Have you & that girl Miskin been whoring among the Daren shoppies for all those goods you are taking up to the pit?" She said, "You are not the only one on a committee in this house." This hint referred to Caib Collection Committee. She said, "If they refuse their names go down in the black book." I said, "What for?" She said, "The future of course." I said, "That's known as blackmail." Kate laughed, "Business is business!" I said, "How do you mean?" She said, "To put it bluntly the shoppies are afraid their wives might find a fancy woman on the doorstep." I said, "But you are in the Pentecostals." Her answer was, "Don't forget the Lord is on the side of charity. I would walk the streets in my bare skin for those poor men down below." "Never Kate," I said, "you would do it for your own satisfaction." She said, "Hark who's talking! Going with you is like going with a fish." "Then why did you marry me?" I said. "I was fed up, wanted to leave home. Now you know," she said. I asked her, "Any names in the black book yet?" She said, "Victor Einon refused chewing twist but Edna Miskin was in the shop with his son Seaton last night so she will be fetching a boxful up to Caib this afternoon. Teach old Vic a lesson in charity." I said, "God help us, there's no scruples left." Kate replied, "Blame yourself, John Vaughan, if you must blame anybody. All I can say is it's up to us to make sure the men down there get the best of everything. If you were on stay-in strike I would come down the pit to you."

"Why, Kate?" "Not for you to go short. Excuse me, we are collecting from Daren Arcade this morning. See you on top pit at two o'clock." I said, "Dewi Benjamin's wife owns the Arcade, you cannot put her name in your black book." She said, "We can find plenty of volunteers, the Howard boys, the Miskin boys, but in Phoebe Benjamin's case it is Dewi Ben who has made arrangements for us to collect bacon, brawn, eggs, mutton chops & cockles if the cockle woman brought supplies on the eleven o'clock train yesterday, if not cockles whatever Phoebe can spare in the way of bara lawr or sweetbreads." Try to imagine Kate on Lodge Number One. By her ruling every collier in the pit would be negotiating his own Price List. Confusion for Joseph Gibby & everyone else. Kate delighted in messiness, chaos in other words. Her & the Miskin girl were back & fore, back & fore to Caib every day like two flags. While we organized from the institute they badgered the banksman to send down food & clothes gathered by the Collection Committee. Women, there they were all hours of the day hanging around the pit head. Wives, fiances, mothers, all demanding to send down messages & so on but the banksman's hands were tied. He had orders agreed upon by the Lodge & the management. After seven days 11 men were raised to the surface, 2 stretcher cases with suspected pneumonia, the other 9 brought up walking sticks cut from Norway posts. What a memento for their self imprisonment. They all had them, 43 walking sticks cut with hatchets & pocket knives. High-ups in our Federation came to thrash out principles & law but thirteen whole days & nights went by before Joseph Gibby gave way. Of course as usual we never spoke to him although we all had his name on our tongues, his photograph there for anyone to see in Caib institute committee room, the full committee facing the camera on May Day 1927 when we officially opened the institute. Eventually Cled Howard was reinstated & Caib returned to normal procedures for wage claims, pennies, threepenny bits, shillings dribbling out of our pockets into Joseph Gibby's bank account. Try as we may the Price List differentials never worked fairly for men cutting coal, on traffic, on day-wages, repairing, labouring or on the surface. Never a Friday without representations to Caib cashier. You had to admire him & Andrew Booth. The light of development in our Scientific Age makes a man realize they were as much victims of circumstances as we were only they did not have to worry about keeping body & soul together. It was a bad time. Bad time. Extremely bad in the thirties. All you have to do is examine the whole development of Society to appreciate that we workers of Daren were just emerging from being little better than clods of the earth. "Six days shalt thou labour" the ministers used to preach from Horeb, Bethany, Salem, Libanus, Calvaria, Siloh, Nebo, St Mark's, Ebenezer, Tabernacle, Rama. "In the sweat of thy face shalt thou eat bread" was another favourite for condemning the working class & very few atheists & so-called free-thinkers in Daren ready to disagree. Ignorance ruins worse, much worse than anything in this world. Ignorance is terrible. Like carrying sin once we REALIZE how ignorant we are. Born completely ignorant, living in ignorance, the struggle for existence going on & on until we perish. Possibly we should thank God for the privilege of struggling towards wisdom. Thank God for wisdom even though I do not believe in God as such. Through Science we shall put an end to man's cruelty to man with time on our side for all the millions & millions of failures in the past.

Discovery upon discovery until the working classes become extinct. Once we were animals snarling over bones, now we fly faster than the birds, travel the oceans faster than fishes, speak to each other across continents. Now education is advancing North, South, East & West. But very often patience comes hard besides wearing thin. The patience of having to go back to the colliery office after a week's toil & plead for the minimum wage. The patience of coping with a wife when you cannot fathom her reckless ways. She rose from her bed two days after the birth of our daughter Ellen on June 9th 1938 when everyone in Daren was dumb-founded, horrified by the explosion in Alf Gilbert's conveyor face on June 7th. Sheer tragedy. 16 colliers & boys killed, wiped out without a chance of survival. Again nobody in Daren set eyes on Joseph Gibby. I said, "Kate, for God's sake stay in bed till the midwife gives permission." She said, "We'll be having visitors after the funeral. I must clean up the place, it isn't as if I'm bad or anything." Will-power, nothing but will-power the way it functions in the wilds. Our visitors were Morgan & Idris Miskin with their loose flag of a sister. Edna & Herbert Prothero & later came Dewi Benjamin & his wife Phoebe & last of all Selina Cynon with a child in arms herself, old Twmws Ivor's grandson by his son Hayden Percival who was killed in the explosion. Proud Selina Cynon in black mourning coming on this visit to see our new baby, desperation written all over her. In Selina's own house the biggest congregation of mourners gathered after the funeral, her husband Hayden Percival being so popular. Selina's baby was named Percival after his father. All the time that poor mite cried & cried. A wild burial morning, cloudburst over Waunwen sending floods down the tip & rushing into Chapel Street where the culvert over-flowed

194

along Lower Terrace & down Thelma Street one side & then on down the main road to Daren river. More thunder & lightning while we were up in the cemetery then sunshine followed & you could smell mud everywhere in Upper Daren. As expected Joseph Gibby sent 16 12/6 penny wreaths. What price a 12/6 penny wreath for a man or a boy's life? Where is the sense in preaching, "The Lord giveth & the Lord taketh away?" The explosion in Alf Gilbert's conveyor face gave every minister in Daren a ready-made sermon. Easy for them. Their great Lord. How can the Lord above have anything to do with those who have never even heard of Him? If He was in Alf Gilbert's face there is not much hope for those who believe in the Lord. As for miners & coal-owners, where does He come into the picture? A man is lucky if he is religious in this day & age.

I thought, dead right old Sioni-boy, right down the line they're sapping the life out of Daren. Down through the Coal Board's sixty-two grade classified hierarchy, with Christ knows how many yes-men and yes-please-women in each department. The time has come for Andrew Booth's daughters-in-law to promote the cause of the Free Wales Army. Choose between the F.W.A. and Ike Pomeroy. Offer Ike a pair of electrodes, Ilya Kuryakin's gat, plus Whitehall sanction to purge and he'll exterminate every redundant miner in Daren. Any man who loses a shift to paddle with his kids in Mumbles, or prematurely hunt relics like Charlie Page, report to Ike Pomeroy for androgen drainage. If the NCB can't have a full complement of brain-washed Stakhanovites, they'll run the industry with unkillable compo cases. Their woe-men.

195

Christmas morning 1966, ten weeks to Caib's dead-line, Ellen shivering out of my Chunky sweater and into her clothes, my eyelids coming down like night skies and Treasurer Vaughan's Account fallen off the bed.

17

Llew Hopkins touched his peak to him as he climbed out of his car. "This way, mister. Full 'ouse waiting for you upstairs there. Listen, mun, will the Coal Board take this place over? See, I been in authority here goin' on forty years."

The area industrial relations officer smiled cheese, shaking his head in mimicry of a doleful marionette.

"Straight up them stairs, mister," Llew said. 'Oi, *you*, Reesy Stevens, show him the way."

He was an egg-bodied man with long-fingered hands and the powerful neckless head of a take-over mogul, late middle age iron greying his stubbed hair and spreading his feet. His dark wine-red knitted tie matched his thin silk socks.

"You're in at the kill, mate," I said.

He grinned saliva-toothed, dead-eyed as a china spaniel. "Wait, friend! Surely you received an offer when I came here a few weeks ago?"

"You were only considering face workers then, butty."

"Ah, of course, but today I've come to finalize an agreement with your lodge regarding grades two and three."

I said, "Our compo sec lives over in Brynywawr."

"He's been notified, friend, I assure you he's been notified."

Luther Howard jumped down off the stage, hand out to usher the Coal Board officer, quiet clamour from all the Caib men in the hall cutting to a polite drone.

"Luther," I said, "ask him if he can find Llew Hopkins a job in a long-life 'stute. Old Llew's sweating cobs down in the billiards room."

"The man isn't our responsibility..."

"Certainly not, Mr Vivian. It's up to the NUM, Mr Vivian. We'll look after the caretaker. Come and take a seat, Mr Vivian."

"Wipe the yellow off, Luther," I said. "When the Caib closes the 'stute closes and Llew's finished."

Luther rushed back from the side steps leading up to the stage. "For Christ's sake, man, face up to the facts. We haven't got a leg to stand on. The Caib's had it, right, but we can't afford to antagonize the Board. We tried that last November. Look, Rees, they're buying our houses, they're giving us fifty quid removal expenses and another fifty quid to settle in. To my mind that's organization. What more can we ask?"

"How many men are they going to down-grade?" I said.

"We're sorting that out today, negotiating... ah, Christ, what's old Shink on about now?"

Before Mr Vivian reached his chair on the stage Luther's uncle, old shellback Shink Patch stepped forward from the front row. "'Scuse me, didn't you work in the Pen-Mawr round about nineteen-twenty-one, after the big strike, I think it was? Let's see now, there was a Jacob Vivian driving that heading up to the low coal, aye-aye, that was him, Jacob Vivian."

"My brother," said the Coal Board officer, slack palm held up for peace, unction damaging his empty smile.

"Bit of a pudding he was," Shink said, "taking him all in all. Ta very much." Shink sank to his chair slow as an old lion sitting in cold water.

I said, "Your father was a better NUM man than you are, Luther."

"Matter of opinion, Rees. From what I hear your opinion don't count for fuck all since you packed in on the coal."

"We can't trust you, Luther."

He went up on the stage. The lodge chairman from Brynywawr called upon the Coal Board officer and we heard the tale from him until St Mark's church bell clanged, coaxing in the faithful handful to evening service.

I was redundant, along with a third of the men belonging to Caib, men over sixty, near sixty, men disabled, the ailing, the worn-out and the half-broken.

Ellen said, "Don't worry, we'll survive so long as we don't have any more children."

"Beaut," I said, "I won't get enough redundancy pay to buy a birth certificate."

"Never mind, I love you," she said.

I thought, thank the Christ—here in Wales it has to be Him by way of exemplar, of acme, zenith, *ne plus ultra*.

Shifts rode down, came up again, trailed off to the baths as if Caib was destined to last indefinitely. We stopped talking about the closure. It was ordained, settled like inheriting Rhesus negative. Colliers trickled away from Daren to long-life pits. New NCB houses, new furnishings, new lives in the old mould. Families vanished: the coal-face Howards, the Miskins, Seward Tremain and two brothers, five from Charlie Page's family, Jesse and Islwyn Morgans, young Dicko Harding, Fred Fransceska, Archie Booth (retired) and two NCB electrician sons, single men and whole families went away. Repeat of the dirty Thirties. Upper Daren gentled into puzzling decay as winter dragged on. Lower Daren buzzed falsely feverish Saturday and Sunday nights. The Social Club cut two bingo sessions. Work slowed on the new council house estate—seasonal, explained the *Clarion*. Bandwagon newspapers splashed appeals: Factories for Daren. Social economics, logical as wetness and dryness. We had vague promises from the Home Office, carrot smells, the radio and television factory working four days a week until April, TO LET notices on Noddfa, Tabernacle and Rama, their stained-glass windows boarded up after schoolboys had used the coloured saints, crosses and bearded shepherds for cock-shies.

Daren police station was condemned, the massive old stone building demolished and rebuilding started before they cleared away the rubble. The housing estate hung fire throughout February, when our council sacked the watchman for flogging flooring timber and electrical conduit. Rollo & Sons continued washing Caib new tip, narrowing the river gulley, leaving it dead, craterous. Charlie Page's name appeared in *The Times*; his courageous wife back-lashed weekend honeymoons with a retired insurance collector.

Caib's new powder magazine was almost completed, its

pillar-box-red steel door lying on the grass behind the carpenter's shop. Someone had stolen the lightning conductor off the roof of the neat, new, useless building.

Ianto Pugh retired before the closure. I fell into his shift on afternoons, a frail bachelor named Amwell Cassam (orphaned since boyhood, only son of an old Daren family) taking my place on night shift. Amwell drank rough cider. He lived with a rheumy black retriever dog in basement rooms below Regent Street. He had high narrow shoulders and the low-slung, tender-looking paunch of an alcoholic. When Libanus chapel sent out a call in 1873, Amwell's great-grandfather answered from Wiltshire, the chapel's first minister, who baptized his flock in Daren river. Amwell attended the pumps by night, stepping into the cage like a caricature of depression unless he'd pepped himself with cider before coming to work. Mornings he stepped out of the cage like a culled zombie. After ten years on NAB and national insurance benefit, Daren labour exchange sent Amwell to qualify the death of Caib colliery. He lasted three weeks, deteriorating after collecting his first pay packet to the fourth night of his absence from work. That night his scabby old retriever crashed through the window of the basement dwelling. Amwell was dead beneath a pile of old overcoats, one of his great-grandfather's wood-wormed poker-work motto placques on the wall above his ex-W.D. camp bed: GOD IS NOT MOCKED. Two men attended Amwell's funeral, myself and the Libanus minister—two declining Baptist chapels kept him off the dole. Or a call.

Walking home from Daren cemetery, I saw Llew Hopkins emptying ashes outside Caib institute boiler-house. Forty years of ashes filling a crescent-shaped hollow, seven feet deep nearest the boiler-house doorway, the extremities of the crescent fortified with winter nettle stalks.

"Amwell Cassam is dead, Llew," I said.

"Aye, so I heard. Fool to hisself, that bloke. Never hurt a soul, only hisself. Listen to me, Reesy, there's rumour they've knocked through the big jump over in Brynywawr. Anythin' in it?"

I said, "They hadn't knocked through yesterday, Llew."

"Ent it fuckin' shameful? Here I been all these years lookin' after this place, for what, boy, tell me for what?"

Llew rarely cursed other than complementary damns, bloodies and buggers. Stiffly motionless under the heatless February sun, canted skew-hipped over his black walking-stick, he personified functional crippledom cast aside, rendered socially worthless. Llew's apotheosis.

"How old are you then?" I said.

"Sixty-two. Thass nothin' to go by, mun! I'm same now as was thirty bloody year ago. Duw, it used to be a man worked on the coal till he was seventy."

"He's slowing down at forty these days, Llew."

Hawking from nose and throat, he spat savagely.

I said, "Will Daren council take over the bowling-green?"

"More'n likely. Two councillors in the team, besides Mr Thorpe from Barclay's and Mr Purcell from Houghton's brewery. They'll have to 'ave one of them pavil-leon places though when we shut the 'stute." He joggled into motion, muttering, "By the Jesus, forty years, been here forty years, aye … for what, for bloody what?"

Up-road from the institute you could see four saloon buses filling with day-shift colliers on Harding's Square. Five double-deckers crowded the Square when we worked the

Four Feet, with as many men travelling by train from Daren Halt to Regent Street station. Llew Hopkins nudged himself through the institute door and I noticed a row of elderly men inside the chest-high reading-room window, leaning impassively like Press box privilegees, gazing up towards Harding's Square. As the buses pulled away they drifted slow-motion as wafted mobiles back into the reading room. Caib pit-wheels spun soundlessly, a tinkling grind swinging downwind from Rollo & Sons' tip-washing plant hidden around the curving breast of Waunwen. The old parish cart-track shot Roman-true slantwise up the mountainside, smooth fawny brown, bordered by lichened rock outcrops, beds of sober green moss and great ragged smothers of dark red fern. I couldn't see the Forestry Commission trees parading the far crown of Waunwen. Failed to see George Thorpe's car coming out from the bungalow road, too, until he hooted a refined warning and I stepped back to exchange nods as he rolled by.

Emily, I thought, dear doldrum-bellied Emily—loitering carefully negligent through the maroon-painted side gate, pausing to glance over the bowling-green fence, justifiably curious Daren citizen, natural, hands flat open in my trouser pockets like a confirmed stroller. But she wasn't in the bungalow garden, neither front nor back. Stiffly gargantuan in the cold sunlight, the winter trees hung like fossilized seaweeds. A quiet mile away up the river the machinery churned out Rollo & Sons' second million pounds. I stared up at the pale sky, pale blue, pale as Cardiganshire watered milk, and heard myself, "Rees, you're looking for trouble."

So I came out from the woods whistling a ragged tempo Julie Felix L.P. number through Senior Service smoke, feeling

203

easy, proud as a bloke tried and exonerated, relieved and empty-headed, Emily's girl-romping, "Hullo-hull-ow!" bluntly hooking somewhere inside me like the back-swing of a sickle.

"*Shwmae*," I said.

"Well, well, Rees Stevens!"

"Hullo, Emily."

Amwell Cassam's Thursday funeral, his dog put down by the RSPCA, last night's ice glittering the fringes of Nant Melyn, pumpsman Ted Mayhew working a doubler (my double turn tomorrow), George Thorpe calmly vultured behind his desk in his sanctum and his wife blooming effulgent as one of her summer dahlias, white woollen dress stretched over her diaphragm by the reaches of her bosom.

I said, "Smashed any good bottles lately?"

"George found your naked monster. There was an awful scene, dreadful really. I had to tell him it was my handiwork. Wishful thinking, he said, afterwards. Do come into the house; it's bitterly cold."

We were moving along the hallway, pleasantly inane like salesman and client with a satisfying deal behind them, when a tall grandfather clock gonged right close to my ear. One clean jump and I buffeted her shoulder, both of us spinning on the tiled floor, my secondary grab mistaken for something else, and we collapsed backwards, slid apart like a divided avalanche. The big clock gonged twice more, chains whirring rhythmically within its polished rosewood trunk, then omnipotently hammered on: tick-tock, tick-tock, as if intelligent life was yet to come, creak out from primeval hopelessness, the bastardized beginning. Time itself spelling out its own sacrosanct fatuity.

Emily said, "Dear me, well, well... are you hurt?"

She wore scarlet thigh-length long-johns with white lace trimmings. "Those are the fashion now," I said.

"What? Pardon, Rees?" bringing her legs together, sharply jerking upright on the tiled floor, guilt quaking her round blue eyes like a *Before* advert for scrambled nerves.

I thought, try not to frighten her, at the same moment spontaneously hypnotized by the skin-tight winter knicks — but Ellen wore them. Ellen wearing them, my indomitable Ellen, prototype of all long-johnned women.

Repeating, "Coffee, I'll make some coffee, yes, coffee", Emily somehow rose from the slippery floor with her knees pressed together.

"Bit of a shambles," I said. "But anyhow we're whole, no cracked bones, nothing splintered."

We sat like low-grade Platonists in the warm bungalow, exchanging cruel inanities, cruel patter, Emily cross-ankled, demure as anaesthetized ecstasy, her neat little mouth taking the coffee like a divine nun habituated to elixir.

I said, "Emily, let's go out to the shed and break some bottles."

"Oh, I daren't any more; no, you see, my husband interfered all the time. I had no privacy."

"Right, what's the attraction these days?" I said.

"I suppose I must tell you, Rees."

"Definitely."

The schoolgirl giggle overwhelmed her. She shook pent-up delight. "I'm painting the attic," she whispered, "with silver paint. It's ever so weird."

I said, "Silver paint?"

"Silver! Next summer I shall start with a pair of Egyptian mouth-breeders and a few guppies in a small tank, not too large, about thirty inches by thirty-six inches by twenty-four inches. You see that power point? The lead comes down inside the wall. I've fixed another socket up there to warm the water. Mouth-breeders must, really must, have an average temperature of seventy-five degrees, eighty for breeding purposes."

I said, "*Duw-Duw.*"

We climbed into the attic off a step-ladder, Emily leading, obliviously brisk, urging, "Hurry, please hurry; my husband will be home soon."

It was like standing inside the prism-shaped hulk of a frozen whale, daylight shimmering phosphorescently cold, scaly off the boarded rafters and ceiling joists, glittering Christmas tinsel silver, Emily herself glowing luminous as a London Palladium chanteuse in her white woollen dress. The casement-type dormer window overlooked the front garden. Beyond the bowling-green you could see the blue-pennant sandstone flank of Caib institute, with two uniform rows of green-painted Georgian windows along the billiards room and upstairs concert hall.

"Your husband doesn't know?" I said.

She swirled her thick brown hair. "It's a secret!"

"Does he know about your scarlet bloomers?"

"George will be home..."

I said, "Show, love, don't be shy."

Emily ducked, running for the trap-door.

She's frightened, I thought, still frightened. Can't blame her either. Me in my cemetery black and this grey hair. Where in the name of Jesus God did I get this grey hair?

"Rees," she appealed from the step-ladder, "please come down."

"What time does he leave the bank?" I said.

"Soon, in half an hour. Scandal would ruin us, ruin us all!"

Forgetting about Jonah, I hauled her back into the silvered attic. "There won't be any scandal, Emily. I promise, love, truly."

"My own home, Rees, it's terrible, really,"—a burst of panic rushing her across to the dormer window and then she spun round, instant erotica, spluttering, "Very well, but you'll have to hurry, be quick, quick! "—stone-killing everything, almost everything, I mean the mutuality, concord, the tenderness.

Hurry, I thought, all right, all right, hurry and return from never-never, and that's how I felt taking a roundabout route through lanes and across waste ground until I came out opposite Waun Arms. Old colliers, some railwaymen, two bus conductors in the bar and Mrs Freda Rowland-Parry fat as a mother-squid behind the counter.

"Pint of Houghton's, please," I said.

"Gone time, Rees. Look, five to four."

"Time for a glass?" I said.

She pulled once, thirty years computering her judgement, the beer climbing to standstill at the brim of the half-pint glass.

"Where you been, wedding?" she said. "Hey, I'm talking to you, Rees."

"Amwell Cassam's funeral."

"Blessing in disguise," she said, genuinely righteous, her pouched eyes glittering humane vengeance. "Never had a fair chance, Amwell didn't, not from the very first day he was born. Many's the time he slept rough, those chapel buggahs coming in here, telling us to report him. Ach, *mochyns* safe inside their own front doors. Me and Wyndham, we know who's who, all the years we've served the public."

Wyndham Rowland-Parry swept floors in the radio and television factory, his right arm permanently kinked by a colliery accident. Their three sons won college places from Lower Daren Grammar School, dour long-headed boys, non-smilers who became civil engineers as if predestined.

"Still losing trade, Freda?" I said.

She growled like a man in a scrum.

I said, "Few more weeks and Ellen will be keeping me."

Her shrug shivered her drop earrings. "Come on, boys, haven't you got homes to go to? Time, gents, tuh-hime, pur-lease!"

Frost tingled the darkening afternoon. My bowels felt trustless as sopping-wet tissue-paper. I thought, if death means Amwell Cassam, if it means Dai Stevens flattened beyond identity, if death means fleecy-haired John Vaughan floating out from Number 9 Thelma Street, or Granny Stevens taking it without hardly feeling it, if death means Daren cemetery with some utility gink mouthing lunacy... ah, by the Jesus, I shouldn't have dragged Emily up into that attic. Shouldn't have, not now, today, not after she's been so good in the past. Always the past, the mortifying past. John Vaughan's past, past time out of mind, all Daren's earthbound past putrefying from uncountable sweats, worshipful feasts, January nights, dried lungs, broken backs, burnt blood, lucifered Christs, ghetto dreams, shanty chapels, tombstone chapels, the first shovelful of muck multiplying into Caib tip-slide, and farther away still those deft Hunter and Fisher Folk (our first ever) chipping flint arrow-heads with the surety, precision of monocled watch repairers. The Folk curled like badgers in mountainside holes, sniffing dawns millions of years after the last pterodactyls sparred fanged mating bouts in humid glades beside hydrolytic swamps, the Coal Board's property virginally seamed down beneath Waunwen, awaiting royal protocol, £164,000,000 to the coal-owners and His Majesty's sanction on 12th July 1946, exactly seven months before Caib killed my innocent, sandy-haired father, at the same time releasing my mother from love, from duty.

"Love first," I mumbled, aching bones carrying my hang-dog guts, immediately forgetting my mother, gathering another private injuction, another palliative: "Rees, as if it matters either that you could, that you could not until Emily lay down in Daren woods and now you can, but today you shouldn't have, because it's made you sick. As if it matters, man, man alive, as if it matters to anyone, except yourself." Tal Harding purring alongside in a brand-new Volvo, calling out like St Christopher reduced to spieling, "Lift, Rees? I'm passing your house. No work this afternoon? Don't blame you, brother, not if you feel the way you look."

The warmed interior trapped perfume and the taint of heated oil.

"What do you think of her?" he said. "She'll run in nicely by the time we get some decent weather."

He enjoyed himself with the gears.

I said, "Remember Amwell Cassam?"

"Of course, poor Amwell. Was Percy there, at his funeral, I mean?"

"Nuh, nobody came," I said.

"You're looking rough, Rees. Anything the matter?"

"Nothing that time won't mend. Your car stinks, Tal-boy, stinks like a bloody whore-shop."

209

He said, "One of the girls brought this spray bottle to the post office yesterday morning. Her father uses it in his Dormobile. I agree, Rees, it's foul. Open the window your side."

"Seen Percy lately?" I said.

"He's letting himself drift badly, old Perce. What's he going to do after Mrs Cynon dies?"

"What did you do after Dicko Harding died? He'll carry on, find some chopsy old cow to look after him. You though, Tal, you ought to get married again. Build another bungalow behind the 'stute, next to the one you sold to Mr and Mrs Thorpe. Good company, Thorpy neighbours while the rest of Daren rots on its feet."

"Emily Thorpe, she's a bit puddled. George is all right, dry old stick but he's quite reasonable, solid business type and all that."

"*Buy* the bloody 'stute," I said, "It'll be empty in a couple of weeks."

"You're in one of your awkward moods, Rees."

"Life's awkward," I said. "Here we are, home sweet womb. Can I interest you in a piece of local history written by Ellen's father?"

"The Account. Ah'm, yes, Ellen mentioned it one time. No, actually I'm meeting someone—girl from Lower Daren post office as a matter of fact. We generally take a spin on our half-day."

"Invite us to the wedding, Tal."

"Maybe, Rees, maybe."

I went into the cold house, just in time to light the fire for Mrs Cynon bringing home the two kiddies.

18

My water-bowelled sickness persisted into next day, a double shift spent hiking between Caib and Brynywawr. The mine-cars were gone, like the best of the coal-face workers. I ate a cooked meal in Brynywawr canteen as the afternoon shift went down, elderly blokes mostly, old-timers and part compo cases riding the cages on both sides of Waunwen mountain. Hard frost from daybreak and brazier fires glowed around the black zone, away from the cleaner administration buildings. I saw Ike Pomeroy entering the canteen. He bought cigarettes, tall, sprightly lean, flat-backed at the counter, then he drove off towards the drift outfall.

"It isn't for the coal coming out on the belt these days," said a Brynywawr surface workman. "Ike's only potching, showing busy like the rest of the officials."

I asked him, "Serving your notice?"

"Aye, two more weeks to go. Twenty-seven bloody years behind the tumblers before they modernized, and before that I worked on the coal. My boy and his young missis, they've gone across to Bedwas. Lovely new house, central heating. Ideal all round. Wouldn't mind goin' myself only the wife's dead set agenst it. She's member of Brynywawr Players, see, been with 'em since leaving school very nigh. Jesus Christ, what do they expect? Mind you, I'll have a fair lump of redundancy out of the buggers."

"Much work here in Brynywawr?" I said.

"There's the old arsenal estate turned into factories since the war. They'll take you on if you're under the forty mark."

"I can picture you working in a factory," I said.

He chuckled, the fantasy echoing around inside his tea-cup.

I rode down in an empty cage, watching my cap lamp brightening fast. Fifteen shifts left. Thirty times around the pumps, I thought, unless my name comes out of the hat in Caib institute tomorrow night. I might draw lucky for a couple of months on demolition. Fitter's labourer on dismantling. Yesterday afternoon I wasn't fit for Emily Thorpe. I've addled a few thousand brain cells, besides liquefying my bottom gut.

But the luck rose to Ted Mayhew.

The suddenly it all came to a stop, ended, men off every shift shouldering loaded toolbars down to Harding's Square on the final day. The last NCB workmen's buses. No more hobnail boots clacking the pavements — some of our modest miner democrats washed at home, they refused to use the pit-head showers. No hooters any more from Caib winding-house. Sunday peace over Daren. A dozen or so familiar faces arrived daily, men whose names were picked out of the hat for dismantling down below and around top pit.

Men on bare day-wages, so absenteeism slowly increased, hung high and steady—they were better off financially as sick or injured citizens, despite accusations and economic jug-tooting from Coal Board leaders puffing safe behind the lines. Economics, aye. Power economics, as if miners were fated servile simmured to endless servility, not simply individuals of all sorts, loving, loathing or negligent towards everything under the sun, from women to television comedians, everything from onion-growing to Das Kapital. But the NCB élite merely issue data and directives. They are the Napoleons of coal-killing, their family lives chimerical. Do they have black-sheep sons, queer Brontë daughters, Electra-bleeding mistresses, nostalgias, cultural afflictions, spites, paradisial moments, depressions? What's their antidote to the disinfected breath of the Holy Ghost? Any oglers among them? Do they have sweaty feet, Pentagon morale, morality, or the yen to grow sideburns, or itches, earache, or lint in their navel-holes? Does Saturn emulsify their zodiacs? Of course, they'll fall to oblivious dust, humanly anarchic like us all. Surely so.

Left-behind day-wage blokes, though, powerless, dismantling pits where they've spent working years, are *on to* nothing from the NCB, nothing promising, no reversal of ends and means. At best they could hope for a win on Littlewoods, while their OMS records gathered dust in Brynywawr offices and in Hobart House, SW1.

Daren allegiances were stretching before breaking, pride found its price in clubs, pubs, chapels, football teams, among dog fanciers, cricketers, pigeon fanciers, gardeners, motorists, social pride, competitive pride, pride of place. The Women's Guild shrank, dwindled to pensioners and the size of its committee. Old age throve, flourishing isolated from Daren's diminishing youth population. Both cinemas closed in March, resorting to bingo one night a week. Our MP opened a plastic bag in the House of Commons to show the members a lump of steam coal. He evoked bumblings worse than cat-calls. Daren's advance factories remained a mirage bubbling comically off the lips of councillors. Two young doctors emigrated; they were replaced by poker-faced Indian doctors. Daren Miner's Cottage Hospital became an old folk's convalescent home. In April old Watt Howard had the sack from the housing site. Afraid of losing their jobs, craftsmen and labourers accepted tighter bonus targets.

Stormy April, Rollo & Sons' filter beds overspilling, the river flooding black for days on end while rumour hardened to reality and one morning the firm's lorries ceased running through Daren. Mr Rollo's crew moved away to more profitable tips.

Meanwhile the Minister of Labour lowered his eyes, entwined his fingers and preached mobility of labour for the sake of Britain, our production, our balance of payments— that modern myth strewn with the fangs and gore of Democracy, Communism, Capitalism, Socialism, Science, Theology, Utopia. But Ministers do not collect their cap lamps at six-thirty a.m. five days a week, fill shuttering with concrete, or bolt up steel girders on power stations, and neither do their wives de-gut cod in Grimsby nor disembowel capons in a chicken-packing station.

The purgatorial kiss upon civilization: They and Us, since the first man trod over his father. Whatsoever any ministerial pundit was isn't what he is. *They and Us* remain inescapably the proof of whatever one happens to *be*.

214

Very nice of course. Nice balance between destiny and dearth.

Long lines of tiny fir trees sprouted uphill, crosswise to the ancient plough-marks above Daren woods. We came through the gnarled, towering old hardwood trees this warm May morning, Mrs Cynon sauntering ahead with the youngsters, Ellen glancing at the cow-parsley spot where we greened the drought of two barren years.

"Emily Thorpe ran into the bungalow," she said. "Did you see her?"

It was better to say, "She seems to be very handy in the garden."

"Rees, why don't we move to Lower Daren? There are plenty of empty houses and it's much nearer the factory."

I said, "Three hundred and seventy-four empty houses according to the *D and D Clarion*."

"Shall we move?"

"I can't imagine anyone wanting to buy our house, Ellen."

"Tal Harding might. I'll ask him."

"When old Dicko bought houses people were still moving into Daren. The market's turned arse-about. Tal won't buy unless he can sell or rent at a profit."

"Let me ask him, Reesy? We'll find a larger house in Lower Daren, away from Caib. It's depressing since all the life has gone. Our street alone—why, it's full of old people. You can hear them coughing at night. Grey, mean old men; they remind me of my father."

"My hair's grey," I said.

"It isn't, boy, not on your chest, and you know, down..."

Her hand resting on my head, walking alongside composed

as a policewoman guiding a child. "The accident made this grey."

"Thanks, beaut."

"Certainly it was the accident. Even before you left hospital I noticed grey hairs coming."

"Thanks, beaut," I said.

"Oh, dammit! Don't be cranky; it's such a glorious day. We're all right now, we're fine. The Caib is dead, but we're loving great,"—her finger-tips probing my head like a bump reader.

I saw Mrs Cynon rubbing spittle over nettle stings on Elizabeth's leg. Song-birds were ringing the woods and big thrusting lambs were lifting their mother's hind legs off the ground. Mrs Cynon waited for us at the stile crossing the forestry fence.

I said, "Why should Tal Harding buy our house, except for the obvious reason?"

"Rees Stevens, you evil waster!"

"I mean for old time's sake, Ellen. He's marrying this girl from Lower Daren post office."

"Some day they'll put up a new factory on Caib colliery, once they clear the old buildings away. The house will be valuable then."

Factory, I thought: imagine a Mayfair politician canvassing votes by promising factories. "Beaut," I said, "*when* will they build a factory on the site of Caib colliery, my love?"

Mrs Cynon answered, "Nineteen-seventy! Not before, as God's my maker. They won't tell us straight from the council chamber, but truth will stand!"

We crossed the stile and climbed the hillside along a forestry haulage road which ran diagonally upwards inside a long, waved slash of bulldozed clay. Underfoot, the loose ballast chippings glared white, the geometrized landscape above and below stirring a peculiar boredom. Man-made mood.

Mrs Cynon moved on ahead again with the children.

"Tal won't buy our house," I said.

"He will if I ask him."

"Threaten him, ah?"

Her smile was power-loaded, the guarantee of an abbess right-armed by the Almighty. "I saved Tal from drinking his money away," she said.

"Saved anyone else, beaut?"

"Yes, matey, back there in the woods with everything soaking wet and you blazing like a box of matches on fire."

"Aye, desperation," I said. "Okay, let's offer him the house. Granny Stevens will turn over in her grave."

"*Me*, Rees, I'll ask him."

"Right, girl, right."

"Come on, put your arm around me. You'd quarrel with the Virgin Mary."

I said, "Aye."

We were high above the bowling-green, two rinks dotted with bunched woods and leg-shortened, tweedy-looking players. Caib institute lay squat as the offices of a Victorian insurance company. The deserted 'stute, doors and windows locked. Old Llew had retreated to the last of his butcher-trading family; he delivered meat for Manny Hopkins in a green three-wheeler van.

Mrs Cynon waited, left forearm across her midriff, right hand on her hip, like a model for a grannies' boutique. "The council is taking over the institute," she said. "Old-age pensioners are having it, mini-bus service picking us up three evenings a week."

I said, "There are two pensioners' halls in Daren already. Anyhow, they've always held meetings in Caib 'stute."

"The worst is yet to come. I warned you to go away last Christmas."

"We're moving to Lower Daren," Ellen said.

The old lady was shocked. "Ell-len..."

"You can stay with us on weekends, Selina. Can't she, Rees?"

Lydia frowned against the glare and adult reasoning. "But Nana Cynon looks after us every, *every* day for daddy to shut himself in the back room."

"We haven't sold the house yet," I said.

Mrs Cynon folded her arms. "Not likely to either! Another five years and the whole street will be knocked down. Yes, Ellen, true. Ask Alderman Griff Thomas."

"That buggers everything. We're knackered," I said.

I saw the old lady's nostrils twitching revulsion. "Come with Nana," she warned, prodding the children forward.

"Must you use underground language in front of Lydia and Elizabeth?"

I said, "Slip of the tongue, beaut."

She pulled free. "Rees, sometimes I hate you," — her new-born scheme already shambled by secret ordinance from Daren council offices.

"I know," I said.

"You know nothing! You think you're Holy Jesus himself!"

"He isn't on twenty-five-per-cent compo, my sulky love."

"Oh, shut your mouth!"

"I'll see you back in the house," I said. "Make some excuse to the kiddies."

"That's right, go home and mope in the back room. You're as bad as my father."

Then I had to slap her face, twice, her fingernails gouging thin scalding furrows down my nose. We turned away from each other like de-polarized magnets.

"Sorry," she said.

"Sorry," I said.

Five men left on Caib pit-head in June. Regular surface workers: banksman, three traffic men and the overman. The cages were tipped over sideways on massive baulks of timber laid across the shaft. Sheep slept in the workshops, eight smithy fires dead since March, buckets of rust-filmed water, tongs, formers, rusted mauls, wedges, chains, jig-plates, bits and pieces scattered in hundreds. Old Derby winners were chalked on the walls. Horses' names, obsolete reminders, alien jargon (BELT CLIPS FOR WEST 12. SEE MWCIN HOWARD RE CUTTER PICKS. BARHOOK PIN FOR RIMMER'S HEADING), film actresses, breasts and thighs, Ike Pomeroy caricatured with his dago moustache among confident illustrations of angle irons, brackets, drilling formulas, pulley ratios. Behind the smithy door, the World's Cup winners named in their respective positions.

Trampled sheep droppings everywhere and thieving beyond precedent in Daren. Street-corner gangs moved in as the five dismantlers came down the tump. Every Monday a storeman from Brynywawr accepted orders for corrugated sheets off the screens, washery and pit-head buildings. Archie Booth's sons brought a lorry fifty miles for two hundred sheets: they ordered two dozen. Schoolboys smashed what their fathers and elder brothers failed to carry away. Every window in the colliery, washery, baths, canteen and flocculation plant was broken; the main winding-house fortressed with breeze-blocks inside the panes, but these, too, were hammered down, further sledge and chisel work removing the engine's brass bearings. A smaller engine house on the surface disappeared entirely, asbestos sheets, windows and doors assiduously stripped to the concrete base which held the engine.

Mrs Cynon privately protested to Seymour Lloyd, the retired Police Superintendent advising her against sending a letter to *Daren & District Clarion*. He assumed the Coal Board wasn't interested in petty prosecutions—everybody knew about the electric motors and haulage equipment abandoned underground. Afterwards Mrs Cynon demanded a vote of bad conscience in the Women's Guild, but too many members were the wives or relatives of looters.

Red painted to last a decade, the steel door of the never-used powder magazine still lay flat on the grass behind the carpenter's shop. Sodden log-books were scattered on the site of the original old stone-and-mortar-built magazine, soiled records of every shot fired in Caib since 1958. Log-books, powder tins and ripped-open leather satchels for carrying detonators. Trodden sheep droppings from the threshold to the four demolished walls.

A weight-training enthusiast named Claude Prosser rolled a pair of tram-wheels through the length of Upper Daren. Next day he fell forty feet off the flocculation-plant tower— Claude the only scavenger who attempted stripping the steeply pitched tower roof. He and his widower father were unemployed, earning a few extra quid doing a song and patter act around the clubs.

Finally on 1st July (black Friday tailing Caib's history) the

220

five surface worken came down the tump for the last time. Bunched in a chatty group, they reached our house without a backward glance, Mrs Cynon standing out on the unmowed lawn, calling each man by name, wishing him good luck.

I thought, the old lady's sad. Her Hayden died in Caib. It's part of her life, Selina's scar, big Percy hobbling on his stick, always there to remind her.

She returned to the kitchen. "That's that, boy, *mae wedi cwpla*. I am now going off down to the infants' school to fetch Lizzie-fach."

"I'll start the dinner," I said.

"*Does dim yn aros, mae wedi cwpla.*"

Nothing to belong to any more, I thought. Change or die. The wheel has turned full circle. Our black and white days are over. Twelve thousand buried in Daren cemetery. Whole families of children from times of diphtheria, tuberculosis, typhoid and smallpox. Daren men killed in the pit, in the soft-coal levels. Men and women who gave up the ghost. Preachers, teachers, miners, aldermen, shopkeepers. Daren's map of the dead. Life is cheap. Change or die. Change direction.

Pilferers softly banged and rapped on Caib colliery while I scraped new potatoes in the kitchen. I remembered ambulance sirens, ambulances since childhood, whining up to the pit-head. Miners tramping the streets in the middle of the night, bringing bad news to wives and mothers. Now, from this 1st July, quietness. Clean, quiet, residential Daren, with twenty per cent of the men on hardship allowance and school-leavers taught to appreciate dereliction as a way of life by fathers and uncles with damaged limbs or lungs. Privilege of the underprivileged.

221

I thought, *we* can't change. If change doesn't come from outside, we'll gradually die off. Fade like a horse-and-cart ghost town. Our compo cases will meagrely survive on street corners or hide, mouldering in bedrooms, despair conquered because despair requires energy. We'll fade, responsibility diminishing to queueing once a week at the labour exchange, to grey mornings in doctors' waiting-rooms. Daren's councillors are feuding via letters to the *Clarion*, and Cledwyn Hughes is engaged in the finesse of double-think diplomacy, lucidly bland as a secular bishop on BBC Wales and TWW. Numbing phrases relating to footage, skills, manpower, a plethora of talk and paper campaigns for generations who have lived by weekly wage packets. In the national press, Coal Board and N U M last words, edited regrets about the closure of Brynywawr colliery: that's where they spent the big money. Unpublicized millions at the command of unknown men. Virtually unknown. Those mining experts with clean lungs, nostrils, toe-nails and finger-nails.

My face lifted unaware in the mirror above the kitchen sink: wooden mouth, inward eyes, greying hair. Mr Rees Stevens, house-man, scratched from the bread-and-butter stakes, scraping spuds for his wife and family.

What kind of a bastard life was I born for? I thought— the simplest curse, damnation against fate swaddling like a winding-sheet.

19

My longings are flowing to an end. Although our man & wife years are cut in my mind like a quarry, Kate remains silent in Portsmouth. Why ever did I come to Winchester in the first instance? Only because she sent Ellen a picture postcard of the cathedral. Jumping to the wrong conclusion I brought the child away from Daren but Kate had already flitted to her second home in Queen's Street. For her Winchester was no more than a bit of a change. She created mysteries around herself. I arrived with hopes that have since become withered, longings that turned to dust. A man can stand so much before he steadies in his tracks. For this reason I feel the end is in sight & the end for me means the way I began under the peaceful ranges of Waunwen. Once more I shall have true friends & neighbours unlike in this cathedral city where I have never made a positive friend in 14 years. When a Welshman loses his hiraeth he is lost for life. The rest of him is a masquerade. Wife finally gone, hope disappeared like the one-way letters I posted off to her every Saturday. I consider myself a sham here in Winchester. Daren calls. Memories of summer evenings come racing full stretch as I walk down Water Lane. Summer evenings with ukelele & mouth organ music in the field by Caib dam where we used to swim. Happy gangs of all ages. Standing on the bridge below the old Mill I see Daren river not the weedy Itchen. I stare at English faces and remember great old Daren characters. All the hiraeth is coming back now. So I give in. Give in to losing Kate. Our daughter definitely does not need a mother any more. From now on the future is plain as an open book. At first Ellen was against the idea of going home. She has her own mind to please. It would not do for me to criticize. She has witnessed our poor example. Now last Monday she marched home from the office & into the flat with that white face of hers guaranteed to remind me of Kate. 'Dad, we shall be ready to leave in a month's time. Why don't you write to some of your friends in Daren? We must find a house & I must find another position.' No disputing Ellen is a girl blessed with a mind of her own but I ventured to ask, 'Are you sure?' 'Why not, dad? I have nothing to lose. After you are settled in perhaps I will come back to Winchester.' I said, 'Daren is a lovely old place.' She said, 'Will you let my mother know we are leaving?' I replied, 'Yes, Ellen, just a few words to explain although frankly I have lost hope as Daren was too small to hold your mother years ago,' & then this amazing daughter of ours placed a £1 note on the table & recommended something completely foreign to her nature & my own, 'Dad, go out & get drunk until you can't stand on your feet. At least have something to remember before leaving Winchester.' I actually tried but after three & a half pints instead of feeling light hearted I went right down to

*bottom ebb unable to breathe & when some strangers brought
me back to the flat they had to abandon me in the lavatory. It
was my stomach & legs then. In the morning I read an appeal
in the MIRROR asking miners to work on Saturdays due to
the coal shortage. What a chance for the N.U.M. If every
lodge in the country took advantage they had the industry
over a barrel. Unfortunately as I know from experience the
average collier like any other worker only turns to politics at
the demand of necessity when his personal economic existence
is all rags & tatters as a consequence of the major curse upon
human nature, namely exploitation. Not one but two deadly
curses working hand in glove, namely privilege & exploitation.
As this last month of separation from home peters out I feel a
sense of renewed purpose, good thoughts of joining in again
with the salt of the earth. My own society back there in Daren.
This Winchester city is riddled with class distinction brought
down through the ages where as the discovery of coal delivered
Daren into being out of a long blank of time with only weak
signs of old agriculture above Daren woods & the tumbledown
remains of three farmhouses left as symbols of civilization.
Food & fuel. Fundamentals of Human Existence. A man has
to get down to fundamentals & it seems to me the Account
should wind up on this principle. So therefore I am content to
state*

THE END

signed
John Vaughan.

Ellen came in as I sealed the Peak Frean's tin.

"Hullo, the new forestry officer is moving into Ike Pomeroy's house. That's definitely the end of the Coal Board in Daren."

"It's a take-over," I said.

Mini-skirted like a teenager, she tapped the biscuit tin. "Have you done with these?"

"As good as. Say, what are you wearing under that imitation of a skirt?"

She tossed her rump like a can-can filly. "I'm a respectable married woman, matey."

"Lovely, too. Lucky waster, whoever he is," I said.

Her rump jigged calculated whimsy. "If you want to know, I'm his beaut."

"Don't trust him, missis. The bastard might be using you. Ulterior motive, see, missis, grafting from right inside, like a maggot."

She froze, grinning like a catalogue doxy. "Hush your mouth."

I said, "The last men came down from Caib this afternoon. As Selina said, *oes dim aros, dim aros*. Do you think we ought to move away from Daren?"

"Not unless you want to, Rees."

"I don't know what's best. Wherever we go I'll have to train for another job."

"Well?"

"I'm unteachable, Ellen."

"Once a miner, always a miner?"

"Aye, something like that."

"Not counting your accident?"

"Only partly. All this crap about miners adapting

themselves to other occupations, it's compulsory bloody sales talk. These big leaders, our administrators, they'd put the same heart into selling ships, mutton, soap powder, anything from rubber goods to radishes. They're like Jews. Jews remain Jews. Once a miner, always a miner. I mean a good, born and bred miner. The best ex-miners are disabled."

"Like yourself?"

"In a way, aye."

"You find some strange ideas, Reesy."

"The man who doesn't carry evidence of his work might as well have stayed inside his mother's guts."

She smiled empty as a yawn. "This back room hasn't left many tell-tale signs on you, matey. Bit greyer, slower, but exactly the same man. My tough guy full of worries."

"It was like dying in the beginning," I said. "But these are early days, early days yet."

She said, "Is that why virgins are valuable?"

"Any sort of virgin. I was bent into mining. I loved and hated it. Who's going to bend me towards something else? Who, ah? The kind of mindlessly productive twats who..."

"Your Caib mouth! Selina and the kiddies are in the kitchen."

"...pitch their rehabilitation centres in depressed areas? The same kind of mindless ass'oles who make us believe we're only suitable for clocking in and out of heavy-industry factories when we finish in the pits?"

"Don't nag at me," she said.

"Nag, by the Jesus. Where are all the Bevin Boys gone? The way of all flesh, like Bevan and Bevin. Ernest Bevin filched the fascist patent to fight a war against it."

She said, "Reesy, for God's sake..."

I said, "Our NUM leaders complain about men thrown on the scrap-heap. We've been fighting losing battles since the Industrial Revolution. Will Paynter took on a scrapheap when he became sec of the NUM. And listen, some years ago—I had this piece of news from Charlie Page—some years ago Arthur Horner gave his signature to a bloody Coal Board advert begging men with a low percentage of dust to go back underground because they'd beaten the dust problem with modern techniques. Aye, beaten the dust problem. Your father thought Horner was the grand daddy of social justice, but he was just a big quarreller. Miners have always quarrelled, against dictatorial bastards sitting in offices and amongst themselves. We've had to quarrel or live like yobs. Now the NUM's beaten by facts and figures, profit and loss statements flowing like bum fodder from Hobart House. We're almost on their side now, competing against gas and oil and nuclear power. Aye..."

"For God's sake," she said.

I said, "Give any man doing a shitty job enough to live on for working two days a week, and he'll spend the other five days enjoying himself and worrying how he can lose the job altogether. The state of the country has bugger all to do with his problem, nor the industry itself. He's out on his bloody tod..."

"You're ranting," she said.

"I was bent to a shitty job when I left school. Thousands of miners like myself, and we stuck our lot. Right then, Daren's a scrap-heap and I'm on it. Most of the disabled men left behind from Caib aren't disabled enough to go to Remploy. Bloody quaint, ah? They're fit for nothing by any bloody arrangement. Whatever the Board of Trade, the Ministry of

Fuel and Power or the Ministry of Labour does will come too late. We should have fought against pit closures from the very beginning, landed ourselves on the scrap-heap of our own accord. Now they've organized us on to the scrap-heap. We're viable waste. Three cheers for economic feudalism."

She said, "Finished?"

"What do you mean?" I said.

"Reesy, you enjoy destruction. Come on, we'll feed the youngsters and take them across to Daren woods."

"I haven't destroyed you, Ellen."

"Certainly not, we're a couple of beauts together. Come on, let's go."

"Away to the woods," I said.

"That's right, away from the coal and muck on your mind. No more *ach y fi*."

"Don't forget I love you, Ellen."

"I love you, too. Come on."

GLOSSARY

p49   *Beth sydd yn bod arnoch chwi nawr, cariad?* – What is the matter with you now, darling?

p221   *Does dim yn aros, mae wedi cwpla.* – There is nothing left, it is finished.

p60, 72   *Brawd* – brother

p87   *Cwtch* – shed, hiding-place

p150   *Dabbo (Da bo' chi)* – All go well with you

p81   *Dere 'ma* – Come here

p23   *Dere mâs o fyna!* – Come out from in there

p98   *Dere nawr* – come now

p80   *Diolch yn fawr* – Thank you very much

p16   *Gwaith, gwaith. Gad 'e fod. Paid a gwneyd dim rhagor!* – Work, work. Leave it there. Don't do any more.

p90   *Gwenwynllyd* – jealous

p61   *Gwt* – queue

p223   *Hiraeth* – nostalgia for home

p93   *Hwyl* – fervour

p110, 182   *Iesu* – Jesus

p106   *Iesu mawr* – big Jesus

p221   *Mae wedi cwpla* – it is finished

p2   *Merch* – girl

p88, 208   *Mochyn* – pig

p161   *Mum-glo* – inferior coal

p13   *Myfi sy'n fachgen ieuanc ffôl* – I am a young foolish boy

p1   *Nefoedd* – heaven

p97   *Nos da* – goodnight

p140   *Pais* – petticoat

p108   *Twti* – excessively small

Foreword by Leighton Andrews

Leighton Andrews is Labour Assembly Member for the Rhondda, and Minister for Education and Skills in the Welsh Government. He was elected to the National Assembly for Wales in 2003. He had previously worked for the BBC in London as Head of Public Affairs. He is an Honorary Professor in the School of Journalism, Media and Cultural Studies at Cardiff University.

Cover photograph by I C Rapoport, Aberfan 1966

I C Rapoport was born in the Bronx, New York. He studied photography at Ohio University, Athens Ohio and began his career as a freelance photo-journalist in 1959.

His photographs have appeared in major publications across the world including the *New York Times, National Geographic, Newsweek* and *Time*. He presented his complete Aberfan 1966 assignment for *Life* magazine to the National Library of Wales in 2005 and the work was published as *Aberfan The Days After: Y Dyddiau Du A Journey in Pictures Taith Trwy Luniau*. He lives in Pacific Palisades, California.

SERIES EDITOR: DAI SMITH

1	*So Long, Hector Bebb*	Ron Berry
2	*Border Country*	Raymond Williams
3	*The Dark Philosophers*	Gwyn Thomas
4	*Cwmardy & We Live*	Lewis Jones
5	*Country Dance*	Margiad Evans
6	*A Man's Estate*	Emyr Humphreys
7	*Home to an Empty House*	Alun Richards
8	*In the Green Tree*	Alun Lewis
9	*Ash on a Young Man's Sleeve*	Dannie Abse
10	*Poetry 1900–2000*	Ed. Meic Stephens
11	*Sport*	Ed. Gareth Williams
12	*The Withered Root*	Rhys Davies
13	*Rhapsody*	Dorothy Edwards
14	*Jampot Smith*	Jeremy Brooks
15	*The Voices of the Children*	George Ewart Evans
16	*I Sent a Letter to My Love*	Bernice Rubens
17	*Congratulate the Devil*	Howell Davies
18	*The Heyday in the Blood*	Geraint Goodwin
19	*The Alone to the Alone*	Gwyn Thomas
20	*The Caves of Alienation*	Stuart Evans
21	*A Rope of Vines*	Brenda Chamberlain
22	*Black Parade*	Jack Jones
23	*Dai Country*	Alun Richards
24	*The Valley, the City, the Village*	Glyn Jones
25	*The Great God Pan*	Arthur Machen
26	*The Hill of Dreams*	Arthur Machen
27	*The Battle to the Weak*	Hilda Vaughan
28	*Turf or Stone*	Margiad Evans
29	*Make Room for the Jester*	Stead Jones
30	*Goodbye, Twentieth Century*	Dannie Abse
31	*All Things Betray Thee*	Gwyn Thomas
32	*The Volunteers*	Raymond Williams
33	*Flame and Slag*	Ron Berry
34	*The Water-castle*	Brenda Chamberlain

WWW.THELIBRARYOFWALES.COM

LIBRARY OF WALES

The Library of Wales is a Welsh Government project designed to ensure that all of the rich and extensive literature of Wales which has been written in English will now be made available to readers in and beyond Wales. Sustaining this wider literary heritage is understood by the Welsh Government to be a key component in creating and disseminating an ongoing sense of modern Welsh culture and history for the future Wales which is now emerging from contemporary society. Through these texts, until now unavailable or out-of-print or merely forgotten, the Library of Wales will bring back into play the voices and actions of the human experience that has made us, in all our complexity, a Welsh people.

The Library of Wales will include prose as well as poetry, essays as well as fiction, anthologies as well as memoirs, drama as well as journalism. It will complement the names and texts that are already in the public domain and seek to include the best of Welsh writing in English, as well as to showcase what has been unjustly neglected. No boundaries will limit the ambition of the Library of Wales to open up the borders that have denied some of our best writers a presence in a future Wales. The Library of Wales has been created with that Wales in mind: a young country not afraid to remember what it might yet become.

Dai Smith

LIBRARY of WALES
FUNDED BY

Noddir gan
Lywodraeth Cymru
Sponsored by
Welsh Government

CYNGOR LLYFRAU CYMRU
WELSH BOOKS COUNCIL